SWORD ART ONLINE

Alicization Invading

VOLUME 15

Reki Kawahara

abec

bee-pee

YEN ON

NEW YORK

SWORD ART ONLINE, Volume 15: ALICIZATION INVADING
REKI KAWAHARA

Translation by Stephen Paul
Cover art by abec

SWORD ART ONLINE Vol.15
©REKI KAWAHARA 2014
First published in Japan in 2014 by KADOKAWA CORPORATION, Tokyo.
English translation rights arranged with KADOKAWA CORPORATION, Tokyo, through Tuttle-Mori Agency, Inc., Tokyo.

English translation © 2018 by Yen Press, LLC

Yen On
1290 Avenue of the Americas
New York, NY 10104

Visit us at yenpress.com
facebook.com/yenpress
twitter.com/yenpress
yenpress.tumblr.com
instagram.com/yenpress

First Yen On Edition: December 2018

Yen On is an imprint of Yen Press, LLC.
The Yen On name and logo are trademarks of Yen Press, LLC.

The publisher is not responsible for websites (or their content) that are not owned by the publisher.

Library of Congress Cataloging-in-Publication Data
Names: Kawahara, Reki, author. | Abec, 1985– illustrator. | Paul, Stephen, translator.
Title: Sword art online / Reki Kawahara, abec ; translation, Stephen Paul.
Description: First Yen On edition. | New York, NY : Yen On, 2014–
Identifiers: LCCN 2014001175 | ISBN 9780316371247 (v. 1 : pbk.) |
    ISBN 9780316376815 (v. 2 : pbk.) | ISBN 9780316296427 (v. 3 : pbk.) |
    ISBN 9780316296434 (v. 4 : pbk.) | ISBN 9780316296441 (v. 5 : pbk.) |
    ISBN 9780316296458 (v. 6 : pbk.) | ISBN 9780316390408 (v. 7 : pbk.) |
    ISBN 9780316390415 (v. 8 : pbk.) | ISBN 9780316390422 (v. 9 : pbk.) |
    ISBN 9780316390439 (v. 10 : pbk.) | ISBN 9780316390446 (v. 11 : pbk.) |
    ISBN 9780316390453 (v. 12 : pbk.) | ISBN 9780316390460 (v. 13 : pbk.) |
    ISBN 9780316390484 (v. 14 : pbk.) | ISBN 9780316390491 (v. 15 : pbk.)
Subjects: CYAC: Science fiction. | BISAC: FICTION / Science Fiction / Adventure.
Classification: PZ7.K1755Ain 2014 | DDC [Fic]—dc23
LC record available at https://lccn.loc.gov/2014001175

ISBNs: 978-0-316-39049-1 (paperback)
       978-0-316-56107-5 (ebook)

10 9 8 7 6 5 4 3 2 1

LSC-C

Printed in the United States of America

"THIS MIGHT BE A GAME, BUT IT'S NOT SOMETHING YOU PLAY."

—Akihiko Kayaba, *Sword Art Online* programmer

SWORD ART ONLINE
Alicization Invading

Reki Kawahara

abec

bee-pee

CHAPTER FOURTEEN

SUBTILIZER, STEALER OF SOULS, JUNE–JULY 2026

The sniper had pale-blue hair.

Her delicate, girlish body fit surprisingly well with the mammoth 50-caliber rifle she used.

She was prone, in firing position, and had her back turned, hiding her face. But she was proud and beautiful and dangerous, surely no different from a lynx.

Her concentration was tremendous. She watched the path below with absolute stillness, her right eye pressed to the scope and index finger on the trigger. It was worth watching for longer than this, but time was limited.

Something came out of a hiding spot and across the floor of the abandoned building. Pebbles, twigs, and scraps of metal littered the ground and had to be avoided carefully to ensure the approach was silent—or else she would hear.

Suddenly, her shoulders twitched.

She must have sensed something that was neither sound nor vibration. Her instincts were impeccable but, sadly, too late.

A right hand reached out, wrapping around her slender neck, while the left pressed on the back of her head. With quiet but undeniable intent, the strangling began.

The Army Combative skill kicked in, and the visual representation of the girl's health, her HP bar, began to drop rapidly. The sniper struggled, but in the VRMMO *Gun Gale Online*, unless the victim had a clear advantage in the Strength stat, it was nearly impossible to break out of a rear naked choke barehanded. In that sense, it was just like the real world.

Of the twenty-nine contestants in the Bullet of Bullets event, the blue-haired sniper was the most desirable target to fight...no, to hunt. She had been expected to snipe from the upper half of this five-story building.

The problem was that both the fourth and fifth story had a clear shot at the main street of the map. The choice had to be made quickly: Which floor to wait on?

Common sense said the fourth because it would be quicker to stop there and get into firing position. But upon seeing the library on that floor, intuition and logic both said otherwise. Intuition said the sniper was probably still young enough to be a student. Logic said that a student would want to avoid shooting in a library, which might be mentally associated with everyday life.

That suspicion was correct. The blue-haired sniper spent the extra thirty seconds or so to climb another floor higher, and she appeared in the fifth-floor storeroom.

And now, like a butterfly that wandered into a spider's web, her fragile life was soon to vanish.

Oh, but if only this was not some calculation of binary data in a virtual setting, but the taking of a real life and soul.

If only it was not her avatar struggling against the chokehold, but her true flesh-and-blood body. How sweet the moment would be when it arrived.

In the upper-right corner, the sniper's HP bar went under 5 percent. But she still struggled desperately to break free.

Though her defeat was certain, she neither wasted energy trying to shout nor went limp in submission. Her refusal to give up on escaping was even rather touching to her foe.

And into her ear from behind, as tenderly as a lover's embrace, came a whisper.

"Your soul will be so sweet."

1

His eyelids rose slowly.

He'd fallen asleep at some point. The new Italian sofa he'd imported last week was a bit too comfortable. Without getting up from the smooth leather surface, he glanced at the smartwatch on his left wrist.

2:12 AM.

He got up, stretched, and walked to the southern-facing wall. It was entirely made of smartglass, and its currently transparent surface afforded him a gaze of the waterfront from his executive room on the forty-third floor.

The port gleamed softly with the reflected light of the downtown skyscrapers. A number of large ships were stationed along the expansive harbor. But their angular, forceful silhouettes were not those of luxury cruise ships. They were battleships of the Third Fleet of the United States Navy under Pacific Command.

For many years, San Diego, the second-largest city in the state of California, had been a military town. It had stationed over twenty-five thousand military personnel and their families at a massive naval base that served as the city's primary economic engine.

But in recent years, new industries had rapidly taken hold—high-tech sectors such as information, communications, and biotechnology.

Some companies straddled the boundary between military and tech. Most of them were private military contractors, or PMCs, that accepted contracts from the military and other large companies for protection, training, and even direct combat on the ground.

The chief tactical officer (CTO) of Glowgen Defense Systems, Gabriel Miller, gazed down upon the darkened port next to downtown San Diego and smiled without even realizing it.

He was still excited from the dream he'd had during his brief nap. It was a dream of the full-dive VR game event he'd participated in just a few days ago from this very executive suite.

Gabriel hardly ever dreamed, but when he did, it always replayed some scene from his past in minute detail. He could still feel the pleasant sensation of the blue-haired sniper struggling against his grip. Almost as though it were real and not a dream...

But it wasn't real. That battle happened in the virtual world, not the real one.

Full-dive technology was a revolutionary invention, and its creator, Akihiko Kayaba, was worthy of respect. If he were still alive, Gabriel would have spent millions to recruit him. Even though he was the most infamous criminal of the century—in fact, *especially* because of that.

But the experience offered by the AmuSphere, as close as it came to providing truth, only made the fact that it *wasn't* real that much more unfulfilling. Like salt water—never truly quenching his thirst, no matter how much he drank.

As Glowgen's youngest officer and major shareholder, Gabriel led a life without any unfulfilled physical wants. Yet, his gnawing mental needs could never be satisfied with money.

"...Your soul will be so sweet..."

He repeated the words from his dream.

In fact, he wished he could have said those words in Japanese, which he'd been studying for the past three years. But because his player account was tagged as an American one, he didn't want to give away any unnecessary details or make himself more memorable. They'd have a chance to speak more intimately someday. And he had many questions.

The little smile playing across his lips went away, and Gabriel used one of the touch sensors at various spots on the glass to lower the translucency of the surface. It turned into a darkened mirror instead, reflecting his image.

His blond hair was loosely pulled back, and his eyes were a piercing blue. On his six-foot-one frame, he wore a white dress shirt and dark-gray slacks. His shoes were custom-made cordovan leather. His image was almost embarrassingly white and white-collar, but Gabriel thought nothing of his personal appearance, instead favoring the essence held within. The flesh was nothing more than a shell that enveloped the soul, after all.

Soul.

Just about every religion contained the concept of the human soul. Christianity, of course, held that the soul was sent to either Heaven or Hell depending on your actions in life. But Gabriel's belief in and fixation upon the soul had nothing to do with being Protestant or Catholic.

He knew it. He had seen and experienced it for himself.

He'd witnessed an indescribably beautiful collection of light particles leaving the forehead of a girl whose life was fading away as he held her in his arms.

Gabriel Miller was born in Pacific Palisades, a suburb of Los Angeles, in March of 1998.

He was an only child and grew up with every material and emotional expression of love from his wealthy parents. They lived in a huge mansion that provided him with many places to play, but young Gabriel's favorite place of all was his father's private collection room.

His father was the owner and manager of Glowgen Securities, the precursor to Glowgen Defense Systems, and he was an avid collector of insects. He had countless glass cases arranged in the large collection room packed with the little things. When

Gabriel had time, he hid in there, magnifying glass in hand, gazing at the colorful bugs as he sat on the sofa in the center of the room, daydreaming.

Sitting in that tall, dim room all by himself, surrounded by thousands upon thousands of silent, unmoving insects, young Gabriel sometimes experienced the strangest sensation.

Until a certain moment, all those insects had once been alive. They'd been on the plains of Africa or in the deserts of the Middle East or the jungles of South America, contentedly building their nests and foraging for food.

And then, a collector came along and caught them, treated them with lethal chemicals, sold them through a series of transactions, until at last they wound up lined in tidy little rows in the Miller household. This was not just a room for displaying a large insect collection. It was a massive mausoleum housing thousands and thousands of defiled corpses...

Gabriel would close his eyes and imagine what would happen if all the insects around him suddenly came back to life.

Six legs, scrabbling in the air for freedom, feelers and wings vibrating and twitching. *Skitter-skitter, skitter-skitter*—individually faint but multiplied times infinity—a wave of scraping and scratching noises that engulfed and bowled him over.

Skitter-skitter, skitter-skitter.

His eyes flew open. He thought he saw one green beetle's leg twitching in a corner of a case directly across from him. He leaped up from the sofa and rushed eagerly to examine the case, but the insect was just a lifeless display sample again.

The emerald-green shell, which gleamed like metal; the legs with sharp little spikes; the compound eyes with their lattice of incredibly tiny photoreceptors. What kind of power had once operated these precise little machines?

His father told him that insects did not have a brain, like humans did. "So how do they think?" he asked. His father showed him a video.

It depicted praying mantises mating. The smaller male held down the much larger, rounded female from behind and pressed the end of its abdomen against hers. The female did not move for a while, until abruptly, without any warning, she grabbed the male's upper half with her forearms and began the unforgettable display of devouring his head. To Gabriel's shock, the male even continued mating, only disengaging once its entire head was gone. Then, when the female released her grasp, she fled the scene.

But despite having no head anymore, the male mantis crawled across the grass, climbed branches, and nimbly continued its escape. Gabriel's father pointed this out and said, "The entire nervous system of insects like the mantis is kind of like their brain. Losing their heads is only the loss of sensory organs. They can still live for a while."

For several days after seeing that video, Gabriel wondered where a praying mantis's soul was. If they could live on even after their heads had been eaten, then losing all their legs probably wouldn't stop them, either. Was it in the abdomen? The thorax? But the insects would still wriggle and writhe, whether you crushed their soft stomachs or pierced them with a pin.

If no part of their body caused instant death when destroyed, then praying mantises' souls must be spread throughout their entire being. This was eight- or nine-year-old Gabriel's conclusion, after he had undertaken numerous experiments on bugs he caught around his home.

Insects ran on a mysterious power that operated their machine-like bodies—a soul that stubbornly clung to its vessel even as parts of it were destroyed. But at a certain moment, it would give up and leave that body behind.

Gabriel eagerly wanted to witness that soul leaving for himself, perhaps even catch it. But no matter how hard he stared through the magnifying glass, no matter how careful his experiments, he never caught or even saw any *thing* leaving an insect's body.

He spent long hours and expended immeasurable enthusiasm in his secret lab deep in the woods behind his house, but he never found the slightest bit of success for his trouble.

Even young Gabriel had an instinctual feeling that his parents would not welcome this interest of his. So after the incident with the mantis video, he never asked his father about it again, and he never told anyone about his experiments. But the more he hid it, the deeper his obsession became.

Around that time, Gabriel had a very close friend his age.

Alicia Clingerman was the daughter of the corporate board member who lived next door to Gabriel's family. The children went to the same elementary school, and their families got to know each other. She was shy and quiet and preferred staying inside and reading or watching videos, rather than going out and playing in the mud.

Gabriel, of course, kept his experiments a secret from her and never once spoke about insects or souls. But he never stopped thinking about them. When he gazed at Alicia's face, smiling angelically as she read her stories, Gabriel pondered where exactly *her* soul was.

Insects and humans are different. Humans cannot live without a head. So the human soul must be in the head, he thought. *In the brain.*

But Gabriel already knew, from browsing the Internet on his father's computer, that brain damage did not necessarily lead to loss of life. There were construction workers who survived despite being pierced from chin to crown with a steel pipe. Some doctors had succeeded in rehabilitating patients with mental illnesses by removing a part of their brain.

So it has to be a specific part of the brain, Gabriel thought as he stared at Alicia's forehead, which was framed by wispy golden locks. Somewhere past her smooth skin, hard skull, and soft brain matter, her soul was hidden.

In his youthful naïveté, Gabriel assumed he would end up

married to Alicia. Perhaps one day, he'd actually get to see her soul for himself. Given how angelic she was, it was certain to be the most indescribably beautiful thing.

Gabriel's wish would come true much sooner than he realized, but only half of it.

In September 2008, a major bank collapse triggered a worldwide financial crisis.

The resulting recession engulfed Pacific Palisades in Los Angeles, too. Several of the mansions around them were sold, and the number of luxury cars on the street visibly dwindled.

Glowgen Securities's cautious business model paid off, and they were able to keep the damage to a minimum, but the Clingermans' real estate investment company suffered huge losses. By the following April, the family had lost all its assets, including the mansion, and was going to move to Kansas City in the Midwest to rely on some farm-owning relatives.

Gabriel was sad. He was wise for a ten-year-old boy and understood that there was no way he could actually help Alicia. He could easily imagine the hardships that awaited her in the future.

All his privileges—a large home kept safe by perfect security systems, every meal prepared by experienced cooks, schools full of other rich white children—would become things of the past for Alicia, replaced by poverty and hard labor. Worst of all, Alicia's pure soul, which was supposed to be his one day, would now be tarnished by someone else, some stranger—and that was the hardest thing of all for Gabriel to bear.

So he decided to kill her.

On Alicia's last day of school, after she said her good-byes, Gabriel invited her to go into the woods behind their houses when they got off the school bus. He guided her there along his secret route, skillfully evading all the security cameras along the roads and fences, ensuring that no one saw them, walking over fallen leaves to hide their tracks, until they reached his secret laboratory, which was hidden in an especially dense area of shrubs.

When Gabriel put his arms around her fragile body, she returned his embrace, having no idea of the countless insects that had perished in this space. The girl sobbed and hiccuped, telling him she didn't want to go anywhere, that she wanted to stay there in that city with Gabe forever.

In his mind, he silently reassured her that he'd make that come true. He put his hand into his pocket and pulled out the tool he'd prepared: his father's four-inch steel needle with a wooden handle, used for killing insects.

He stuck the sharp end into Alicia's left ear, pressed his other hand against her right, then rammed the implement all the way in to its base.

Alicia blinked in wonder, not realizing what had just happened, and then her body abruptly went into violent spasms. A few seconds later, her blue eyes lost their focus.

And then, Gabriel saw *it* happen.

Something luminescent, like a tiny gleaming cloud, emerged from Alicia's forehead. It floated gently toward him, right between his eyes, and passed without sensation directly into his head.

The soft sunlight of the spring afternoon around them vanished. Instead, powerful beams of light shot down through the branches of the trees directly overhead. There was even the faint sound of bells.

Gabriel's eyes welled up with tears of unfettered joy. He was viewing Alicia's soul…and not only that, he understood that he was seeing what her soul was seeing.

The tiny glowing cloud, over a few seconds that seemed like an eternity, passed through Gabriel's head and rose, higher and higher, guided by the light of Heaven, until it disappeared. The spring sunlight and the chirping of the birds returned.

As he sat there, cradling Alicia's lifeless and soulless body in his arms, Gabriel wondered whether what he'd just experienced was true or merely a hallucination brought about by his extreme excitement. But whichever the answer, he knew that for the rest of his life, he would be seeking that experience again.

He took Alicia's body to an oak tree he'd found with a deep, gaping pit beneath its roots and tossed her body down into it. Then he examined himself very carefully, plucked two long golden hairs from his body, and dropped them into the hole, too. After carefully washing the needle, he returned it to his father's tool kit.

The local police never succeeded in finding any clues to Alicia Clingerman's disappearance, and the case went cold.

Twenty-eight-year-old Gabriel Miller awoke from this brief but deep reverie. He pulled away from the reflective-mirror glass and headed to his work desk on the western wall of the room. The instant he sat in the Norwegian reclining chair, a phone icon began to blink on the thirty-inch display panel embedded into the desk's glass surface.

He tapped the icon, which brought up the face of his secretary, who began to speak.

"I apologize for disturbing you, Mr. Miller. Mr. Ferguson, the company COO, would like to have dinner with you tomorrow. Shall I make the arrangements?"

"Tell him my schedule's full," Gabriel immediately replied. His usually implacable secretary looked a bit startled by this. The chief operating officer was the vice president of the company, the number two man at Glowgen DS. Gabriel was just one of ten executives, and he wasn't important enough to turn down an invitation—under typical circumstances.

But the secretary's expression faded in a second, and she said, "I understand. I will let him know."

The call ended. Gabriel sank back into his chair and crossed his legs.

He had an idea of what Ferguson wanted. He was going to try

to convince Gabriel not to participate in a particular exercise that was on the schedule. But secretly, the COO's intention was the exact opposite. The wily old badger was *hoping* he would venture into danger and wind up on the KIA list. After all, Gabriel was the son of the previous CEO and was the company's biggest shareholder.

For his part, Gabriel understood how stupid it was for a corporate executive to take part in a live-combat scenario with actual gunfire being traded. Even if he had combat experience of his own, the CTO's job was to draw up overall tactical plans from the safety of the company office. There was zero need to expose himself to the danger of the battlefield.

But for the sake of his top-secret master plan, he couldn't sit back and miss out. This was a strategy that directly linked to the life goal Gabriel had had since the day he saw Alicia's soul leave her body.

The client in this case was not their primary partner, the Department of Defense. Instead, it was the National Security Agency, a department they'd never dealt with.

When two NSA agents visited this very office last month, they succeeded on multiple fronts in stunning Gabriel, who did not experience normal emotions as others did.

For one thing, the operation would be extralegal, completely off the books. This made sense, as the plan was to send Glowgen's combat team on a naval submarine and attack a ship belonging to an allied nation, Japan. And if casualties resulted on the other side because of combat, so be it.

The point of the operation was to steal technology.

When he heard the details, Gabriel was so stunned—or perhaps elated—that he gasped. Fortunately, the agents didn't notice.

It was called Soul Translation technology. A stunning machine, developed by a tiny arm of the Japan Self-Defense Force named Rath, that could scan and read the human soul.

As a devout seeker of the soul, Gabriel had been keenly fascinated by the full-dive tech coming out of Japan. It was what drove him to play against Japanese players in *Gun Gale Online* and study the Japanese language. He even spent tens of thousands of dollars to get his hands on one of those hellish devices that were supposed to have been destroyed: the NerveGear. But not so *he* could wear it, of course.

After the controversy over that deadly game, Gabriel expected that continuing development in full dive would taper off. But no, they'd continued clandestine research, and now they were on the verge of unlocking the secrets of the soul.

To Gabriel, this NSA offer was as good as fate.

For one thing, Glowgen DS was big but still just a PMC. There was no way they could spurn an offer from the NSA, which was more powerful than the CIA at this point. They convened a quick board meeting and chose to accept the contract by a margin of two votes. To maintain the secrecy of the mission, they chose operatives with dirty pasts and expertise in wet work whom they could lean on for the combat team.

And Gabriel nominated himself to be CO.

Naturally, they would hide Gabriel's role as company executive from the combat team. They were the types of people who, if they found out his identity, would take him hostage and demand ransom from the company instead.

And Gabriel *had* to undertake this risk in order to go.

The NSA agents told him that not only had Rath's STL tech succeeded at reading the human soul, they could even make clones of it. Once the artificial intelligence code-named A.L.I.C.E. was complete, its soul would be loaded onto Japanese drones that would overturn the balance of military power in East Asia.

He didn't care about war in Asia—or anywhere in the world, for that matter. But the moment he heard the name Alice, Gabriel's mind was made up.

She would be his.

He would do whatever it took to get the soul contained in that tiny medium called a lightcube.

"Alice...Alicia...," he murmured, leaning back into his chair. That faint smile had returned to his lips.

When Gabriel's grandfather founded Glowgen, he intended it to mean "generating glow." He thought of it as the glow of prosperity and happiness, but to Gabriel, his heir, it conjured only the image of that golden glow emerging from Alicia's forehead as she died.

What generated that glow? The soul, obviously.

It was all fate at work.

A week later, Gabriel and eleven squad members flew to Guam, then took a nuclear submarine from the local naval base into Japan's territorial waters. Right before the operation began, they switched to a tiny ASDS submarine that ferried them to their assault on the *Ocean Turtle*, a massive marine research craft.

He didn't know whether they'd take the vessel bloodlessly or whether one side—or both—would suffer losses. But Gabriel was certain that Alice and the STL tech would be his. He could give the NSA some random lightcube and a copy of their research.

Soon…very soon. He'd done his experiments on a number of people since Alicia, and he never got any closer to the true nature of the soul—but it would be in his grasp before long.

He would get to see that beautiful cloud of light once again.

"…Your soul…will be so sweet…"

This time, as he closed his eyes, Gabriel said the phrase in perfect Japanese.

2

Captain Dario Ziliani, commanding officer of the Seawolf-class nuclear submarine *Jimmy Carter,* was a true submariner, who rose through the ranks from cleaning out torpedo tubes to his current position. His first sub was a Barbel-class diesel, an extremely cramped vehicle, the meager interior of which was largely occupied by oil stench and clangor.

Compared to that, the Seawolf class, the most expensive submarine ever developed, was more like a Rolls-Royce. Since being named captain in 2020, Ziliani had given his sub and crew all the care he could provide. The harsh training paid off, and now the high-tensile body, S6W reactor, and crew of 140 were unified into a single organism fast enough to swim freely in any sea, provided it had the depth.

In a way, the *Jimmy Carter* was like Ziliani's baby. Sadly, he would soon be phased out of active service, forced to choose between working on land or early retirement, but he knew that if his recommendation, XO Guthrie, was put in charge next, she would be in good hands.

But then, like some dark cloud over his impending change in life, Captain Ziliani got a strange and ominous order just ten days ago.

Jimmy Carter was designed to support special-operations missions, and it had systems that worked with Navy SEAL forces.

One of them was the presence of a miniature submarine on the aft deck.

On several occasions, she'd sailed deep into foreign waters with SEALs on board. But these missions were always to support peace for the United States and the world at large, and the men who rode on those missions shared the same sense of duty as Ziliani and his crew.

But the men who'd boarded in Guam two days ago…

Ziliani went back to meet with them once, and he nearly ordered his officers to launch them out of the tubes. A dozen-plus men lounging around in disarray, blasting music from headphones, playing poker for keeps, littering beer cans around the place. They were not regimented sailors. They could barely pass for proper military.

Only one of them, their tall commander, who apologized for the mess, seemed to have any sense of decorum at all. But his stunningly blue eyes…

When Ziliani took his outstretched hand and gave him a hard stare, he felt a sensation he hadn't had in many years.

It was from his childhood, long before he enlisted in the navy. He'd been swimming at the beach in his hometown of Miami when a great white shark swam directly past him. He didn't get attacked, fortunately, but he did look into the shark's eyes as it swam by. They were like bottomless pits that absorbed all the light that touched them.

And in this man's eyes was that same dark void…

"Captain, I've got something on the bow sonar!" said one of the techs, pulling Ziliani out of the memory. "It's a nuclear turbine. Identifying now…Match. That's the megafloat, sir. Distance to target: fifteen miles."

He snapped back to attention. He was in the command center and needed to give orders.

"Maintain depth. Speed one-five knots."

The helm repeated his order, and then there was a brief sensation of deceleration.

"Do we know where the Aegis defense ship is located?"

"Gas turbine–engine signal at forty-three miles southwest of target…Match. JMSDF *Nagato*."

Ziliani stared at the two dots on the large display screen. The Aegis ship would be armed, but the megafloat was just a research facility, as he understood it. And their orders were to send that band of armed ruffians for infiltration. To a Japanese ship—an allied nation. It didn't seem like the kind of operation the president or DoD would approve.

Then he remembered what the black suits who'd brought him the orders straight from the Pentagon had said.

Japan is undertaking research on that megafloat that will put them at war with America again. The best way to maintain peaceful relations is to bury that research in the darkness, where it belongs.

Ziliani wasn't young enough to take them at face value. But he was also old enough to know that he didn't have any option other than to follow orders.

"Are our guests ready?" he murmured to his executive officer, who was standing nearby.

"On standby in the ASDS."

"Good…Maintain speed, depth to one hundred feet!"

Compressed air cleared the ballast tanks of seawater, lifting the considerable hull of the *Jimmy Carter* toward the surface. Slowly but surely, their distance to the dots on the sonar shrank.

Would Japanese scientists die? Most likely. And he wasn't going to forget his part in this operation until the day he died.

"Distance to target: five miles!"

Ziliani steeled himself and cast aside his misgivings. "Disengage ASDS!" he commanded. He felt a minor vibration—a sign that the cargo on the aft deck had been released.

"Disengaged…ASDS is autonomous."

The little submarine containing a pack of wild dogs and one shark picked up speed, charging toward the belly of the giant turtle floating on the sea.

CHAPTER FIFTEEN

IN THE FAR NORTH, OCTOBER 380 HE

1

Alice Synthesis Thirty placed the freshly washed plates in the drying basket and wiped her hands on the bottom of her apron before looking up.

Beyond the window, tree branches had scattered many of their yellow and red leaves with the chill of the last few days. The winter really did arrive here much earlier than in Centoria.

Still, the light of Solus looked warm in the first blue sky they'd had in days. On the thickest branch of the closest tree, a pair of climbing rabbits could be seen pleasantly sunning themselves.

Alice smiled as she watched them, then turned and said, "The weather's so nice today; perhaps we should pack a lunch and go to the eastern hill."

There was no response.

In the center of the little wooden cabin's main room, which combined a living space with a dining room and kitchen, there was a plain, unfinished wooden table. Seated at one of the matching chairs was a young man with black hair. He did not react to Alice's suggestion. He simply gazed, expressionless, at a nondescript point on the table.

He wasn't solidly built to begin with, and by now, he was noticeably thinner even than Alice was. His bony structure was clearly visible through his loose clothing. His empty right sleeve, hanging limply from the shoulder, only added to his pitiable appearance.

His eyes, black as his hair, were empty. They reflected no light and suggested his mind was distant, completely shut off from the outside world.

Alice stifled a pain in her chest that never dulled, no matter how many times she felt it. In a cheery voice, she said, "There's a breeze today, so we should bundle up. Hang on—I'll get your coat for you."

She put her apron on the hook next to the sink and headed to the bedroom. She gathered up her long blond hair and covered it with a cotton scarf. A faded black eye patch went over her vacant right eye socket. One of the two wool coats on the wall was hers, and she carried the other one under her arm as she returned to the main room.

The young man hadn't budged. She put her hand against his scrawny back, and he awkwardly got to his feet.

But that was all the black-haired boy could do. He couldn't even walk a single mel. She put the coat over him from behind, then circled around and tied the strings at his neck tight.

"Just one more thing," she told him, rushing to the corner of the room.

Sitting there was a sturdy chair made of a light-brown wood. Instead of feet, it had metal wheels—two big and two small. An old man named Garitta who lived alone in the forest made it for them.

She grabbed the handles on the back of the chair and rolled it over to the young man. Before he could start wobbling or topple over, she sat him down on the leather seat, then threw a heavy lap blanket over his legs to keep him secure.

"There! Now we can go."

She patted his shoulders, took the handles, and rolled the chair toward the door on the south side of the cabin.

Suddenly, he tilted his head and reached toward the east wall with his left hand, fingers trembling. "Aaah…aaah…"

They were no more than guttural vocalizations—nowhere close to words. But Alice could sense what he wanted right away.

"Oh, I'm sorry. I'll get them for you."

Hanging on sturdy hooks on the wall were three swords.

On the right was Alice's golden longsword, the Osmanthus Blade.

On the left, the pitch-black sword he had once worn, the Night-Sky Blade.

And in the middle, the masterless white weapon, the Blue Rose Sword.

First, Alice took the Night-Sky Blade off the wall and tucked it under her left arm; it was nearly as heavy as the Osmanthus Blade. Next, she lifted up the Blue Rose Sword. This one was only half as heavy as the black sword—inside the scabbard, there was just one half of a blade.

And the owner of this sword, the flaxen-haired boy who was the black-haired boy's best friend, was no longer among the living...

She closed her eye briefly, then took the two swords back to the wheelchair. Once they were laid over his knees, the young man placed his hand on top of them and looked down. The only time he expressed his will with vocalizations or movements at all was when he asked for the black and white blades.

"Hold them tight, so they don't fall off," Alice told him, trying to ignore the throbbing in her chest. The painful memories were as fresh as ever, even after several months. She pushed the wheelchair and its extra weight out through the doorway.

Instead of stairs, the porch had a thick slab leading to the ground. Down in the garden, the soft breeze was a bit chilly, but the gentle sunlight wrapped around them.

The log cabin was located right in the middle of a little clearing deep in the woods. Alice had chopped down the trees herself, stripped the bark, and put it together. It wasn't pretty, but she'd used the highest-quality trees she could find, so it was sturdily made. Old Man Garitta had shown her how to build it from the ground up, and the entire time, he'd remarked about how he'd never seen such a strong girl.

Apparently, this clearing had been Alice and Eugeo's secret playground during childhood. Sadly, she could not remember any of it. The Synthesis Ritual that had turned her into an Integrity Knight had robbed her of all memory before that point.

All she told Garitta and the other villagers was that she had forgotten her past. But the truth was that Alice Synthesis Thirty, the Integrity Knight, was an entirely new personality—an imposter inhabiting the body of Alice Zuberg. She would have given this body back if she could have, but like Eugeo, the real Alice's memories were gone from this world forever.

"...All right, let's go."

She set forth, pushing the wheelchair onward to drive away the moment's recollection.

The round clearing, about thirty mels in diameter, was covered in a soft undergrowth, but on the east side, underneath a large, jutting branch, there was a thick pile of dead grass. It looked like the nest of some giant creature—which, as a matter of fact, it was—but the owner was not here. She glanced over, wondered where it was off playing now, then headed down the path that split the clearing north to south into the woods.

After about fifty mels, the path split into east and west branches. To the west was the village named Rulid, but she did not want to visit when she didn't have a reason. Instead, she turned east, strolling through the radiant pockets of sunlight where they broke the canopy overhead.

They proceeded through the forest, which, at the end of October, was now transitioning from fall leaves to fallen leaves.

"Are you cold?" she asked, but he didn't reply. He wouldn't say a thing, even if they were in the midst of a raging blizzard. She glanced over his shoulder to make sure the coat was tight around his collar.

Naturally, a heat element or two would warm him up. But Rulid already had its share of suspicious residents, and she didn't want to get into the habit of relying on sacred arts around here, lest it lead to rumors.

After fifteen minutes of travel along the beaten path (adding new wheel ruts along the way), the road ahead began to lighten. The trees steadily gave way to a steep little hill. The path began to incline, but the extra strain didn't bother Alice.

Once they reached the top of the hill, the view opened up.

Just to the east was the blue surface of Lake Rul. On the far side was vast marshland. To the south, endless forest. Looking north, there was nothing but the snowcapped End Mountains, jutting upward to pierce the sky. Her days flying over those peaks on her dragon were nothing but distant memories now.

She wanted to see beautiful vistas with her own eyes. The bountiful blessings of earth and sun here should be enough to heal the eye that she'd lost at Central Cathedral half a year ago, but Alice was not yet ready to use sacred arts to fix her own shortcomings.

Because even with this breathtaking view of late autumn before them, the young man with her could only gaze dully into nothingness. She sat next to the wheelchair and leaned on one of the large wheels.

"It's beautiful. More beautiful than any painting hanging on the walls of the cathedral," she said, smiling. "It's the world you saved, Kirito."

A single white waterfowl ran across the surface of the lake, sending up concentric ripples, and took off into flight.

How long had they sat there?

The next thing she knew, Solus was high overhead. It was time they got back to the cabin so she could fix lunch. In his current state, Kirito ate only a small amount at a time, so if she missed any of his meals, it would have an effect on his maximum life value.

"Let's head back," she said, getting up and taking the wheelchair handles.

Just then, she heard the sound of footsteps on the grassy

hillside and turned around. A girl in a black monastery robe was approaching. There was a dazzling, sunny smile on her young face as she waved wildly.

"Sister!" she cried out, her voice traveling on the breeze. Alice broke into a smile herself and raised her hand to wave back.

The girl raced up the last ten mels, skidded to a halt, and paused to catch her breath before bursting out with "Good morning, Alice!"

Then she hopped to the side and greeted the wheelchair-bound boy. "Good morning, Kirito!"

She beamed at him, seemingly unbothered by his lack of response, but the moment her eyes drifted down to the swords resting on his lap, a note of sadness crept over her expression.

"...Good morning, Eugeo," she whispered, reaching out to brush the scabbard of the Blue Rose Sword. If an unfamiliar person attempted to do the same thing, Kirito might give the faintest bit of a defensive reaction, but he allowed this to happen without comment.

With her greetings finished, the girl straightened up again and turned to Alice.

Conscious of the odd warmth within her now, Alice replied, "Good morning, Selka. I'm surprised you knew we were here."

It had taken over a month for her to refer to the girl by name without feeling strange about it.

Ever since Kirito had told her about the existence of her sister at Central Cathedral half a year ago, Alice had been desperate to meet her. But now that this wish had come true, the more she cared for Selka, the more she had to wonder whether she—not Alice Zuberg, but Alice Synthesis Thirty—was fit to be this girl's sister.

If Selka was aware of this inner turmoil, she didn't let it show through her beaming smile. "I didn't use sacred arts to search for you. I went to your house, and you weren't there, and since the weather's so nice today, I figured you would be here. I left some fresh milk and an apple-and-cheese pie I baked just this morning on your table. You should have them for lunch."

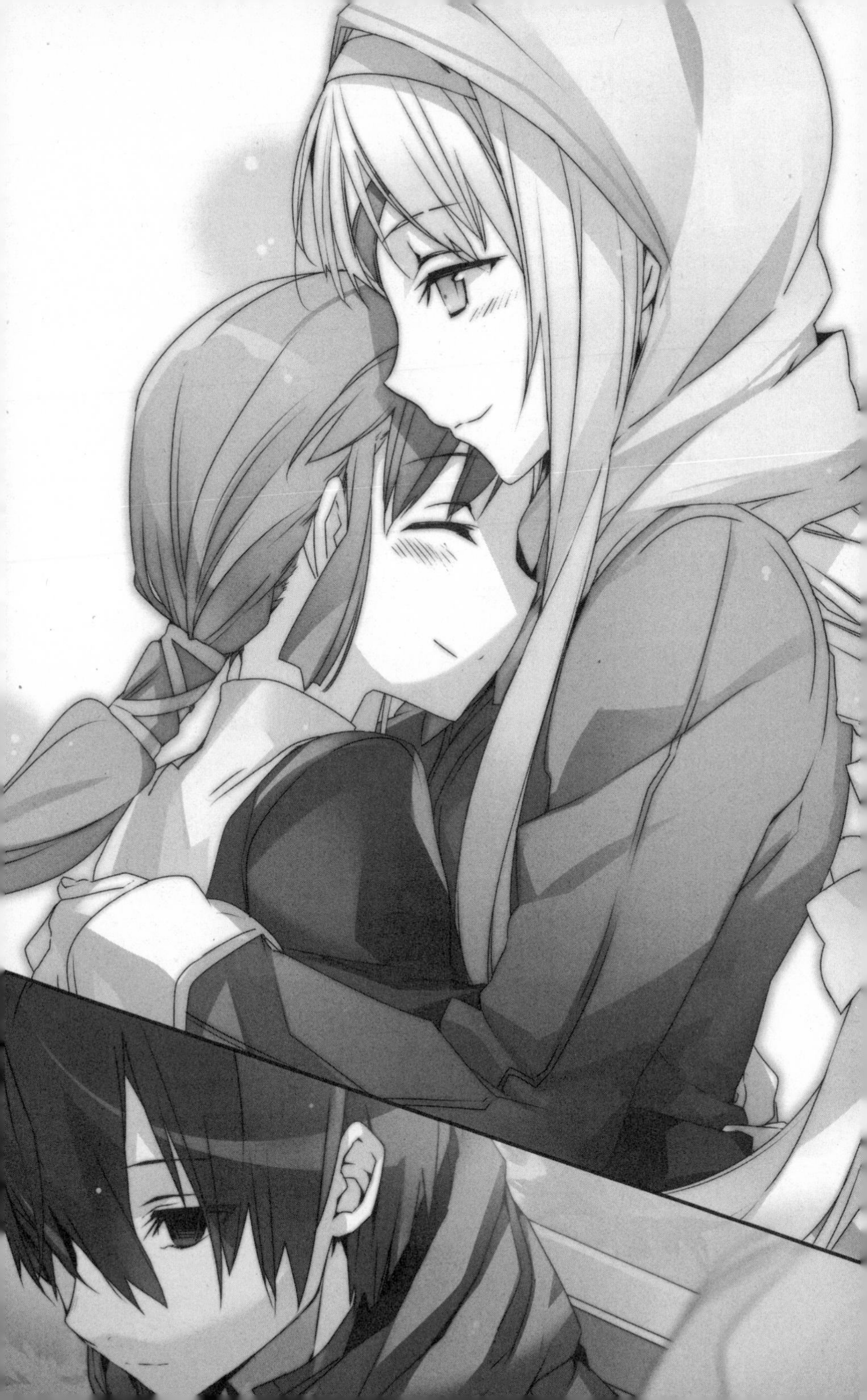

"Thank you. I appreciate that; I was just wondering what to prepare."

"If he has to eat nothing but *your* food, Kirito's going to up and leave you at some point!" Selka laughed.

Alice smiled back at her. "How dare you! I'll have you know that I can make pancakes without burning them now."

"Do I dare believe you? The first time, you tried using heat elements on them and turned them into charcoal!"

Alice tried to flick her forehead with a finger, but Selka dodged and went right in for an embrace. She pressed her face against Alice's chest, and Alice circled her arms around her sister's back.

It was for this moment alone that Alice wished she could be free from the pressure that weighed on her heart.

How much easier life would be if she could forget the guilt of abandoning her duty as an Integrity Knight to live in this quiet cabin in the remote forest. But Alice knew that she would never be able to forget it. Even as she embraced her sister here, the end was approaching from beyond the mountains—the tick of each passing second bringing it ever closer.

At the end of the ferocious battle at the Axiom Church's Central Cathedral half a year ago, Alice had fallen to the marble floor, suffering wounds severe enough to kill her and only vaguely aware of what happened in the fight.

A duel to the death between Administrator, pontifex of the church, and Kirito, who was wielding two swords at once.

Administrator, incinerated by the flames of Prime Senator Chudelkin's obsession.

Kirito witnessing Eugeo's passing, then screaming into a crystalline board that appeared at the north end of the chamber. At the end of an exchange that Alice did not understand, Kirito's body suddenly stiffened, and he fell to the floor—leaving the rest of the world in silence.

By the time Alice had recovered just enough life to move again,

Solus's first rays of morning were shining from the east window. With that light as her source of sacred power, Alice was able to heal Kirito's wounds. But he did not regain consciousness, and she was forced to leave him there and use healing arts on herself next before she examined the crystal board at last.

But the glowing purple surface was now dark, and no amount of touching or commanding would provoke any response from it.

At a loss, Alice sat.

She had taken Kirito's word and fought against the absolute tyrant Administrator for the sake of the people and her distant sister, but deep down, she hadn't actually expected to survive.

When the horrific soldier that Administrator called a Sword Golem ran her through—

When she used her body as a shield against the devastating thunderbolt—

When she flung herself in front of the sword that attempted to end Kirito's life—

Alice had been ready for death at several moments throughout the fight. But through the sacrifices of the little sage Cardinal, the peculiar spider named Charlotte, and Eugeo, as well as Kirito's awe-inspiring tenacity, she had survived.

You saved my life! Now accept the responsibility for your actions! she had screamed at the black-haired youth lying on the ground beside her. But he never opened his eyes. It was as though he were telling her, *Now you have to think for yourself and choose your own path.*

After many minutes of cradling her knees, Alice finally got to her feet.

With the disappearance of the room's master, the levitating disc was just as powerless as the crystal panel, so she had to destroy it with her sword. Then she put Kirito over her back and jumped down to the ninety-ninth floor.

From there, she descended the long staircase, past the senators— who were still mindlessly chanting their sacred arts—to the grand stairs of the cathedral and headed straight for her sword master, Bercouli Synthesis One, whom she'd left in the great bath.

The bathwater that Eugeo's Perfect Weapon Control art had frozen was almost completely melted now, so Bercouli was floating, splayed out in the water. Fortunately, Chudelkin's petrification art had been undone.

She heaved his large body onto the walkway and smacked his cheeks, calling out, "Uncle!" and the knight gave one huge sneeze before opening his eyes.

He greeted her lazily, asking whether it was morning already, and Alice tried to explain everything that had happened. When all was said and done, Bercouli looked stern and alert, but in a comforting voice, he said, "You did well, Little Miss."

From there, the commander of the knights moved quickly. Starting with Vice Commander Fanatio, who was unharmed in the rose garden despite her defeat to Kirito and Eugeo, he gathered up the other Integrity Knights who'd been petrified in punishment, such as Deusolbert and Eldrie, then took them to the Great Hall of Ghostly Light on the fiftieth floor and told them all he could of the truth.

That after a battle with two disciples from North Centoria Imperial Swordcraft Academy, Administrator had been defeated and eradicated.

That the pontifex had been working on a terrifying plan to transform most of the citizens of the realm into monstrous weapons with swords for bones.

That the senate, the body that controlled the knighthood, was essentially composed of just one man, Prime Senator Chudelkin, who had perished along with the pontifex.

The only thing that wasn't explained was the truth of the Integrity Knights—of how they were "produced." Bercouli had been skeptical of Administrator's tale that they were summoned from the celestial realm, so he was able to withstand the shock of the truth, but he determined that more time and care would need to be taken to reveal this to the other knights.

Even then, Eldrie, Fanatio, and the others were absolutely stunned. It was impossible to blame them. The absolute ruler for centuries, who exhibited godlike powers, was suddenly gone, just like that? It was not an easy thing to accept.

At the end of a fierce, chaotic debate, the knights decided to follow the commander's orders for the moment. Perhaps much of that was due to the presence of not just Bercouli's charisma and leadership, but the continued function of their Piety Modules. Despite the changing situation, they were still knights who served the Axiom Church, and now that Administrator and Chudelkin were gone, Commander Bercouli was undoubtedly the highest-ranking member of the church remaining.

The moment Bercouli was entrusted with leading, his mind began working toward his original duty of protecting the human realm. He, too, would have had his own doubts, naturally. He had just learned that stolen memories of his beloved had been close at hand for all those years.

Yet, he decided to firmly seal off the hundredth floor with its thirty swords for the Sword Golem and the hundreds of memory crystals inside and to hide everything from the knighthood except for the death of their sovereign. He prioritized the mission to prepare for the coming invasion from the Dark Territory over recovering the memories of all the Integrity Knights, himself included.

Bercouli started rebuilding the broken knighthood, as well as reforming and retraining the Imperial Knights of the four empires, which had had armies in name alone. Alice helped him with this, of course. With Kirito's impromptu eye patch tied around her head, she whizzed north and south all over Centoria.

But she could not remain at the cathedral forever. Among the other Integrity Knights and the church's rank and file that were unaware of the pontifex's death, there was a growing demand that the traitor who'd rebelled against the Axiom Church—the still-comatose Kirito—be put to death for his crimes.

One morning, after her work was done for the time being,

Alice took Kirito onto a dragon with her and left the city. It was two weeks after the bloodshed of that fearsome battle.

But that was only the beginning of her labor. While they camped out, an experience she was unfamiliar with, Kirito remained unconscious. She knew he needed a good set of walls and a roof over his head, not to mention a nice warm bed, but she didn't have enough money for them to stay at an inn, and she was unable to bring herself to make use of her Integrity Knight status for personal gain.

That was when she remembered the name of Rulid, a place Kirito had mentioned while they were stuck on the outside wall of the tower.

Even if her memories were gone, surely the people who lived in Alice and Eugeo's hometown would welcome them, or so she hoped. And thus, she guided the reins of the dragon north. She flew only a bit at a time to minimize the strain on Kirito's body, so the trip across Norlangarth to the village at the foothills of the End Mountains took three whole days.

She landed in the forest a distance away from the village so as not to startle the inhabitants, then commanded the dragon to watch her cargo and carried Kirito toward Rulid on foot.

Along the way from the forest down the footpath through the fields, she met a number of villagers. They were all shocked and wary, and none of them called out to her.

The moment she arrived at Rulid, which was built on a little plateau, and passed through its wooden gate, a large young man leaped out of the nearby guard station. His freckled face was flushed as he blocked her way.

"Stop! Outsiders are not allowed in the village!" the young man-at-arms bellowed, making a menacing show of placing his hand on his sword. Then he noticed Kirito's face, slung over Alice's shoulder, and he stopped in his tracks, suspicious. He started mumbling something to himself before he then got a better look at Alice, and this time his eyes bulged.

"You...*you*! It can't be...!"

This reaction actually came as a relief to Alice. After eight years, this man-at-arms seemed to still remember her. Choosing her words carefully, she replied, "I am Alice. Please call the elder, Gasfut Zuberg."

Perhaps she should have called herself Alice Zuberg, but she couldn't bring herself to do it. Her first name alone seemed to suffice, however. His face instantly went from red to blue, his mouth flapped wordlessly, and he dashed off into the village. He didn't tell her to wait there, so she went through the gate and walked in after the guard.

Pretty soon, the village was buzzing like a beehive that had been disturbed. Dozens of villagers crowded the sides of the path, exclaiming with shock as soon as they saw Alice in the afternoon sunlight.

But none of them appeared to be rejoicing in the return of one of their own. If anything, they were suspicious of the woman in her metal armor and the young man sleeping on her back—even fearful.

The gentle slope eventually met a round open space at the center of the village. There was a fountain and well in the center, and at the north end, a small church with a circled cross on its roof. Alice came to a stop at the start of this clearing as the villagers looked on and whispered in fear from a safe distance.

Minutes later, the crowd parted from the east, and a man strode forward with firm intent. He was of advanced age, with a cleanly kept gray beard, and it was clear to her at once that this was the village elder of Rulid, Alice's one-time father, Gasfut Zuberg.

Gasfut came to a stop a short distance away and examined both Alice and Kirito without expression.

Ten seconds later, he spoke in a voice that carried well despite its softness.

"Is that you, Alice?"

Alice merely said, "Yes." But the elder did not approach her or reach out to her. In a sterner voice than before, he asked, "Why are you here? Have your crimes been forgiven?"

She didn't have an immediate answer. She didn't actually know what her crimes were, nor whether they had been forgiven or not.

Young Alice Zuberg had been taken by Deusolbert to Centoria for the crime of entering the Dark Territory, according to what Kirito had told her. That was indeed a violation of the Taboo Index. But as an Integrity Knight, Alice was no longer bound by that taboo. The only law to a knight was the order of the pontifex. And now that pontifex was gone. From now on, she would have to define sin, forgiveness, good, and evil for herself...

With this thought weighing on her mind, Alice stared into the elder's eyes and replied, "As punishment for my crimes, I have lost all memory of my life as a resident of this village. I do not know if this counts as forgiveness, but I have nowhere else to go."

It was Alice's true, unvarnished opinion.

Gasfut closed his eyes. Deep furrows appeared along his mouth and brow. When his thoughtful frown disappeared, his eyes were harsh—and his words, even more so.

"Begone. We cannot allow a criminal to stay in this village."

Selka seemed to sense Alice's momentary tension. She looked up, confused.

"Sister...?" she whispered.

But Alice just smiled down at her. "It's nothing. Come, let's head back."

"...Okay," Selka said, releasing her hold but giving Alice a concerned look before her joyful smile returned. "I'll push the chair as far as the fork in the road!"

She stood behind Kirito's wheelchair and gripped the handles with her tiny hands. Not only was the chair itself heavy, it also held the weight of one (admittedly gaunt) adult person and one and a half Divine Object swords resting on it. It should have been too heavy for a fourteen-year-old apprentice nun who wasn't used to physical labor—but the first time Selka had tried it, leaning forward with her feet firmly planted, the wheelchair rolled slowly forward.

"It's a downward slope, so be careful."

Selka hadn't toppled the wheelchair yet, but it was still hard not to be concerned.

"I'm fine, Sister. You're just too much of a worrywart," she said. Apparently, when Alice had lived in Rulid, she'd done plenty of exploring and experiments with Eugeo but had been overly protective of her younger sister.

Did her basic personality remain the same even without her memory, or was it just a coincidence? Alice couldn't help but wonder about this as she walked alongside Selka, who was absorbed in her job of pushing the wheelchair.

Once they reached the foot of the hill, the downward slope became a flat path. Selka did her best to push the chair along, now that it was heavier. As she stared at her sister hard at work, Alice found her mind drifting again into the past.

The day she was denied entry to the village, she had resigned herself to her fate as an outsider, feeling lost and dejected until Selka found her and called out to her at the tree line. Selka knew she was acting against her father's wishes, and without her bravery and the benevolence of Old Man Garitta, Alice would surely still be wandering in the wilderness today.

Certainly, the story would have been difficult for Selka to accept, too—that her sister had finally returned home and yet didn't remember anything of the past. That Kirito, who had spent a brief but memorable stay at the village, was now in a coma. And that Eugeo, who had been like a brother to her, was dead...

But the only time Selka cried was upon hearing the news that Eugeo would not be coming back. Since then, she had never been around Alice without a smile on her face. The strength of her heart and breadth of her benevolence never failed to amaze Alice. It was a strength more powerful and divine than any priest's sacred arts or knight's sword.

It was also a daily reminder of just how powerless Alice was now that she was no longer a member of the Axiom Church.

With Garitta's help, she built a small but sturdy cabin in the woods just two kilors away from the village. Her first order of business after that was to apply powerful healing arts to Kirito, who was still in a coma.

On one cloudless day, she had headed to the most verdant spot in the forest to receive the greatest possible blessing of both Solus and Terraria, using the vast sacred power to generate ten light elements and apply them to Kirito's body as treatment.

The healing art took Alice's entire being and soul to produce, and it was powerful enough to heal not just a human, but the life of a massive dragon all the way to full in a single instant. No matter how deep Kirito's wounds were, she knew that even his severed arm would immediately be restored, and he would wake up in perfect condition at once.

Once the brilliant spiritual light dissipated, Kirito's lids did indeed open—but without any illumination in those vacant pools of black. Alice said his name over and over, shook his shoulders, even clung to his chest and screamed, but all he did was stare blankly at the sky. She couldn't even restore his missing arm.

Four months had passed since that day, and there had not been a single sign that Kirito's mind would ever return.

At every opportunity, Selka said that with how diligently she was caring for him, the old Kirito was sure to return someday. But silently, Alice feared this might never happen. It might be beyond her means.

Especially for a person who was nothing but a creation of Administrator.

Alice was pulled out of her reminiscence when Selka finally broke her silence and said, "I need…a break" and stopped pushing the wheelchair.

She reached down and put her hand on her younger sister's back as the girl panted and glistened with sweat.

"Thank you, Selka. I'll push it from here."

"I was gonna try…to get it all the way…to the fork…"

"You got it a hundred mels farther than the last time. You've been a huge help to me."

Since coming to the village, Alice had learned that a much older sister was supposed to show her appreciation by giving the younger one a bit of an allowance, but she didn't have a single copper in her pockets now. With her current finances, losing even a single *shia* in the forest would be devastating, so she did not carry coins unless she was heading to the market to buy something.

Instead, she smoothed Selka's brown hair with her palm. Her sister gave her a happy smile, breathing normally again, but there was a trace of sadness there as well.

"What's wrong, Selka?" she asked, taking the wheelchair handles. "Is something troubling you?"

Selka hesitated. "Um…Mr. Barbossa wanted you…to take down a tree in the clearing again…"

"Oh, that's all? You don't have to feel bad about bringing that request to me. Thank you for letting me know," Alice said, favoring her with a smile.

But her sister's expression went from a downcast gaze to genuine sadness. "It's just…they're so selfish, aren't they? Don't you agree, Kirito?"

Naturally, the boy in the wheelchair did not react. But Selka carried on with renewed conviction anyway.

"Mr. Barbossa and Mr. Ridack won't let you live in the village, but they're more than happy to ask you for help when they need it. I know I'm the one passing on their message, but you don't have to do this. I can bring you all the food you need from home."

Alice giggled at the outraged pout on her sister's face and said, "I appreciate your offer, but honestly, it's all right, Selka. I like the home I have now, and I'm grateful that I'm still allowed to be close to the village…Once I've fed Kirito his lunch, I'll be right there. Which area was it?"

"The one to the south," Selka mumbled, then walked alongside the wheelchair in silence.

When they were nearly to the fork in the road that led to the log cabin, Selka spoke up again. "Sister, my training period will be over next year, and I'll receive a small stipend after that. You won't need to help them anymore at that point. I can take care of you and Kirito...I can do it for as long as..."

She lost her words then, and Alice hugged her gently. She pressed her cheek against the girl's brown hair, which was a different color than her own but felt very similar, and whispered, "Thank you...But I'm happy enough just knowing you are nearby, Selka..."

Selka left, turning back to wave again and again in obvious reluctance, and Alice returned to the log cabin with Kirito at last, to prepare for their lunch.

She'd learned how to handle the household chores after much practice, but cooking was still a skill that eluded her. Compared to the Osmanthus Blade, the knife she'd bought at the village general store was so flimsy and weak that it took twenty or thirty minutes just to chop up the ingredients.

Thankfully, she had Selka's fresh-baked pie today, so she cut a small piece to feed Kirito. She had to put the forkful of pie next to his mouth and wait patiently for him to part his lips so she could stick it into his mouth. Slowly, slowly, Kirito would chew the food, merely reliving distant memories of eating.

While he chewed, she, too, tasted the apple-and-cheese pie. It was probably baked by Elder Gasfut's wife, Sadina Zuberg—Selka and Alice's mother.

When she lived in Central Cathedral, the tables of the dining hall were laden with every delicacy from all over the world. The flavor and appearance of Sadina's pie paled in comparison, but it seemed far more delicious. She didn't particularly like how Kirito's reaction was slightly more enthusiastic for the pie than it was for her own cooking, however.

After the meal was done and she'd cleaned up, she put Kirito back into the wheelchair and laid the swords across his knees.

Outside the cabin, the afternoon sunlight shone golden upon their approach. The days were much shorter now, and evening snuck up fast. She rushed them back to the fork to the south and headed west this time.

Eventually, the forest gave way to a barley field nearly ready for harvest. Beyond the heavy stalks was the sight of Rulid on its hill. In the midst of the red-brick roofs was a spire that jutted above all else: Selka's church.

Neither Selka nor Sister Azalia, the nun who ran the church, was aware that Central Cathedral, the seat of power for the Axiom Church, which presided over the four empires, was now just a hollow structure without a master. Still, that didn't prevent the little church and its orphanage from running smoothly.

If the cathedral was in chaos after the death of Administrator, it had no effect whatsoever on the lives of the populace. The Taboo Index still functioned, constricting the minds of the people. Would they be able to pick up swords and protect their lands from disaster?

If the order came from the Axiom Church and the emperors, they would presumably obey. But that alone would not be enough to defeat the forces of darkness. At the very least, Commander Bercouli was wise enough to recognize that glaring truth.

What would decide the battle to come was not priority level of weapons nor authority level of arts—it was willpower. Kirito's battle had proven that with the way he overcame a devastating disadvantage of strength to defeat multiple Integrity Knights, Prime Senator Chudelkin, and even Administrator.

As she approached the village, proudly absorbing the gazes of caution and fear from the residents working in the barley fields, Alice sent a silent message to her sword mentor.

Uncle, peace might not be a thing to fight for, according to the common people, but a thing that is constantly and eternally given to them. And the ones who did that...are the Axiom Church, the Taboo Index, and us, the Integrity Knights.

At this very moment, Commander Bercouli was probably

busy in Centoria, training the armies of the four empires and arranging production of arms. Perhaps he was already sending troops to the Eastern Gate at the far end of the Eastavarieth Empire, where the battle would likely be the most intense. He must want every last knight he could marshal, whether for their assistance in management or just for pure battle ability.

But here I am now...

Reflecting on her current situation, she passed through the barley fields into where they were clearing the forest south of the village, and she stopped the wheelchair before a huge mound of dirt so she could survey the vast area.

Just two years ago, this had been a massive forest, even larger than the one to the east where they lived in the cabin now. But after Kirito and Eugeo cut down the monstrous Gigas Cedar that ruled over the woods and absorbed every last bit of its holy power, the men of the village were obsessed with expanding their fields, Selka had told her with annoyance.

At the center of the clearing was the tremendous black stump of the tree, and at the south end, there were dozens of villagers industriously chopping away. One of them, a burly man busying himself with orders rather than using an ax for himself, was Nigel Barbossa, the owner of the biggest farm in the village.

Reluctantly, Alice rolled the wheelchair down the small footpath. Kirito showed no reaction as he passed the stump of the enormous tree he had once cut down. He simply stared downward, cradling his swords.

The first to notice the approaching pair were the youngsters of the Barbossa clan, who were resting atop the stumps of newly felled trees. The trio appeared to be around fifteen or sixteen years old and gazed greedily at Alice with her golden hair and scarf, then glanced at Kirito in the wheelchair. They muttered to one another and chuckled.

After she passed without paying them any heed, one of the youths lazily called out, "Uncle, she's heeeere."

Nigel Barbossa stopped yelling orders and spun around, hands on his hips, a wide smile across his plump face. Something about his large mouth and beady eyes reminded her of Chudelkin.

Alice returned his smile to the best of her ability and bowed. "Good afternoon, Mr. Barbossa. I heard that you wanted me for something…"

"Ah, yes! Thank you for coming, Alice," he said, stomach jiggling as he approached, arms outstretched. She prepared herself for a possible attempt at a hug, but fortunately, the sight of the wheelchair in front of her made him reconsider.

Instead, he stood just fifty cens to the right of her and twirled around, indicating a huge tree that stood at the border of the forest and the clearing. "Do you see that? We've been working round the clock on that infernal platinum oak since yesterday morning, but even ten grown men with axes have barely been able to nick it."

He made a gesture with his index finger and thumb to describe a small semicircle.

The enormous oak, a good mel and a half across, stood thoroughly rooted in place, resisting the woodcutters' efforts. Two men were trading strikes from either side of the cut, which was indeed less than ten cens in depth.

Sweat was pouring off the shirtless men like waterfalls. The muscles of their chest and arms were thick, but it was clear from the inconsistency of their swinging that they did not have regular experience with an ax.

Even as she watched, one of the men's feet slid a bit, and the blade hit diagonally. The handle of the ax broke about halfway up, and he fell hard on his backside to uproarious laughter from the others in his vicinity.

"What are those fools doing…?" growled Nigel, then he turned back to Alice. "At this rate, there's no telling how many days it will take to get rid of this one tree. And in the time we've wasted on this, Ridack's team has added another twenty mels of land in each direction!"

Barbossa was referring to the next most-wealthy farming

family in the village. He kicked at a pebble in frustration and snorted, nostrils flaring. But his scowl quickly transformed into his massive smile again as he wheedled, "So while I know our arrangement is for once every month, I was hoping you might give us some help in this one special case, Alice. You may not remember that on several occasions when you were young, I reluc—er, generously gave you sweets to enjoy. You were such a sweet young girl back then. Er, as you still are now, of course…"

Alice avoided rolling her eye as she cut him off. "I understand your problem, Mr. Barbossa. But only if it's this one time."

It was currently Alice's calling—no, just her means of making a living—to clear out trees and rocks, like this platinum oak, that proved especially difficult to the process of clearing the forest for farmland.

Naturally, this was not an official job. About a month after they'd settled into the cabin in the woods, there was an incident with fallen rocks blocking the path to the pasture to the west. When Alice came across it and moved the boulder all on her own, word spread throughout the village, and people started coming to her for help.

If she was going to live with Kirito like this, they'd need at least *some* money, so she was grateful to have a job to do. But Selka was worried that if she kept accepting any task, the men would never stop coming to her, so she set up a system: Each farm could ask Alice for help only once a month.

Despite being beholden to the Taboo Index, Norlangarth Basic Imperial Laws, and the village precepts, Nigel was asking for a second task within the month in violation of that agreement, but Alice was not surprised by this. It wasn't because, like Alice and Eugeo, he'd broken through the seal in his right eye—what the pontifex had called Code 871. It was simply that he viewed Alice as being beneath him. In other words, the powerful farm owner didn't need to waste his time upholding a deal with some former criminals who lived in a dismal shack on the outskirts of town.

Meanwhile, Alice nodded to Nigel again and left the wheel-chair behind. She checked on Kirito just in case, but he seemed unconcerned with the fuss around them, so she gave him a silent reassurance that it wouldn't take long and headed for the platinum oak.

When the men spotted her, they leered and made a show of clicking their tongues in irritation. They were all aware of her strength by now, however, so they silently moved away from the tree.

She took their place and drew a quick sigil of sacred script with her right hand, bringing up a Stacia Window. The tree's life value was tremendous, which explained why ten grown men had struggled to cut it. Its priority level was too high for her to borrow their axes this time.

Instead, she trotted back to the wheelchair, crouched, and whispered, "I'm sorry, Kirito. I need to borrow your sword for a little while."

She brushed the black leather scabbard with her hand and sensed his arm tensing as it cradled the weapon. But when she stared patiently into the blank pools of his eyes, his arm eventually went limp, and from deep in his throat, he croaked, "...Aaah..."

Rather than an utterance of will, it was more likely the echo of some memory, Alice interpreted. The only thing controlling Kirito now was not conscious thought, but whatever memories still lingered in his heart.

"Thank you," she whispered, retrieving the black sword from his lap. Once she was sure he would be fine without it, she returned to the oak tree.

It really was a beautiful specimen. Not quite as grand as the ancient trees scattered around Centoria, perhaps, but easily more than a century old. Mentally, she apologized to the tree, then took a stance.

She placed her right foot forward with her left in the rear. She held the Night-Sky Blade in her left hand and placed her right hand on its leather-wrapped hilt. With her one good eye, she gauged her distance to the tree.

"Come on, now, are you really going to cut down that massive oak with your flimsy little sword?" one of the men shouted, prompting a gale of laughter from those nearby. Others chimed in, claiming her sword would break or the sun would set first.

Eventually Nigel said, with great consternation, "Er, Alice, it would be appreciated if you could do the task in about an hour…"

She'd cut down over ten trees since she'd started her job, and they always took no more than thirty minutes. This was because she had to carefully limit her strength so as not to destroy the axes they gave her to use. This time, however, there was no need. The Night-Sky Blade was a Divine Object with the same priority level as her own Osmanthus Blade.

"It will not take that long," she muttered, squeezing the hilt.

Then she shouted, "Haaah!!" An explosion of dust burst up from her right foot in front.

It had been a long time since she had last swung a real sword; fortunately, she hadn't forgotten any techniques. The level slash shot from the sheath like black lightning.

None of the men around her actually saw it, apparently. Once the sword was fully outstretched to her right, Alice straightened up and met their baffled gazes.

The smooth bark of the platinum oak was unmarred aside from the mark the men had been chipping away at for the past day—or so they thought.

At last, one of them wondered, "Did she miss?" and a few of them cackled.

Alice turned back to the one who'd spoken, lowering her sword. "It's going to fall your way."

"Huh? What are you—?"

The man paused, his eyes bulging. The trunk of the oak was very slowly starting to tilt. Like those around him, he suddenly wailed and started running the other way.

With a tremendous rumble, the gigantic tree toppled onto the place where the men had been standing just three seconds before.

Alice made her way back to the stump, waving away the dust. The rings of the tree were thick on the fresh cross section and shone as though polished. There was just one end of the stump that was still jagged and torn.

She wondered whether that was because she was losing her edge or whether it was due to the lack of depth perception with only one eye. As she turned away, she nearly jumped out of her skin. Nigel Barbossa was rushing toward her with a huge grin and arms wide.

Her rough handling of the sword made for a menacing clink as it slid back into the sheath, which brought Nigel up short. But the smile never left as he rubbed his hands together.

"Won…wonder…wonderful! That was incredible! So much for Zink, the chief man-at-arms! That was simply divine!" he babbled at a distance of a mel—his expression equal parts delight and greed. "Wh-what do you say, Alice? I'll double your pay if you work once a week for me rather than once per month…No! Once a day, even!"

He was rubbing his hands at high speed now. Alice merely shook her head.

"No, thank you. What you are paying me now is enough."

If she brought the Osmanthus Blade and used its Perfect Weapon Control art, she could do more than one tree a day—she could reduce this entire forest to flat land as far as the eye could see in a matter of minutes. But if she did so, it would only change their demands into tilling the land, breaking the rocks, even making the rain fall.

Nigel grumbled at her rejection and didn't seem to remember she was there until she said, "My payment."

"Ah, yes, of course, of course." He put his hand into his pocket and pulled out a bulging sack, then plucked out a 100-*shia* silver coin, as he had promised her, dropped it into her palm, and tried his luck again. "Alice, how about this? If I pay you another silver, would you consider retracting your offer to Ridack for this month…?"

She held her breath, preparing to turn him down again, when a heavy thud caught her attention. She looked up with a start and saw that the wheelchair had toppled over, sending Kirito to the ground.

"…Kirito!" she shouted, running past Nigel to him.

Kirito was reaching forward desperately with his left arm as he lay on the ground. In that direction, the loafing young men had balanced the longsword in its white-leather sheath upright on the ground and were exclaiming over it.

"Whoa, why is it so heavy?!"

"No wonder she could cut down a platinum oak in one swing with it."

"Hey, you guys, hold it straight!" cried a third, who grabbed the hilt of the Blue Rose Sword with both hands so he could pull it out.

Alice actually heard the sound of her jaws grinding. A cry left her throat before she was even aware of it herself. "You scoundrels—!"

The boys turned to her, mouths agape. She crossed the twelve mels between them in an instant and came to a stop with dust swirling around her. The three backed away when they saw the look on her face.

Alice took a deep breath and used it to stifle the explosion threatening to erupt from within her. She helped Kirito get up first, put him back in his wheelchair, then hissed, "That sword belongs to him. Give it back now."

Suddenly, the young men looked aggrieved. The large one who'd been about to draw the sword pointed at Kirito, his lip curled. "We asked him to let us borrow it."

Even sitting in the wheelchair, Kirito was reaching for the white sword, moaning weakly.

One of the youngsters holding up the sheath said mockingly, "He was happy to lend it to us. He was like, 'Aaah, aaah.'"

The last of them nodded and agreed, laughing.

Alice had to keep her hand tight on the handle of the wheelchair—if she didn't, she would grab the handle of the Night-Sky Blade and draw it instead.

Half a year ago, she would have cut off all six arms that dared to touch the sword without a moment's hesitation. An Integrity Knight was not bound by the Taboo Index and its rules against harming others. As a matter of fact, without the seal in her right eye to bind her, there was no law at all that limited Alice's behavior.

But...

Alice clenched her teeth painfully, fighting against her urges. These young men were the common folk that Kirito and Eugeo had sacrificed their lives to protect. She couldn't harm them. It wasn't what *they* would have wanted.

She stayed absolutely still and silent for several seconds, but she didn't do a very good job of hiding the fury that blazed in her remaining eye. The three boys stopped laughing, their smiles replaced by fearful looks.

"...All right, all right. Geez, you don't have to get so mad," the largest boy said, sulking as he released the handle. The other two followed his cue and let go of the sheath, almost relieved that they didn't have to support its weight anymore. It toppled heavily to the ground.

Alice walked over without a word, crouched, and easily lifted the white-leather sheath with no more than three fingers. As she turned back, she paused for a moment to glare at the little imps before returning to the wheelchair.

After quickly dusting off the sheath with the hem of her cloak, she placed the black and white blades on Kirito's lap. He clutched them tight and went still.

Nigel Barbossa was absorbed in giving orders elsewhere, seemingly with no interest in the situation here. Alice gave him a little bow for propriety's sake—he wasn't paying attention—and wheeled the chair back to the path going north.

The surge of hot, stormy anger that had filled her for the first time in ages had turned into cold helplessness. This wasn't the first time she'd felt it since moving into the forest near Rulid. Most of the villagers avoided talking to her, and they hardly even treated vacant Kirito like a human being.

She wasn't blaming them. From their point of view, she was still the criminal who broke the Taboo Index. She ought to be grateful they allowed her to live close to the village and sold her essential goods and food.

But all the while, in a corner of her mind, she wondered, *To what end?*

To what end had she undergone all that suffering and fought with Administrator? What exactly was the thing that the other administrator, Cardinal; her intelligent spider, Charlotte; Eugeo; and Kirito had made such sacrifices to protect?

Those thoughts led her to a question that she knew she could never voice: Was there truly a point in protecting people like Barbossa's family?

That question was one of the reasons Alice had put down her sword and traveled to this distant region. Even now, on the far side of the Eastern Gate at the edge of Eastavarieth Empire, the forces of darkness were marching closer. It was a question of whether Commander Bercouli could get his new Human Guardian Army arranged and in place in time. She hadn't been stripped of her status as Integrity Knight—only the late Administrator could do that—so perhaps Alice ought to head for that gate as soon as possible.

But the Osmanthus Blade was far too heavy for her now.

The celestial realm she thought she had come from did not exist. The Axiom Church she swore fealty to was full of hypocrisy. She'd learned far too much of the ugliness and pettiness of the people of the human realm. The days when she could pray to the gods and swing her sword believing in the righteousness of her cause had long passed.

Now there was only a handful of human beings that Alice

truly wanted to protect. Her mother and father, Selka, Old Man Garitta, and Kirito. As long as she could keep them safe, she would be content to turn her back on the knighthood and live her days here in peace…

When they were out of the clearing and onto the path that wound through the barley fields, Alice stopped and whispered to Kirito, "Can I do some shopping in the village, since we're here? I won't let those nasty children mess with you again."

He didn't answer, but Alice took that as agreement and wheeled the chair north.

Her 100-*shia* silver coin bought her a week's worth of food and necessities. By the time they were heading back to their cabin in the forest, the sun had begun to set.

As she approached the porch, she detected the low hum of wind. Once the wheelchair was safely out of the way, she waited for the source to arrive in the center of the little clearing in the woods.

Eventually, an enormous flying dragon almost skimmed the treetops as it soared by—its massive wings, long neck, and silver tail all adding to its regal aspect. It was Alice's dragon, Amayori, who had flown them here from Centoria.

The dragon did two turns above the grassy clearing, then floated down to land. It folded its wings and stretched its neck until its nose brushed Kirito's chest, then it rested its large head against Alice.

She scratched at the silky, faintly blue hair under the dragon's chin, eliciting a purring gurgle from the beast.

"Amayori, you're getting fat. You've been eating too many fish at the lake," she scolded with a grin. The dragon snorted guiltily and began plodding toward its nest on the east side of the cabin. It curled up atop the bed of thickly stacked hay so its neck was intertwined with its tail.

Half a year ago, on the day she'd decided to build this cabin here in the clearing, Alice had undone the leather harness on

Amayori's head and removed the sacred arts of binding. She'd told the dragon, *You are free; go back to your nest in the western empire*, but the dragon would not leave her side.

The dragon collected grass to make its bed and spent the days on its own, frolicking in the forest and catching fish in the lake—but it always came back in the evening. The sacred arts that suppressed the dragon's proud, fierce nature and forced it into servitude to its knight's commands was gone. So why didn't it return to its home?

Still, the continued and willing presence of Amayori, who had been with her ever since she became an Integrity Knight, was a welcome development, and Alice did not try to drive it off. Occasionally, the sight of the dragon overhead caused more rumors about Alice among the villagers, but it was pointless to worry about that now.

Amayori began to snore softly atop the hay, so Alice bade it a good night and pushed the wheelchair into the cabin.

Dinner that night was a stew of half-moon beans and meatballs. The beans were too hard, and the meatballs were all different sizes, but the flavor was really coming together, she thought. Kirito didn't offer any comments, of course. He just let her stick the spoon in his mouth and chewed and swallowed as if that was all he could remember how to do.

If only she at least knew what he liked and didn't like to eat. Moments like this reminded her that the total amount of time she had really spoken to this young man was not even an entire day. Two years ago, Selka had lived in the church with him for a period, but she said that he seemed to enjoy everything he was served, regardless of what it was. It seemed fitting for Kirito.

At last, Kirito finished his stew, so she moved his chair over to the small heater, then washed the utensils and placed them in the basket.

Just then, she heard Amayori, who would normally sleep outside until dawn, growling in a soft trill. She paused and listened intently. With the whisper of the breeze coming through the forest was the unseasonal frail rustle of dead branches, then the sound of large wings beating.

"...!"

She leaped out of the kitchen, made sure that Kirito was behaving in his chair, then threw open the front door. Able to hear more clearly now, she determined that whatever was slicing through the wind was coming closer. She descended the porch and looked up at the night sky.

Against the backdrop of the stars, a black shadow was descending in a spiral—a dragon. She glanced to the east, just in case, and saw that Amayori was still on the bed, of course, looking up at the sky.

"Could it be...?"

She was about to turn back for her sword, thinking that a dark knight from over the End Mountains had invaded, when she saw the scales of the dragon gleam silver in the moonlight. Her shoulders relaxed just the tiniest bit. The only ones who rode dragons with silver scales were the Integrity Knights of the Axiom Church.

But it was still too early to be completely at ease. Who would have flown out all this way? Were they still discussing the idea of punishing Kirito the traitor? Had they dispatched an agent of justice from the cathedral at last?

Amayori crawled out of the bed, sensing Alice's worry, and lifted its head high to growl again. The threatening noise soon made way for a much sweeter purr.

Alice understood why very quickly.

The dragon did three more circles before landing on the south end of the clearing. Its own fuzzy beard was colored similarly to Amayori's. This was Amayori's older brother, Takiguri. Which meant that its rider was...

A knight clad in platinum armor and helmet leaped smoothly to the ground. Alice called out to him in a hard voice. "I'm impressed that you found me. What do you want, Eldrie Synthesis Thirty-One?"

The only Integrity Knight with a number younger than Alice's Thirty did not speak at first. He put his right hand to his chest and bowed deeply. Then he stood up and removed his helmet. His lustrous pale-purple hair wafted in the night breeze, and his city-boy good looks came into view. His voice was higher and softer than the average man's.

"It has been too long, Master Alice. While you are dressed differently than I remember, your beauty still amazes me. The thought of my mentor's golden hair gleaming in the moonlight was so captivating, I could not help but pay a visit with an excellent vintage from the collection."

His left hand emerged from behind his back to reveal a wine bottle. Alice did her best not to sigh, and she answered her strange disciple, "I'm happy to see that your wounds have healed—sadly, your personality has not changed for the better. In fact, if anything, your way of speaking reminds me a bit more of Prime Senator Chudelkin's."

Eldrie gurgled a bit. She turned her back on him and walked toward the cabin.

"Erm, Alice...?"

"If you have something important to say, I'll hear you out inside. If not, you can drink your wine alone and return to the city."

Takiguri and Amayori were rubbing their necks together, delighting in their first family reunion in half a year. Alice gave them a brief glance and returned to the cabin.

Eldrie followed her obediently inside and looked around the interior in wonder before his eyes stopped on Kirito, who was sitting motionless by the heater. He made no comment on the rebel who had once crossed swords with him. Instead, he slid around the far side of the table and pulled out a chair for Alice.

"..."

It felt silly to thank him for this, so she just exhaled instead and plopped onto the seat. Eldrie sat himself down across from her and placed the wine bottle on the table. A hint of a dark expression crossed his face the moment he got a good look at her, probably from seeing the black bandage that still covered her right eye. The agitation was gone the next instant, however. He looked around curiously, his nose twitching.

"...Something smells nice, Alice. Incidentally, I was in a hurry, so I haven't eaten dinner yet."

"How is that 'incidental'? And who would fly from Centoria to the distant mountains bearing wine but taking no travel rations along?"

"I swore to the trinity that I would never eat that limp, tasteless mush again. I'd rather starve and let my life drain away than survive on such—"

She rose from her seat before she was forced to listen to his entire answer. In the kitchen, she ladled the remaining stew from the pot on the stove onto a wooden plate and brought it to the table. Eldrie stared at the plate with a mixture of elation and suspicion.

"...Forgive my impertinence in asking, but...did you make this yourself...?"

"Yes, I did. Why do you ask?"

"...No reason. To eat my sword master's home cooking is a greater honor and joy than learning the secret ways of my weapon," he said nervously, grabbing the spoon and shoveling beans into his mouth.

As he chewed, Alice asked, "So how did you find this place? It's far enough from Centoria that no sacred art should reach here... And I don't imagine the knighthood is in a state to be sending dragons all over the realm just to find me."

Eldrie didn't answer her question right away; instead, he murmured about how surprisingly good the dish was, working the spoon quickly until his plate was clean. He looked up and dabbed at his mouth with a napkin that she hadn't seen him pull out.

"I followed the bond that exists between our souls," he said, fixing her with a look. "If only that were so. No, it was simple coincidence." He spread his hands theatrically. "A knight patrolling the

End Mountains sent word that the goblins and orcs to the north have been active. On the commander's orders, we collapsed the caves to the north, south, and west, and I was sent to confirm that they're not stubbornly trying to dig them out again."

"The...caves...?" Alice murmured. Of the four caves that went through the End Mountains, the south, west, and north caves were very narrow, and the ogres and giants that made up the bulk of the dark army's strength couldn't pass through. Therefore, it was assumed they would amass at the Eastern Gate, but Bercouli was thorough and decided to collapse the other three caves after he took full command.

It was with this knowledge that Alice had made the far north her hideout, but if the enemy dug the cave up again, that situation would change. Rulid would go from being a peaceful, sleepy village to the front line of a bloody war.

"And...did you confirm the actions of the forces of darkness?"

"I flew over the vicinity of the cave for an entire day, and I did not see a single goblin, much less any orcs," Eldrie said, shrugging. "I'm guessing it was all a big mistake, and they were confusing packs of wild animals for monsters."

"...Did you check inside the cave?"

"Of course. I examined it from the Dark Territory side, but the rocks filled it to the roof of the cave. They'd need an enormous platoon to dig that all loose. I was set to take us back to Centoria with that information in my pocket, when Takiguri started acting strangely. I let him fly where he wanted to, which turned out to be this place. I'm just as stunned as anyone. It's quite a coincidence... Or should I say, the work of fate?"

He finished with a dramatic flourish and the bravado of a bold knight.

"It is at such a time, when granted this rare opportunity, that my duty compels me to speak my mind. Please, Alice...return to the fold! We need your sword more than we need the addition of a thousand soldiers!"

She looked down to avoid his insistent gaze.

She knew.

She knew the fragile walls around the human realm were set to crumble to the ground, as well as how hard Commander Bercouli and his new Human Guardian Army were fighting to keep them up.

There was no way Alice could ever truly repay her mentor for protecting and guiding her, and it wasn't as though she'd completely abandoned her sense of solidarity with Eldrie and the other Integrity Knights. But these loyalties alone were not enough to bring her to fight.

Strength was the power of will itself. The battle in the cathedral had taught her this truth. If by sheer willpower, one could gain the advantage in the face of odds that spelled certain defeat, as Kirito had done, then willpower could also turn the greatest divine weapon into nothing more than a sad hunk of metal...

"...I cannot," she said, barely above a whisper.

Without missing a beat, Eldrie demanded, "Why not?"

He didn't wait for her answer. Instead, his gaze whipped to the young man sitting in the chair next to the heater.

"Is it because of him? Is the man who broke out of his cell in Central Cathedral and fought back against the knights, the prime senator, and even the pontifex herself still ensnaring your heart somehow? Because I will gladly seize the honor of cutting out the root of your uncertainty."

He squeezed hard on the edge of the table. Alice's remaining eye shot him a venomous glare. "Stop that!"

It wasn't very loud, but there was enough authority in her voice to bring the other knight to attention.

"He fought for the sake of the justice that he believed in," she snapped. "If not, how do you explain that he was able to defeat the supreme Integrity Knights and even our exalted commander? You fought against his blade. You should know its weight."

Creases of frustration formed on the bridge of his proud nose, but Eldrie did relax his shoulders. His eyes dropped to the table, and he confessed, "It is true that I find it difficult to accept the truth of Administrator's plan to turn half the population into

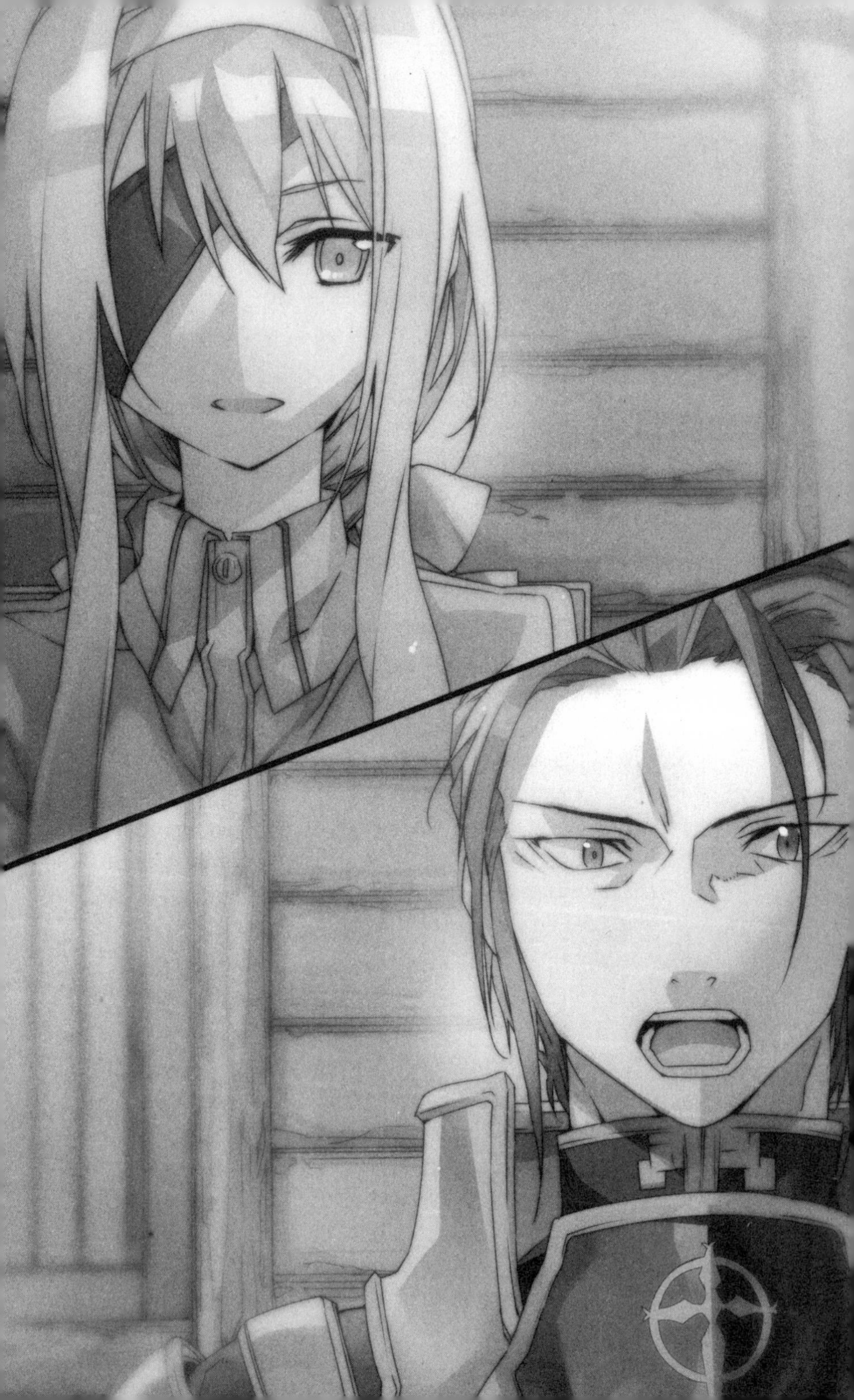

soulless soldiers with swords for bones. And without Kirito and his friend Eugeo, no one would have been able to stop that plan from becoming reality. And if Bercouli's story is true that their guide was the other pontifex, Cardinal, who once stood on equal footing with Administrator, then I have no desire to see Kirito's crimes tried and judged. But...but that only makes his actions harder to understand!"

His voice was plaintive and insistent—a confession of thoughts kept hidden until this moment.

"If Kirito the rebel is, as you claim, a greater warrior than we Integrity Knights, why does he not take up his sword and fight *now*?! Why has he become so feeble and tied you down to this remote place? If he struck down Administrator to protect the people of the realm, then why does he not proceed to the Eastern Gate at once?!"

Nothing about Eldrie's fervent outburst seemed to reach Kirito. The only thing his heavy-lidded eyes reflected was the flickering flame in the heater.

It was Alice's gentle voice that broke the stifling silence that followed.

"...I'm sorry, Eldrie. I cannot go with you. It is not because of Kirito's condition; I have lost my ability with the sword—that is all. If we were to fight now, I would not last three strikes into the duel."

Eldrie's eyes bulged. The proud knight's face crinkled up like a young child's. Eventually, he managed to form a resigned little grin.

"...I see. Then I have nothing more to say..."

He reached out his hand and muttered the initiation of a sacred art, followed by a quick incantation of two crystal elements that he formed into delicate wine glasses. Then he picked up the wine bottle, plucked the firm stopper out with his fingertips, poured an equal amount of the red liquid into each glass, and set it down.

"...If I'd known we'd be drinking to our final meeting, I would have brought a two-hundred-year vintage from the western empire's private cellar."

Eldrie lifted one of the glasses, drank it down in a single gulp, then put it back on the table. He saluted her, stood, and turned, his white cloak flapping.

"This is farewell, Master. Your student Eldrie will never forget your lessons on the sword and arts."

"...Be well. I will pray for your safety," she managed to reply. The Integrity Knight nodded back at her, then strode away, boots clicking. There was unassailable dignity in his gait, and Alice had to look away.

The door opened, then shut. Outside, Takiguri cried once, followed by the flapping of wings. Amayori hummed sadly over the sudden parting, a thorn that pricked Alice's heart.

The powerful wings grew more distant until the sound eventually faded away. She sat motionless all the while.

Before the delicate crystal glass could run out of life and fall apart, she picked it up and put it to her mouth. Her first taste of wine in half a year was not sweet; it left only a puckering tartness on her tongue. Mere seconds later, the two empty glasses vanished, leaving a few brief beams of light behind.

She put the cork back into the bottle, which wasn't empty yet, and stood up. Over by the fire, she told the silent Kirito, "I'm sorry about that. You must be tired. It's past our bedtime. Here, let's get you over there."

Alice helped him stand up, hands on his shoulders, and guided him toward the adjacent bedroom. Once she'd changed him from his black indoor shirt to a plain pajama top, she helped him lie down on the bed by the window.

Near his feet, there was a folded blanket, which she spread out and placed up to his neck. But Kirito's half-open eyes just stared up at the ceiling without blinking.

She blew out the lamp on the wall, filling the room with bluish darkness, then sat next to him and stroked his sunken chest and bony shoulders for several minutes until he finally closed his eyes as though running out of power.

Once she was sure his breathing was quiet and steady, Alice got up and changed into her own white nightgown. She went back out to the living room to check on Amayori at the window, then extinguished the two lamps there and returned to the bedroom.

After lifting the blanket and lying down next to Kirito, a faint warmth enveloped her body. Normally, she only had to close her eye to immediately drift into slumber, but that sensation was elusive tonight.

The shining white of Eldrie's cloak hanging behind him stubbornly refused to vanish from the back of her eyelid, distracting her and keeping her awake.

There was a time when she had been filled with the same pride that he now felt. It was the certainty that her sword was protecting the world, the people who lived in it, and the might of the Axiom Church—and the power that this knowledge gave her actions.

But now she had lost every last bit of that power.

She wanted to ask something of Eldrie, her former disciple. *What do you believe in now that the hypocrisy of the church and pontifex are revealed? What do you fight for?*

But she couldn't. Aside from her and Bercouli, none of the Integrity Knights had been told the entirety of the pontifex's horrifying plan. Eldrie didn't know about the existence of his Memory Fragment trapped in the sealed-off top floor of Central Cathedral, or the fact that his most beloved person had been turned into a piece of the Sword Golem there.

So he could still have faith in the Axiom Church itself. He could wait in faith for the day that the three goddesses sent a new pontifex to Central Cathedral to guide humanity with infallible wisdom once again.

But what should *she* do, knowing now that the existence of the gods and their celestial realm was all a big sham? Whether he had much of a choice or not, Commander Bercouli was preparing for the coming war by revealing only half of the truth to the other knights. If she joined them now, the conflicts she carried within her would surely spread to the others.

Nobody knew whether a hastily assembled defensive army would be able to repel an all-out invasion by the forces of darkness. If they broke through the Eastern Gate, the blood-starved monsters would eventually reach this distant village, too. When she wondered whether there was no way at all left to avoid this tragedy, a voice replayed itself in her mind from memory.

Her mind fixated on two sentences that had come from the mysterious crystal panel after the battle against the pontifex—and before Kirito had collapsed for good.

Head for the World's End Altar.

Leave the Eastern Gate and head far to the south.

She didn't recognize the sacred term *World's End Altar.* But she knew what she would find by leaving the Eastern Gate. Land as black as ash and skies the color of blood over the Dark Territory. Once she made her way into that place, it would not be easy to advance or return.

So once she made the unfathomably difficult journey through the land of darkness and reached this altar, what would be there? Was there really someone—or something—that could protect the people of the world from the dark army...?

Alice craned her head on the pillow and glanced at the boy sleeping on the other side of the bed. She wriggled through the blanket to be closer to him. After a moment's hesitation, she reached out and clung to his body, like a child frightened by a nightmare.

No matter how hard she pulled on his painfully thin frame, the boy whose burning righteousness had moved her so deeply made no response. His sluggish heartbeat did not pick up, nor did his dark eyelashes even twitch. Perhaps all that remained was a husk—a pitiful vessel that had once contained a soul.

If she had a sword in her hand now...

...she would run through both of their hearts in one go and end it all.

But the moment passed, and the idea slipped from her mind like the tears falling onto Kirito's neck.

"Tell me, Kirito...what should I do...?"

She received no answer.

"What...should I......?"

The moonlight shining through the parted curtains collected in the droplets as they fell, one after the other.

2

The next day, the twenty-second day of the tenth month, was the coldest of the fall.

She decided not to go on their usual walk but stayed inside by the stove with Kirito. She was planning to learn from Garitta how to split logs for firewood before winter really arrived, but that didn't seem like it was going to be necessary.

She took an entire day to write a letter on just two sheets of parchment and, after some waffling, finally decided to sign it with her last name Zuberg in common script, then added *Synthesis Thirty* in sacred script below it.

Alice folded it carefully, wrapped it, and addressed it to Selka. She wrote another one to Old Man Garitta and placed the two on the table.

The letters were of parting and apology. Now that Eldrie knew about this house, she couldn't stay here. Next, it wouldn't be Eldrie coming to try to recruit her, but Commander Bercouli himself. And Alice didn't have the words she ought to say to her sword master.

So she was going to run away again.

She exhaled a long, long breath, then looked up at the black-haired young man sitting across from her at the table.

"Say, Kirito, where would you like to go? I've heard that the highlands of the west are beautiful. Or perhaps the jungles of the south? It's warm year-round, and you can pick all sorts of fruit there."

Her voice was bright and conversational, but Kirito did not respond, of course. His empty eyes just stared at the surface of the table. Her heart ached at the idea of forcing this wounded young man into a life of wandering again. But that didn't mean she could leave him here in Rulid. Selka was a nun in training, so she couldn't force that burden on her, and Alice didn't want to do it anyway. Taking care of Kirito was her only reason to live right now.

"...You know what? I'll leave it up to Amayori. Shall we go to bed a bit sooner than usual? We'll need to wake up nice and early tomorrow."

She changed Kirito and got him into bed, then put on her own pajamas, extinguished the lights, and got under the covers.

In the darkness, she listened closely to Kirito's breathing. When he was completely asleep, she squeezed closer to him. Her head rested against Kirito's bony chest, and through the perfect seal of her ear, his slow heartbeat was audible.

Kirito's heart was not here anymore. His heartbeat was just an echo from the past. It had seemed that way for all the months she had fallen asleep next to him like this. But at the same time, a part of her wondered whether there might still be *something* contained within that quiet beating.

If Kirito was actually conscious but unable to display it in any way, how would she explain what she was doing now? The thought brought a little smile to her lips as she sank into a light sleep.

Abruptly, a small tremor ran through their bodies.

She lifted her heavy eyelid and looked toward the window to the east, but the sky through the curtains was still black. She got the feeling she'd slept for only two or three hours at most.

Kirito's body twitched again, so Alice whispered, "It's still the middle of the night…Let's go back to sleep, okay…?"

She closed her eye again and stroked his chest, hoping to put him back to sleep. But then she heard a quiet voice near her ear and finally realized something was wrong with the boy.

"A…aah…"

"Kirito…?"

Kirito didn't have any spontaneous desires at the moment. He would not wake up if he was cold or thirsty or had some other physical need. Yet, his body was trembling, harder and harder—his legs moving as though he might try to get out of bed.

"What's the matter…?"

For a moment, she wondered whether he was actually coming to his senses, so she got up in a hurry and generated a light element to save her the trouble of going to turn on a lamp.

But when the pale light lit up Kirito's eyes, they were just as dark and empty as ever, to her disappointment. So what had caused this…?

This time, it was a sound outside the window that caught her attention.

"*Krr, krrrr!*"

It was from Amayori, who should have been sleeping at the edge of the clearing. The dragon's cry was hard and high-pitched in warning.

Alice got out of bed and raced through the living room to open the front door. Instantly, there was a rush of cold night air. Rather than the scent of the forest, it contained something alien. The stench stung deep in her nostrils, burning, charring…

She raced barefoot through the door. After a brief survey of the night around her, she gasped.

The sky to the west was burning.

The eerie red light was undoubtedly the reflection of some great blaze. Upon closer examination, she noted a number of plumes of smoke splitting the view of the stars above.

A wildfire?! she wondered at first, then dispelled the notion. What was coming on the ashy wind was the sound of striking metal—and many screams.

Enemy attack.

The army of the Dark Territory was attacking Rulid.

"...Selka!!" she shrieked, racing back to the cabin. But the moment she reached the porch, she suddenly had doubts.

She had to save her sister and parents at all costs.

But what about the other villagers?

If she tried to save as many of them as possible, she'd have to fight the dark army directly. Did she even have the strength to do that anymore?

The source of Alice's power as an Integrity Knight was her nearly blind loyalty to the Axiom Church and its pontifex. Now that her faith was lost along with her right eye, could she actually swing the Osmanthus Blade and cast sacred arts anymore?

Then, while frozen in place, she heard a *thunk* from inside the cabin.

Her left eye widened. In the center of the darkened living room, a chair was overturned, and beside it, a young man with black hair was crawling along the floor.

"...Kirito..."

Alice entered the cabin with wilting legs. There was still no willpower in Kirito's eyes, but there was a clear purpose in his sluggish actions. His arm extended straight ahead to the three swords on the wall.

"Kirito...are you...?"

Something hot and hard blocked the passage from Alice's chest to her throat. It took her some time to realize that the cause of her blurring vision was tears.

"...Ah...aaah...," he croaked, not stopping his determined crawl toward the swords for an instant. Alice rubbed at her eye and raced straight for the boy, picking his skinny body up from the floor.

"It's all right—I'll go. I'll save the villagers. Please, don't worry. Just stay here," she whispered quickly, clutching Kirito.

B-bmp. B-bmp. She could feel his heartbeat as their chests met.

Even if his mind was absent, that sound contained the unstoppable strength of burning will and purpose. Faint though that flame might be, Alice could feel its heat.

After pressing her cheek to his for a moment, Alice easily lifted him up and put him in the chair.

"Once I've saved everyone, I'll come right back," she said again, getting the armor and sword belt she kept in the wardrobe and putting them on over her pajamas. Then she rushed to the eastern wall and grabbed her sword without a second thought.

The powerful weight of the Osmanthus Blade pushed against her palms for the first time in half a year. She fastened the sheath to her belt, tossed a cloak over her shoulders, and stuck her feet into boots, then raced back outside.

"Amayori!!" she called toward the dragon's bed on the eastern end. Instantly, a huge shadow surged forward with its head low. She leaped onto the base of the long neck and commanded, "Go!!"

Silver wings beat the air, and after a short run, the dragon soared up into the night sky.

Just gaining a bit of altitude made the state of Rulid very clear. It was mostly the northern end of the village that was burning. The invaders must have come from the Dark Territory through the northern cave.

Last night, Eldrie had claimed there was nothing wrong with the cave, which had been sealed on Bercouli's orders. If they had removed all the rubble in a single day, they must have marshaled far more than just ten or twenty soldiers for this raid.

Since ancient times, it had been common for small groups to infiltrate the three caves in the End Mountains under cover of night so they could work mischief in the human lands. Kirito and Eugeo had said that before they'd come to Centoria, they'd fought goblins in the northern cave. But she'd never heard of such a huge and brazen attack. Perhaps the entire Dark Territory really was preparing for an overall invasion of the realm.

As Alice pondered this topic, Amayori promptly crossed the thick forest and reached the airspace over the barley fields surrounding Rulid. She didn't have reins, but a light slap on the dragon's neck with her palm got her orders across; she told it to hover.

Alice leaned forward and focused on the village. The northern end of the main road that ran north to south through Rulid was glowing with fire, casting the silhouettes of the attackers into relief. They were goblins, leaping lithely back and forth. A short distance from them, much larger orcs were approaching.

Just to the north of the center clearing was an impromptu defensive wall made up of furniture and lumber supplies, but the goblins were already there, and she could make out the glinting of blades clashing just beyond the obstacles.

The village's men-at-arms were fighting back. But their numbers, gear, and experience were inferior even to the goblins'. When the rumbling orcs marched up to them, the humans would be utterly crushed.

She kept watching, avoiding the urge to leap directly into the midst of battle. There were a number of fires burning on the east and west edges of the village, too, but the central clearing and south side were unharmed for now. All the villagers aside from the guards—including Selka—must have escaped through the south gate into the forest, she presumed.

So when she looked more carefully at the central clearing, Alice gasped.

"Why...?!"

Surrounding the fountain at the center of the round empty space in front of the church was a tightly packed crowd of figures. There were so many of them that she at first didn't recognize what she was seeing. It had to be the entire population of Rulid.

Why weren't they evacuating the village?

If the main force of the invaders reached the defense line, the guards would be scattered in an instant. If they didn't get moving *now*, they wouldn't be able to evacuate in time.

Alice slapped the dragon's neck again, intending to ride it directly over the clearing. "Amayori, wait here until I call for you!"

Then she leaped from her mount's back, dozens of mels off the ground, cloak flapping wildly as she split the cold night air.

The circular mass of three-hundred-plus villagers had the adult men on the edges bearing farming tools like plows and scythes, indicating their willingness to fight. Alice landed right near two men who seemed to be giving constant orders.

The paving stones split outward from her landing point with a rumble like thunder. An incredible impact ran from her soles to her crown, indicating some loss of life value.

The two men—Nigel Barbossa, the farm owner, and Gasfut Zuberg, the elder of Rulid—fell silent in shock at the sudden arrival of a visitor from above.

Alice felt a tiny twinge of pain in her breast at the sight of her father's face, but she used the moment of silence that resulted to shout an order to the crowd. "You cannot fight them off here! All of you, take the path south and escape the village at once!!"

Nigel was the first to recover, however. "Don't be ridiculous! We can't leave my mansion—the village behind!!" he bellowed, veins bulging on his forehead.

Alice shot back, "You have enough time to make a clean escape from the goblins if you move now! What's more important to you, your riches or your life?!"

Nigel only mumbled under his breath, so it was Gasfut, the elder, who spoke up next. "It was Chief Man-at-Arms Zink who ordered that we shore up our defenses in a ring at the center of the village. In this situation, even I am at the mercy of his instructions. That is imperial law."

Now it was Alice's turn to be speechless.

In times of emergency, whoever had the calling of chief

man-at-arms gained the right to temporarily issue orders instead of the village or town elder. It was indeed a part of Norlangarth Basic Imperial Laws.

But Zink was still very young and had just inherited the position from his father. He couldn't possibly give wise, rational orders in the midst of such an abnormal situation. The anxiety on Gasfut's pale face made it clear he was thinking the same thing.

But to the villagers, imperial law was absolute. In order to begin a prompt evacuation, she'd have to grab Zink from the northern defensive line where he was giving orders so he could change his tune—but there clearly wasn't time for that now.

What to do? What could she…?

It was then that a young but strident voice piped up.

"We should do what Sister says, Father!!"

Alice gasped and looked at the interior of the circle, where a young apprentice nun was using sacred arts to heal burned villagers.

"…Selka!"

Relieved that she was alive and well, Alice started heading for her beloved sister, but Selka stood up and marched through the crowd for the trio first.

Selka spared only the barest hint of a smile for Alice as she approached Gasfut, all business. "Father, has Sister ever been wrong about anything in her life? Even *I* can tell that at this rate, we're all going to be slaughtered!"

"B-but…," Gasfut stammered, pained. His graying mustache quivered, and his eyes wandered.

Nigel Barbossa filled the silence for the elder instead. "Children should mind their tongues! We will protect the village!" he exploded, his bloodshot eyes fixed on his mansion located close to the clearing. Nigel was only thinking of his fresh harvest of barley and the sacks of coins he'd amassed over the years.

The rich farmer glanced back at Alice and Selka and screeched, "Oh…oh! I understand now! *You* brought those monsters down upon the village, Alice!! When you crossed the End Mountains years ago, you were despoiled by the power of darkness! You witch…This girl is a witch!"

He jabbed a fat finger at Alice. She was stunned. The murmuring of the villagers, the sound of battle at the defensive barrier, even the incoming war shouts of the monster army to the north all faded away.

Since she'd begun living outside the village, Alice had cut down a number of huge trees on Nigel's behalf. Every single time, he positively writhed with delight and gratitude. And now he was making these accusations out of the pure desire to protect his own wealth.

The middle-aged man's expression was as ugly and hateful as an orc's. Alice looked away from him.

Then do as you will. And I will do the same. I'll take Selka, Garitta, my parents, and Kirito and leave this place to find a new home, far, far away.

She clenched her teeth and closed her eye. But even then, her mind kept working.

But if Nigel Barbossa and the other villagers seem stupid to me, it is the centuries of the Axiom Church's rule that made them this way.

The Taboo Index and the countless other laws and rules beneath it constricted the people, giving them the lukewarm bath of safety, while robbing them of something much more important.

The power to think independently. The power to resist.

Over that eternal length of time, where had that invisible power of humanity been collected?

Into just thirty-one Integrity Knights.

She sucked in a deep breath, exhaled, then opened her left eye so wide, it was practically audible. When it focused on Nigel, his face went pale with fright.

But at the same time, Alice felt a strange sense of power welling up from within. It was like a pale flame—quiet but hotter than anything. It was the power she'd thought she'd lost for good at the end of the battle atop Central Cathedral—the power that had helped Kirito, Eugeo, and Alice face off against the greatest ruler of humanity.

She took a deep breath and said, "I am annulling the order of Chief Man-at-Arms Zink. I order all the people in this clearing to evacuate to the forest south of here, with those of you who are armed in the lead."

Her voice was calm and controlled, but Nigel was bowled over, as if struck by invisible hands. It was a credit to his spirit that he even managed the mewling argument he did. "Wh…what authority gives a runaway girl like you the right to—?"

"My authority as a knight."

"Wh…what do you mean, knight?! There is no such calling in this village! You cannot simply call yourself a knight because you can use a sword! If the great knights of Centoria found out, they would…," he stammered, spraying spittle.

She stared him right in the face, then moved her left arm across her body to grab the cloak on her right shoulder.

"I am…My name is Alice. I am third among the Axiom Church's Integrity Knights in the central district of Centoria: Alice Synthesis Thirty!!" she announced, throwing off her cloak.

The moment the heavy cloth was free, the blazing fires reflected in a dazzling array off her golden armor and Osmanthus Blade.

"Wha…? An I-I-Integrity Knight…?!" Nigel shrieked in falsetto, falling to his ample bottom in shock. Gasfut was equally stunned.

Alice's introduction could not have been false. There was no one in this entire world who could lie about being an Integrity Knight—and thus defy the very authority of the Axiom Church. If anyone could, it would only be Kirito and Alice, but even having escaped from Centoria, Alice had not abandoned the sword that marked her as a knight.

The murmuring villagers went utterly silent. Even the shouting and clashing from the battle to the north and the bellowing of the guards and goblins got quieter.

It was Selka who first broke the silence.

"Sis...ter...?" she whispered, clutching her hands before her chest. Alice smiled kindly back at her.

"I'm sorry for hiding this from you for all that time, Selka. This is the true punishment I've been given. And...my true duty."

Large wet orbs collected in Selka's eyes. "Sister...I...I believed in you. I knew you weren't a sinner. You're so...so beautiful..."

The next to act was Gasfut. He fell loudly to a kneeling position on the paving stone, and with his head down, he called out, "I hear and obey your order, Lady Integrity Knight!"

Then he swept to his feet and turned to face the villagers. "On your feet, everyone!" he commanded. "Run to the south gate, with those of you armed at the front! Once out of the village, head into the forest south of the cultivated clearing!"

An uneasy murmur ran through the crowd. It lasted only a moment, however. They had no possible alternative to obeying the elder's orders, especially if he was speaking for an Integrity Knight.

The hardier farmers at the perimeter of the crowd stood and motioned for the women, children, and elderly to get to their feet, too. Before Gasfut could stand at the head of the group, Alice beckoned him over and said quietly, "Father, take care of everyone... and of Selka and Mother."

For just an instant, Gasfut's expression softened, and he replied simply, "Please...do take care, Lady Knight."

Alice knew he would never call her his daughter again. That, too, was a price of the power she'd been given. It was with this thought weighing on her that Alice pressed Selka to stand next to Gasfut.

"Sister...don't get yourself hurt," Selka said through teary eyes. Alice favored her with a smile and turned to the north. Behind her, the villagers all began to move.

"Oh...oh...my...my poor mansion...," wailed Nigel Barbossa, who was still sitting flat on the ground. He glanced back and forth between the retreating villagers and the fires approaching his home. Alice decided to ignore him and focus on the state of the village as a whole.

She'd succeeded at moving the villagers, but there were three hundred of them. It would take time for all those people to leave the village. Meanwhile, the defensive line was bound to break soon, and the marching footsteps of the enemy were approaching from the east and west, too.

Then there was a scream from a young man at the north end of the clearing.

"It's no use! Pull back! Run awaaay!!"

That would be Zink, leader of the guards. The shout seemed to spur Nigel Barbossa on; he leaped to his feet and snapped at Alice, "There…you see? We ought to have stayed here and defended! We'll be killed! We'll all be slaughtered!!"

Alice shrugged and said quietly, "You'll be fine with the head start you've got. I will hold them off here."

"You cannot! You cannot possibly do such a thing! Even…even if you *are* an Integrity Knight, what can one person do against such a numerous horde?!"

The fearsome sight of goblins was visible to the east and west by now, but Nigel remained, shrieking invectives. Alice ignored him and glanced behind her. The last row of villagers was still in the clearing, but they were a good distance away from the center, where she was standing now.

Alice grabbed Nigel by the collar and hurled him southward. Then she thrust her hand into the night sky and called her mount.

"Amayori!"

Instantly, there came a tremendous bellow from above. As she waved her hand from west to east, she commanded, "Burn them all!!"

There was a storm of wings beating as Nigel and the inhuman goblins who were racing into the clearing all looked up at the same time. The massive dragon plunged toward them, its shape dark against the fire-reddened sky, and opened its jaws wide. There was a bright flicker in its throat, and—

Shwoom!!

Brilliant light shot forth. The beam of heat landed on the street to the west and passed right before Alice's and Nigel's eyes, sweeping over to the street east of the clearing.

After the briefest of pauses, a line of tremendous flames erupted from the ground toward the sky. Engulfed, the goblins shrieked and screamed as the force of the eruption threw them off their feet.

The dragon's breath had dispatched over two dozen attackers all at once, simultaneously evaporating the water of the fountain in the center of town and turning it into a cloud of steam. Amayori skimmed over the vapor as Alice gave the order to wait, then glanced behind her.

Nigel Barbossa was back on the paving stones in terror, his beady eyes bulging. "Wh...wha...? A d...d...d-d-drag...?!"

The middle-aged man's pudgy cheeks quivered pathetically. Just then, the steam gave way to reveal Rulid's men-at-arms sprinting forward, wearing matching leather armor. The timing of the order to retreat had paid off in the end, as while the dozen or so guards had wounds here and there, none of them seemed too serious.

Admirably, the large chief named Zink was running in the very back row. When he noticed that the clearing was empty, he was stunned. "Wh-where did the villagers go?! Didn't I tell them to shore up our defenses back here?!"

"I sent them into the southern forest," Alice answered, and he blinked as if finally noticing her presence. Once he had looked her up and down from head to toe, he gasped, "Are you...Alice...? Why are you...?"

"I don't have time to explain. Is this all the men-at-arms? There are no stragglers left behind?"

"N...no, there shouldn't be..."

"Then I want you all to join them and escape. And take Mr. Barbossa there with you."

"B-but...they're nearly upon—"

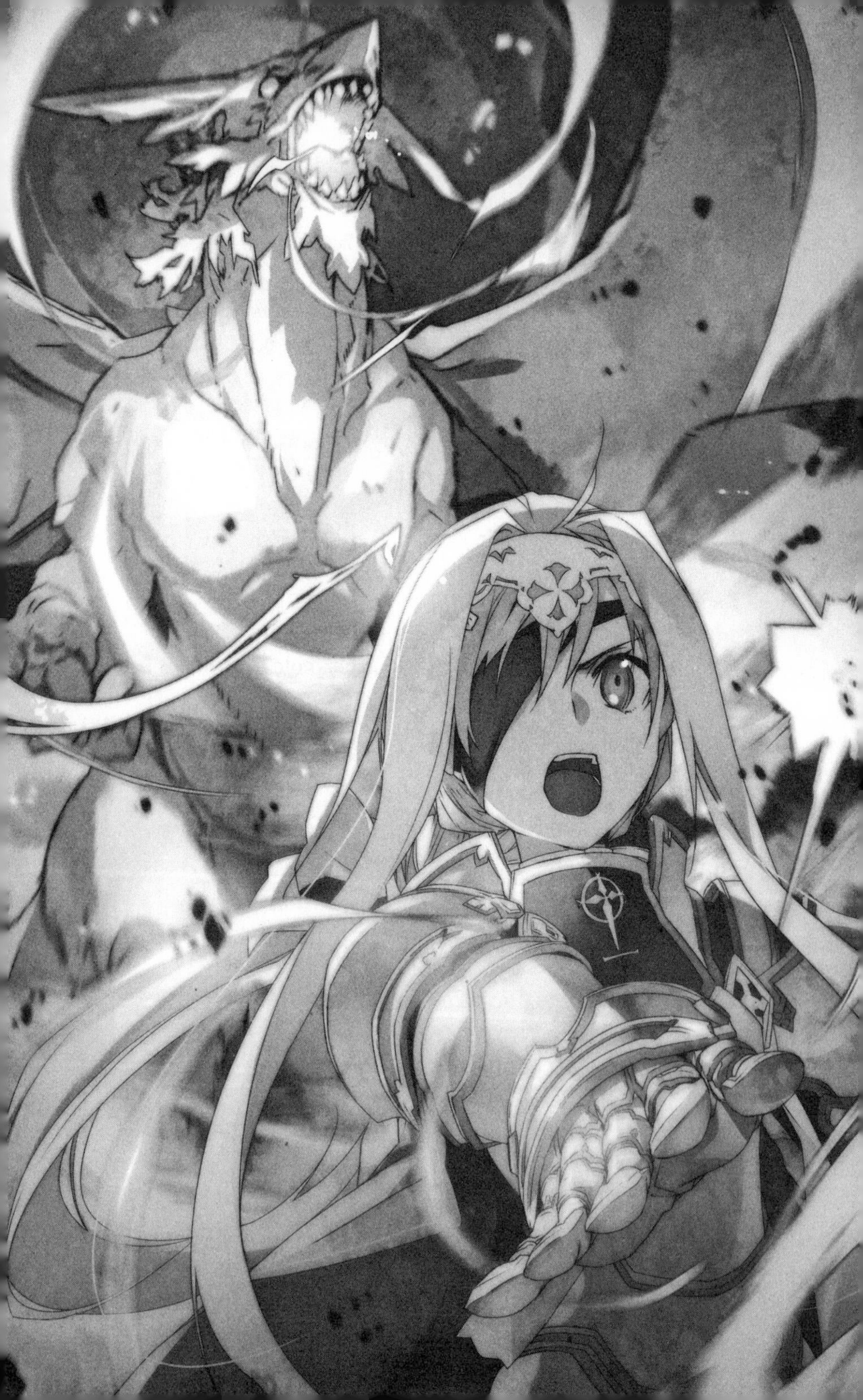

Before he could even finish his sentence, the open space rumbled with a fierce growl.

"Gee-heeee!"

"Where are they?! Where have the miserable white Iums run off to?!"

Charging through the vapor mist into the clearing was a group of goblins wearing crude armor of metal plating, wielding barbaric blades like hunks of steel, and sporting long feathers on their heads. They were apparently from a different tribe than the ones who'd been burned by Amayori's flames along the side roads—a bit bigger and better built.

Alice sized up the demi-humans and put her hand on the hilt of her sword. The dragon couldn't use its flame twice in a row. Alice would have to fight them off by herself until Amayori could restock its flame elements.

One of the goblins noticed Alice in her golden armor and turned its greedy yellow eyes with all their cruelty and avarice upon her. "Gee-hee!! An Ium woman! Kill her! Kill and eat her!!"

It swung its sword with freakishly long arms, sending the other creatures racing straight for her. Alice waited as they approached.

What incredible power I've been gifted. Almost as though my entire existence is a sin.

This Integrity Knight's body.

"Giyaaaa!!"

A thick machete came leaping toward her, but Alice neatly and efficiently blocked it with her left hand. It left a dull impact on her bare palm, but her bones didn't break; her skin didn't even split. She grabbed the lead weapon in her fingers and crumpled it as if it were made of thin ice.

Before the twisted shards of metal could even fall to the ground, her other hand had the Osmanthus Blade loose, swiping sideways through the goblin's body.

The golden breeze of the sword caught the handful of goblins behind it, too, eliminating the heavy block of water vapor in the air, too. The four hostiles looked around with their yellow eyes, uncertain of what had just happened until, without a word, their upper and lower halves separated and fell to the ground.

She took a step back to avoid the sprays of blood that erupted a moment later.

You were wrong, Administrator, she grumbled to herself. *You concentrated all this power into just thirty-one knights and turned us into your puppets. In doing so, you had the collective power that should have gone to all the people of the realm in the palm of your hand instead. But such a grotesque power misleads the one who wields it and those around them. You were consumed by a power that was too great and became something no longer human...*

With the pontifex now dead, there was no way to rectify that mistake.

So if she could at least use this power to the utmost, for the sake of others, then it was what she would do. She would fight not as an Integrity Knight of the church but as an individual swordswoman, of her own free mind and will. Just as those two brave warriors had done.

Alice's closed eye flew open as she paused at the end of her swing.

At the same moment, the impromptu defensive line built at the north end of the clearing was splintered into pieces from the other side.

The main invasion force plunged through, filling the wide main street from end to end. There were at least fifty goblins and a smaller number of much larger orcs bearing tridents, their round bodies covered in thick metal armor.

At the sight of their flashing yellow eyes and the sound of their roars of hatred and greed, Zink and his guards and Nigel Barbossa all let out desperate wails.

But Alice's mind was calm.

She wasn't simply relying on her battle ability as an Integrity Knight. Even a knight would suffer if so many spears managed to surround and pierce them.

It was one new piece of understanding that was giving Alice her power.

I'm about to fight for a cause that I accepted and wanted. To protect my sister, my parents, and the common people that Kirito and Eugeo fought to save.

She could practically feel that lingering self-doubt and powerlessness evaporating inside her, engulfed in the blast of that pure white light. The light raced throughout her body, eventually gathering in the eye hidden behind her black bandage and giving off an incredible heat.

"……!"

A fierce pain shot from her eye socket through the back of her head, causing her to grit her teeth. But this pain was old, familiar, and almost like a long-lost friend. With her left hand, she grabbed the scrap of cloth that crossed her head and ripped it loose.

Her right eyelid, which had remained closed for nearly half a year, now lifted. In the middle of her darkened vision, red light was spreading and pulsing, until it turned into a flickering flame. The sight of the burning houses from her good eye overlapped the image until the discrepancy eventually dissolved—and the image became whole.

With both eyes, she looked down at the black cloth in her free hand.

The bandage, faded from repeated washing, was a piece of Kirito's clothing that he had ripped loose for her. It had protected her right eye for months after the seal had blown it out of her head, and just now, its life had been exhausted. The cloth began to vanish into thin air, starting at one end. Watching the precious, delicate scene play out helped Alice understand.

She thought she'd been protecting and caring for Kirito for the past months, after he'd lost his mind and arm. But she was the one who'd truly been under protection.

"…Thank you, Kirito," she whispered, pressing the black cloth to her lips just before it could vanish entirely. "I'm…all right now.

I'm sure I'll still be uncertain. I'll worry and come close to falling apart…but I'm moving onward. For what you—and I—really want."

As the scrap vanished, she looked up. With her improved vision, she could see nearly a hundred goblins and orcs roaring and charging into the open space. To the rear, she heard the sound of the guards and Nigel Barbossa running away.

There was no fear in Alice's heart as she faced the enemy army by herself.

She sucked in a lungful of scorching air and shouted, "I am Alice, knight of the human realm! As long as I am here, you will not find the blood and slaughter that you crave! Go back through the cave and return to your lands!"

The goblins running at the lead slowed down just a bit, as though blown back by the force of her ringing statement. But then an especially large orc at the middle of the pack, apparently their commander, lifted his two-handed ax and roared back, "Graaaah! Morikka the Foot Harvester will make quick work of one little white Ium girl!!"

His roar emboldened the goblins once again. They washed forward like a black wave. Alice tensed in preparation.

"Amayori!" she shouted, and a huge shadow plunged from the sky above. It didn't have enough accumulated fire elements to use its fire breath again just yet, but it did intimidate the enemies with its size and tremendous cry as it flew so close to the ground, it nearly clipped their heads. The creatures were even more rattled than they'd been before.

Determined not to lose her advantage, Alice brandished the Osmanthus Blade high overhead and shouted, "Enhance Armament!!"

It was the first time in half a year—and merely an initiation of an abbreviated version of Perfect Weapon Control—but the sword obeyed her anyway. With a crisp, clear, ringing sound, the golden blade split into countless tiny pieces, reflecting the light of the fire as they danced up into the air.

"Storm and churn, my flowers!"

With a buzzing rush, the golden petal blizzard pelted down on the enemy.

The first fountain of blood rose from Morikka, the orc leader. Numerous little flowers pierced his body, wiping out his life and sending him falling straight backward with a terrible crash. The other orcs around him wailed and prostrated themselves.

The Osmanthus Blade was one of the greatest divine weapons, born from the oldest tree in the world, which grew at the center of the human realm. Like its other name of everlasting eternity implied, Perfect Weapon Control could split the weapon into hundreds of flower petals, and each one had a priority level that was equal to one or more famed master blades. You couldn't block them with simple cast-iron armor.

With their main force and leader lost in an instant, the other invaders quickly lost spirit. The speed of their charge slowed until they came to a stop about ten mels into the clearing. The goblins in the very front row couldn't decide whether they wanted to give in to desire or fear, so Alice swung the sword in her right hand one more time. The weapon's hundreds of petals scattered through the air, lining up into a strict grid pattern between her and the enemy army.

Alice stared down the demi-humans through the sparkling golden fence and quietly announced, "This is the wall that separates the human realm from the dark lands. Dig up the cave if you will, but as long as we knights live and breathe, you will not be allowed to defile this land! Now choose—come forward and drown in a sea of your own blood or back away and flee to your land of darkness!!"

It took less than five seconds for the goblin in the lead to turn the other way.

3

A pleasant chorus of hammer strikes rose up into the stark winter sky.

Alice put a hand to her forehead and glanced across the barley fields at the jutting silhouette of Rulid.

A week had passed since the invasion by the army of darkness. Many of the homes on the northern side of the village had burned down, but because the elder ordered that almost the entire village put their callings on hold to work on construction, the rebuilding was proceeding quickly. Sadly, twenty-one villagers had been too slow to escape and had lost their lives. Three days ago, there had been a ceremony at the church to mourn them all.

Alice was asked to join in the funeral, and after it was over, she rode on her dragon to inspect the northern cave. The long cavern, which Bercouli had ordered sealed, had been excavated to a width large enough for a burly orc to fit through comfortably, and the part that was closest to the Dark Territory showed signs of a longtime camping area.

The invaders hadn't opened up the entire length of the cave in a night. They must've sent in a team of engineers from the dark side and then resealed that end. When Eldrie checked on the status of the cave, he had no idea that behind the cave mouths, a team of goblins was already inside and working on reopening both ends.

It was a level of tenacity and prudence that was unthinkable from goblins and orcs in the past. Just this one incident alone made it clear that this was not at all like the simple scouting raids that used to happen time and again.

Rather than recollapsing the cave mouths, Alice temporarily blocked the brook that flowed from the center, where the white dragon made its nest. Once the cave was flooded, she unleashed the multitude of frost elements she'd prepared, sealing the cave with ice rather than rock.

Now, unless an arts caster on Alice's level used heat elements to melt the ice, no one would be able to pass through.

Alice looked from Rulid back to the snowcapped mountains in the distance and attached the last sack she had to Amayori's left leg.

"Um…Sister?" asked Selka, who'd been helping her pack for the journey with a brave and unfaltering smile. "Father…wanted to see you off, too. He's seemed absent all day, ever since he woke up. I'm…I'm sure that deep down, he was happy that you came home. Please, I want you to believe that."

"I understand that, Selka," Alice whispered, hugging her sister's little body. "I left the village as a criminal and came back as an Integrity Knight. But the next time…if I finish all my duties, I will come back as Alice Zuberg. And then I'm sure I'll be able to say, 'I'm home, Father,' like I should."

"…Yes. I'm sure that day will come," Selka said with a sob, looking up and rubbing at her face with the sleeve of her habit. Then she turned to the black-haired young man sitting in a nearby wheelchair and energetically told him, "Be well, too, Kirito. Get better soon, so you can help my sister."

The young nun put her hands around his downturned head, made the sign of blessing, and stepped back a few paces.

Alice approached Kirito, gently took away the swords he was holding, and placed them in the sack fixed to Amayori's saddle.

Next, she easily lifted the slight young man and sat him on the front part of the saddle.

She'd considered leaving Kirito behind in the village and asking Selka to take care of him. If she headed for the Eastern Gate, where the real battle against the forces of darkness would commence, Alice would be overcome with duties as one of the guardians of the human army. She wouldn't be able to care for Kirito all day long like she did now.

Even still, she decided to take him along.

The night of the attack last week, Kirito had taken his sword and tried to go to the village. He still had the will inside of him to fight for others. It only made sense that the key to getting his old self back would be at the battle to protect the human realm.

She would tie him to her own back with ropes if that was what it took to protect him. Alice embraced her beloved sister one more time.

"…Well, I should get going, Selka."

"I know. Take care…and make sure you come back, Sister."

"I promise. And…say good-bye to Old Man Garitta for me, too. Be well…and study hard."

"I will. I'll be a good and proper holy woman…and then… one day…"

Selka couldn't finish her sentence. She put on a brave smile, her face crinkled and tearstained. Alice caressed her head, then let go and walked over to her dragon, feeling her reluctance to go, and got onto the rear of the saddle, behind Kirito.

She nodded down to her sister, then turned her gaze to the blue sky. With a light crack of the reins, the dragon began bounding powerfully through the barley field, scarcely affected by the weight of two humans and three swords.

One day, she would return here.

Even if she fell in battle, at least her heart would come back.

Alice brushed aside the droplets stuck in her eyelashes and barked, "*Hah!*"

She felt weightless as the dragon left the ground.

Amayori caught the updraft, circling as it raced up into the sky.

She burned the images into her mind: vast fields and forest, Rulid with its brand-new roofs sparkling in the sun, Selka racing after her with both arms waving.

Alice tapped the dragon's neck, directing it to the east.

CHAPTER SIXTEEN

ATTACK ON THE *OCEAN TURTLE*, JULY 2026

1

Even Takeru Higa, who was well aware of his first-class genius status, couldn't have predicted the various events of the last two hours. But what was playing out before his eyes at the present moment was by far the most shocking of them all.

A delicate girl, only eighteen or nineteen years old, was lifting a man six inches taller than her by his collar. His flashy Hawaiian shirt was stretched enough to tear, and the soles of his sandals hung in the air.

As she glared at Lieutenant Colonel Seijirou Kikuoka with radiant fury, Asuna Yuuki's shapely lips formed a razor-sharp ultimatum. "If Kirito doesn't wake up, I'll make sure you regret it."

From Higa's position, the lenses of Kikuoka's black-framed glasses reflected the lights in the ceiling, so he couldn't make out the man's expression. But the Self-Defense Force officer, who was a black belt in both judo and kendo, swallowed as though intimidated by her threat. He lifted up his hands in a sign of surrender.

"I know, I know. And as it is my responsibility, I will absolutely see that Kirito is restored."

A tense silence filled the gloomy sub-control room. Neither Higa, sitting before the control console, nor Rinko Koujiro, who stood next to him, nor any of the other Rath staffers in the room could speak a word before the overwhelming force of the youngest person present. In the back of Higa's mind, he recognized that she was indeed a true survivor of life-and-death battle.

Eventually, Asuna slackened her grip. Finally free, Kikuoka nearly fell to the floor, exhaling heavily. The girl faltered, too. Rinko leaped forward, white coat flapping, to put a hand on her back for support.

The physicist, who was Higa's friend and mentor from their college seminar, clutched Asuna to her chest and murmured, "It's all right. It'll be all right. He'll come back to you."

Asuna's tension finally broke, and her face crumpled.

"......Yes, of...of course. I'm sorry...I went too far..."

Tears formed at the corners of her eyes; she hadn't cried even during the attack. Rinko gently rubbed them away.

The mood in the room eased up at last, only for the tension to return when the sliding door opened manually. Lieutenant Nakanishi raced inside.

His white shirt was stained with sweat and dust, and the grip of his large pistol was visible in the shoulder holster. He glanced at the women first, then found Kikuoka in the back and said, "Report, sir! Primary and secondary pressure-resistant barriers are closed, and noncombatant evacuation to stern block is confirmed complete!"

Kikuoka strode forward, fixing his collar. "Thank you. How long will the barriers hold?"

"Well...it depends on what they brought with them, but they are indestructible to small firearms. If they've got circular saws, you're looking at no less than eight hours to penetrate. They could break through with explosives...but I doubt that's an option. After all, the center barrier is very close to..."

"The Lightcube Cluster," Kikuoka finished, pushing his glasses up the bridge of his nose.

He stopped to think, then lifted his head and looked around the cramped Subcon room. "Let's get a picture of the situation. Lieutenant Nakanishi, give me a casualty report."

"Sir! Three minor injuries to researchers on the civilian project team, recovering in the stern medical bay. Two heavy and two minor injuries to our combatants. They are also recovering, nothing life-threatening. Including the two who sustained minor injuries, we have six sailors in battle condition."

"It's a damn fortunate turn of events not to have any deaths, for all that fighting...Next, damage report on the ship."

"Control room on the bilge dock is Swiss cheese, sir. No way to open or close it remotely. Same for the corridor from the dock to Main Control, but it's more scratched than anything. The real trouble is that the main power line has been cut...Our power's still stable because it's coming through auxiliary lines, but if we don't reactivate the control systems, we can't rotate the screws."

"We're like a turtle without fins—and with a shark clinging to its belly."

"Yes, sir. All twelve sectors of the lower shaft and the bilge dock are under enemy control."

Nakanishi's chiseled features twisted in frustration. While his hair was close-cropped, Kikuoka had longer bangs like a teacher. The superior officer rested on top of the nearby console and let his wooden geta sandals dangle from his toes.

"So they've got Main Control, STL Room One, and even the nuclear reactor...I guess the silver lining is that they don't seem to be intent on destruction."

"You...think so, sir?"

"If they just wanted to destroy this facility, they didn't need a sub and a grand infiltration plan; they could've just shot it up with cruiser missiles or torpedoes. So the question now is, who are these people? Any thoughts, Higa?"

Higa blinked, not expecting to have the conversation thrown his way. Eventually, he was able to get his brain running again after the shock of their recent experience.

"Ah. Right. Um...," he murmured unhelpfully. He turned to his console, grabbed the mouse, and opened up the ship's security camera footage on the large monitor.

The video clip was dark and unclear, so he stopped it at a random point and adjusted the brightness and contrast. It brought into focus a group of figures moving through the ship interior in a crouching position. They wore black combat suits and helmets with multifunction goggles that covered the top half of their faces, and they carried menacing assault rifles.

"...So as you can see, they've got no flags or other identifying features anywhere on their helmets or suits. The color and shape of their gear isn't official military hardware of any country on Earth. The rifles look like Steyrs, but those are everywhere... About the only thing I can estimate is that, based on their average size, I don't think they're Asian."

"So at the very least, they're not our country's special forces. What a relief," Kikuoka deadpanned. He scratched his chin, his normally gentle eyes narrowed and hard as he stared at the monitor. "There's one more thing we can tell...These people know about the existence of Project Alicization."

Higa agreed. "Yes, that would be true. They came in from the bilge dock and raced straight up for Main Control. They've got to be after the STL... No, they're after the true bottom-up artificial intelligence, A.L.I.C.E."

That meant they'd had a very serious, long-term information leak. But Higa didn't say that out loud, and he suppressed the urge to examine the faces of every last Rath employee in Subcon, choosing to be optimistic instead.

"Fortunately, we did lock Maincon up in time. In other words, I made it so they can't directly interface with the Underworld—much more reliable than just smashing the console. They can't interfere with the simulation or eject the light-cube containing Alice's fluctlight from the cluster."

"But the same goes for us, doesn't it?"

"Sure does. We can't perform any operations requiring admin access here in Subcon, either. It's impossible to eject Alice's light-cube from the outside, either at Main or here...Doesn't that mean we've essentially won, Kiku? They can't access the cluster either physically or electronically, and once our defense ship cruises in with backup, those punks are toast!"

"I'm not sure what makes them toast...but you've actually hit on the problem," Kikuoka said, frowning. He asked Nakanishi, "Will *Nagato* come for us?"

"Well...sir...," Nakanishi replied, lines deepening around his stern jaws, "*Nagato* has orders from fleet command in Yokosuka to maintain its present distance and remain on standby. Command seems to think we've been taken hostage by the attackers."

"Wha...?" Higa gaped, his jaws open. "Hostage?! But all the crew evacuated to this side of the barrier, right?!"

Kikuoka said calmly, "I suspect those men in black have a channel to the top brass of the SDF. *Nagato* left the side of the *Ocean Turtle* at eight hundred hours, six hours before their attack. By the time *Nagato* gets the order to engage, they'll already have secured Alice's lightcube. Of course, they probably have a time limit of their own..."

"So those guys definitely aren't garden-variety terrorists, then. That's bad...If they've got experts, they might actually be able to figure out the trick to recovering Alice..."

"An operation from within the Underworld, you mean...? They've got the first STL room under control, and you can perform the eject command from the virtual console within the Underworld..."

"What happens if you make that command?" Rinko Koujiro asked.

Higa made a gesture with his hands. "The corresponding cube will be extracted from the Lightcube Cluster in the center of the main shaft and sent to the requested control room through the air tubes. That's where it can be retrieved."

He pointed at a square hatch in the corner of the console desk and looked at the door on the wall behind it.

The aluminum alloy door had a small metal plate screwed into it. The letters engraved on the plate said STL ROOM TWO.

On the other side of the door were two Soul Translators. One of them was under supervision by the nurse Sergeant First Class Natsuki Aki—it contained a young man. He'd played a major role in Project Alicization since the early stages and was now practically responsible for the outcome of the project itself: Kazuto Kirigaya.

Kikuoka looked forward once more, folded his arms, and said heavily, "Once again, our final hope rests with him…Higa, how is Kirito's condition?"

There was an intake of breath, and Higa looked at Asuna Yuuki, who was still being held upright by Rinko. Their eyes met.

She was the girlfriend of Kazuto, aka Kirito. How could he explain the present situation? While it was hoarse, her voice *was* firm.

"I'm fine. Please, tell me the truth."

Higa took a deep breath, exhaled, and said, "Summed up as briefly as possible…he's holding steady one step short of the worst-case scenario…Miss," he said, trying to soften the blow.

He grabbed the mouse and took down the still image of the attackers, opening a new window instead. This one displayed a colorful, three-dimensional graph that swayed and rolled gently.

"This is a visualization of Kirito's fluctlight," he explained. Everyone in the room stared at the screen in silence. "In Tokyo, one week ago, he was injected with a muscle relaxant and fell into cardiac arrest. He did survive, fortunately, but he suffered brain damage…technically, fluctlight-network damage. It's something that existing neural medicine finds very difficult to treat, but there is the possibility of recovery with the STL. So we put Kirito into the STL without any limitations, hoping it would prompt the growth of a new network and restore his fluctlight to wholeness."

He took a breath and grabbed a bottle of mineral water off the desk, quenching his dry throat after the unfamiliar act of continual talking.

"In order to make use of this treatment, he needed to dive into the Underworld. It won't take hold unless the fluctlight is active the same way it is in the real world. So like we did when he went on a test dive at the Rath office in Roppongi, we blocked his memories and dumped him into the outer regions of the Underworld...or we tried to. For reasons that remain unclear, probably having to do with the damage to his fluctlight, his memories weren't blocked. Kirito was sent into the Underworld as himself—Kazuto Kirigaya. And we didn't know this until we received his contact from within the simulation..."

"W-wait a moment," interrupted Rinko. "Are you saying that in the Underworld, with time accelerated, he's been living as himself, as Kirigaya? For...how many months...?"

"...About two and a half years."

Higa's answer caused Asuna to twitch in Rinko's arms. It was a shocking thing for her to hear, no doubt, but he had to trust in her earlier reassurance.

"For all that time, Kirito's been around artificial fluctlights in the Underworld. And probably with the knowledge that they are bound to be erased with the conclusion of the current simulation...So he would have headed for the console that makes contact to the real world, which is located in the center of the Underworld, where the first village was installed. To petition you to preserve all the fluctlights, Kiku."

Higa glanced sidelong at Kikuoka, whose glasses reflected the graph on the screen he was reading. The researcher turned back to Rinko and Asuna.

"...It couldn't have been an easy task," he continued. "The console was incorporated into the base of a ruling organization known as the Axiom Church. The fluctlights belonging to the church have absolute numerical superiority, far beyond any common citizen's, which is what Kirito was assigned to be. Normally, he should have died soon after infiltrating the church and gotten logged out of the Underworld...but instead, he survived. I couldn't check the event log while the attack was going on, but it turned out that he had a number of helpers—artificial fluctlights, of course...He had friends. Most of them died in the battle against the church, but when he finally succeeded in opening the circuit to the outside, he was strongly blaming himself. In other words, he was attacking his own fluctlight. Just then, our shady attackers cut the power line, and the momentary power surge caused an instant spike in the STL's output. The result was that Kirito's self-destructive impulse was actualized...and his ego was deactivated..."

"What do you mean...his ego was deactivated?" Rinko asked.

Higa turned to the console. "Just look at this."

His fingers flew across the keyboard, enlarging the real-time graph of Kazuto Kirigaya's fluctlight activity. At the center of the erratically undulating rainbow-colored cloud, there was a small, persistent void, like a dark nebula.

"Unlike a fluctlight contained in a lightcube, a human being's organic fluctlight is still far from being fully understood, but we've still got a pretty rough map of the structure. The part here, at this black hole, is what should normally contain the subject... the self-image."

"Meaning...the actualization of the self, as determined by the individual?"

"That's right. When we express our will, it happens through simple yes/no logic pathways in the fluctlight: whether I will or will not do this thing in this situation. For example, Rinko, have you ever ordered seconds at a beef-bowl restaurant?"

"...I haven't."

"Even if you wanted to or thought you had the room?"

"Correct."

"So that was the result spit out by your self-image pathways. Virtually none of our decision-making leads to proper action *unless* it happens through those circuits. In Kirito's case, the majority of his fluctlight is unharmed. But because the area in question isn't functioning, he cannot process exterior input, and he cannot output his own actions. I would guess that all he's capable of is...reactions, things based on traces of familiar, rote memories. Eating, sleeping, things of that nature."

Rinko bit her lip, considering this for a moment. Then she

whispered, "And...what is the status of his conscious mind right now?"

"...I'm afraid to say...," Higa started to answer, then paused and looked away. "He might not be aware of who he is, or what he should be doing...unable to say or do anything..."

Yet again, silence filled every inch of the melancholy control room.

2

"Fu—"

Heavy combat boots slamming against thick steel wall drowned out the second half of the word.

Vassago Casals, one of the Hispanic members of the assault team, was not satisfied with just putting a few dents in the wall, so he stomped on a package of snacks left behind by one of the Rath engineers who'd occupied this control room less than an hour ago. Only then did his stream of obscenities stop.

He brushed back his wavy black hair, marched to the console desk, and grabbed the collar of the man standing there.

"Say that one more goddamn time."

Hanging from Vassago's whip-strong arm was a scrawny-looking young man. His blond hair was shaved short, and his skin was almost pathologically pale. Thick, metal-framed glasses rested over his sunken cheeks.

This was the team's only noncombatant. He was a hacker named Critter, a nonregular employee of Glowgen Defense Systems's cyber operations (CYOP) division.

He had an arrest record for cybercrime, and his name was obviously a handle, not given. The same was true of Vassago. That name came from one of the seventy-two demons listed in the infamous medieval demonology tome *Ars Goetia*, where

Vassago was described as one of the princes of Hell. No parent would actually give their child such a name. He, too, was a member of the CYOP division, but his specialty was not in computing but in active combat—in a full-dive setting, that is. Like Critter, he had a sordid past record, but his ability to fight in VR was unparalleled.

As a matter of fact, outside of the leader, Gabriel Miller, the rest of the twelve-man *Ocean Turtle* assault team were pet dogs with sordid pasts who were promised new, secure identities for their work.

As one of those dogs, Critter didn't seem particularly scared, hanging from Vassago's grip. He continued chewing his gum. "I'll say it as many times as I want. This system's locks are tougher 'n dried shit. I could have this laptop work on cracking it, and you'd die of old age before it got in."

"That's not what I meant, Four-Eyes! You said it got locked because the rest of us were taking too long to break through, you son of a bitch!!" Vassago snarled back. He had the kind of wild good looks that might've actually earned him a living as a model, and because of that, he was positively feral when angry.

"I'm just stating the facts."

"Yeah, you talk a real big game now, but you were shivering in the back during the action!"

The other members just sat and watched, grinning, rather than stepping in to stop the argument. Once he determined it had gone on long enough, Gabriel snapped his fingers to draw their attention.

"That's enough, you two," he said. "This isn't the time to be placing blame. We need to focus on what to do next."

Vassago's head swiveled around, his lips pouting like a child's. "But, Bro, I just *gotta* teach this punk a lesson, or…"

Gabriel swallowed his usual demand not to be called bro. Vassago called Gabriel his bro out of respect for his VR combat-training chops, but it was an oddly displeasing moniker to Gabriel. To him, friends and comrades and other human relationships based on fickle and indistinct things like emotions were indecipherable.

When humanity finally had the means to extract and save the soul, all human emotions could be neatly described and arranged by the color and shape of that cloud of light. That would be a very good day, indeed.

Gabriel assumed the tone of a team leader as he announced, "Vassago, Critter, I'm happy with the work of the team so far. We've taken over the control room, our primary target, with the only damage being a little scratch to Gary."

Begrudgingly, Vassago let go of Critter's collar and put his hands on his hips. "Okay, Bro, but what's the point if the actual control system we're after is locked? Our final target, the Lightcube Cluster thingy, is on the other side of a wall of steel, yeah?"

"My point is that now we merely have to think of a way to break through that wall."

"You don't think those JSDF guys are just gonna hide in their safe space the whole time, do ya? Once the defense ship that patrols for this turtle busts in with a whole platoon of soldiers, the eleven of us plus one extra ain't gonna get far."

Vassago had a better grasp on the situation than your average stray dog, which was why Gabriel had selected him to be the vice-captain of the team. Gabriel thought it over and shrugged.

"It would seem that our client and the higher-ups of the JSDF arrived at a deal of some sort. The defense ship isn't going to act for a whole twenty-four hours after the start of our operation."

"...Ooh," Critter said with a little whistle. His glasses were thick as goggles, magnifying his pale-gray eyes narrowed in eagerness. "Meaning this ain't just a simple smash-and-grab job...Actually, I'm bettin' I'd be wiser not to call it that at all."

"I would agree with you there," Gabriel replied with a thin smile. He addressed the team. "Let's reexamine the situation. At present, it is 14:47 hours Japan Standard Time, forty minutes after we breached the ship. We are now in the *Ocean Turtle*'s main control room. We succeeded at taking over the desired location but did not capture any Rath engineers, and we're now locked out of the system. Our next goal is to take over the sub-control room... Brigg, can we break through the door in the pressure-resistant isolation wall?"

The hefty team member sauntered forward. "It'll be tough. It's made of the latest composite material. With the portable cutters we brought, it's gonna take more than twenty-four hours to break."

"Japanese money's not dead yet, huh? Can we blow a hole in it with C4, Hans?"

This time, a tall man with a neatly groomed mustache spread his hands in a flamboyant gesture. "I wouldn't try it, honey. The containment chamber for the Lightcube Cluster's right beyond that wall. No guarantees we can destroy that door without harming what's beyond it."

"Aaah," Gabriel murmured, folding his arms. "Well...our mission is to identify just one of those countless lightcubes and retrieve it, along with the interface. We already have that cube's unique ID. So as long as we can use the console, it should be easy to search for that cube and eject it from the cluster. We could be enjoying a beer on the return voyage right now."

"Can you believe this dickweed in the glasses bragged that he broke into the Pentagon's servers, and now he can't crack one stupid little server lock?"

"Those are real big words coming from a gamer whose entire gunfighting career is virtual and online."

Gabriel glared at Vassago and Critter before their argument could resume at full force and cautioned them, "Do you want to go home empty-handed and get mockery for your bonus pay?"

"No!!" they all shouted.

"Are you a collection of incompetents who are going to get shown up by a bunch of amateur engineers?"

"No!!"

"Then think! Prove to me you've got something other than oatmeal above your shoulders!!" Gabriel ordered, acting out the hard-assed commander routine half out of habit. On the inside, however, his thoughts went elsewhere.

As a searcher of the soul, Gabriel's greatest goals were to gain Alice, humanity's first bottom-up artificial intelligence, and to have exclusive access to Soul Translation technology. Once he had them both, he could eliminate the rest of the team with his secret stash of nerve gas and escape to Australia, like he'd planned.

Up to this point, the operation the NSA hired him for perfectly matched Gabriel's own goals. Now that they were locked out of the admin access they needed to operate the system, he had to gain Alice's lightcube through some other means.

Alice...A.L.I.C.E.

The NSA had found out that code name through their mole within Rath. He didn't know the personal data of the mole. But if the reason for betraying his company was a massive sum of money, he wasn't likely to make any actions now that would put himself at risk.

In other words, they couldn't rely on the mole on the other side of the pressure-resistant barrier to help them out. They'd have to achieve their goal with the information and gear they had, and they didn't have much time to do it.

Time. Time was the problem.

Gabriel was capable of entirely controlling pointless emotions like stress and anxiety, but even he couldn't avoid feeling a certain unpleasant pressure at the knowledge of their time limit, about twenty-three hours and closing fast.

When the NSA agents asked him to undertake a top-secret theft, they told Gabriel, *Rath's activities represent a clear threat to the interests of Japan's military-industrial complex. Therefore, a faction exists in the upper echelons of the JSDF that does not think highly of Rath—and might even seek to actively sabotage it.*

The core of Rath was a group of young SDF officers who had little political power. The NSA made use of that, sending a CIA agent with the embassy's office to make a deal with a high-ranking minister of the Maritime SDF. The *Nagato* defense ship for Rath's de facto headquarters, the *Ocean Turtle*, would stand down for twenty-four hours following the attack, under the guise of prioritizing hostage safety.

But once that grace period was over, the ship would have to move, as a defense against the media. Once the fully armed soldiers burst in, they'd wipe out the outmanned and outgunned team Gabriel had assembled.

Even in that worst-case scenario, he was planning to escape on his own with the miniature submarine. However, if he failed to gain the lightcube in question, he would be retreating from his grand journey in search of the human soul without any means of getting back.

Gabriel already had a detailed plan for the rest of his life after the conclusion of this mission.

First, he would escape to Australia with Alice and hide the lightcube and STL tech at his mansion on Sovereign Islands. Then he'd fly back to San Diego and report to the NSA that the mission was a failure. When everything had cooled down, he would return to Australia, install an STL machine in his mansion's spacious basement, and create a virtual world of his own design and tastes.

The first residents of the world would be just Alice and Gabriel. But that was *too* lonely. For the sake of his soul research, he would need to expand the materials he was working with.

He'd go to Sydney or Cairns and find the owner of some soul full of youthful vitality, kidnap them, rip the soul out with the STL, then discard the unnecessary husk. And someday, he might even cross the sea to visit his homeland of America—or Japan, the place where full-diving was born.

Gabriel was deeply charmed by the unique mentality of Japan's VR gamers. A number of them—but not all—treated virtual reality like it was more real than real life and spared none of their actual emotions within the game. Every time he recalled the sniper girl he met in *Gun Gale Online*, a powerful desire throbbed within him, even now.

That couldn't be unrelated to the "real virtual world" that had existed for only two years in that country. Those young players, hacked by the creator of the device, experienced a game of real life and death. The souls of those survivors had an aptitude for the virtual world that others did not share.

If possible, he wanted as many of their souls—especially the Progressors, if you will, the ones who stood at the forefront of the game. He didn't know whether that sniper girl belonged to them or not, but he wanted her soul, too. When a lightcube contained such a precious thing, it would surely shine with a brilliance greater than any jewel's.

The ultimate luster—something that even billions of dollars from the world's richest people could not purchase. And he would gaze at them, lined up in his secret chamber, load those souls into whatever world he wanted, and do with them as he liked.

Best of all, the souls extracted from a human being and contained in a lightcube could be copied or saved however he wanted. A broken or warped soul could easily be rewound until Gabriel fashioned it into the shape he wanted. Until he had given it the perfect cut, like a gemstone, for maximum brilliance.

Once he reached that stage, Gabriel's long, long journey would finally circle around to where it all began. To that moment in his youth, under the big tree in the forest, when he saw the beautiful shine of Alicia Clingerman's soul as it left her body.

Gabriel's eyes closed, and his spine shivered as he indulged in a brief moment of fantasy. When he opened them again, his ice-cold logical mindset was back.

If the souls of these young people from around the world were rubies, sapphires, and emeralds lining a crown, then the giant diamond that deserved to be set front and center had to be Alice. As the ultimate, pristine soul, she was the only one truly worthy of being his eternal partner. Which meant he *had* to find and gain her lightcube for himself.

However, it would be physically impossible to seize it without breaking the pressure-resistant door to the Lightcube Cluster room.

That left system manipulation as his only option. But even the first-rate hacker Critter claimed that he couldn't overcome the defenses on the main console.

Boots clicking against the ground, Gabriel walked over to stand behind Critter, whose fingers were flying over the keyboard.

"How goes it?"

His response was raised hands, palms up.

"Absolutely no way to get in on an admin account. All we can do is steeple our fingers and peer into the little fairy-tale kingdom where all those fluctlights in the cluster are enjoying themselves," Critter said. He tapped some keys, and a window opened on the big screen on the wall, displaying a rather odd sight.

It was not at all what you would define as a fairy-tale kingdom. The sky was an eerie red color, and the ground was as black as fresh asphalt. A number of primitive tents constructed of simple tanned hides sewn together sat at the center of the image. Next to them, there were about ten creatures with squat bodies and bald heads squalling about something.

They were vaguely humanoid but not human. Their backs were hunched, their arms long enough to drag along the ground, while their twisted legs were much shorter.

"Goblins...?" Gabriel muttered.

Critter gave him a little whistle of surprise and delight. "Bingo, Captain. Got it in one. They're not quite like orcs or ogres, so they would have to be goblins."

"I dunno, they're pretty huge for goblins. They gotta be hobs. Those are hobgoblins," commented Vassago, hands on his hips. Given his expertise in VR combat, it came as no surprise that he'd know his fantasy RPG design tropes.

As they watched, the clamor of the ten hobgoblins escalated, until two at the center grabbed each other and started grappling.

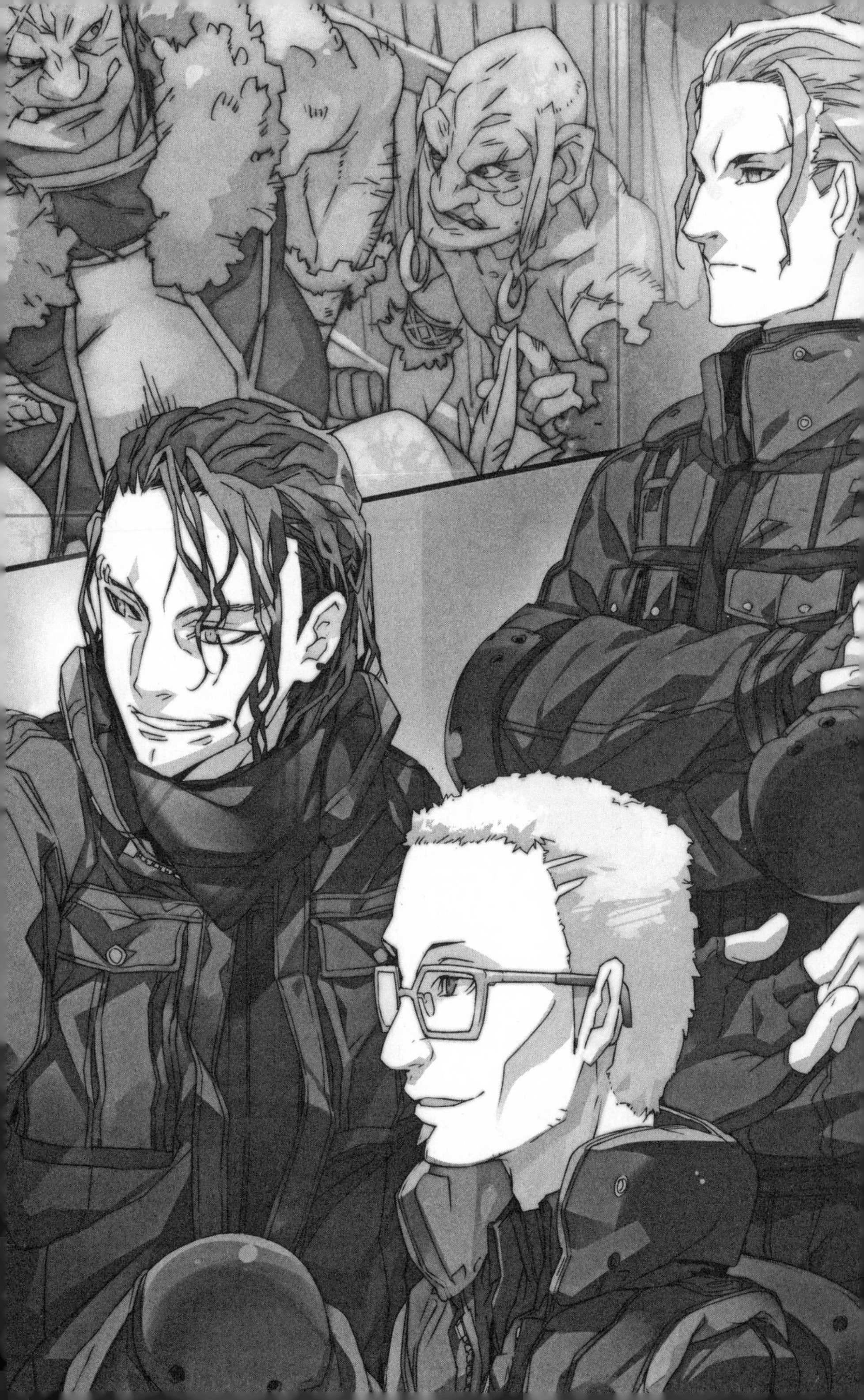

The others formed a perimeter around the fight, waving their arms and screeching in excitement.

"...Critter," Gabriel said to the buzz-cut man on the chair as an idea took shape in his mind.

"Yeah?"

"Are these...these monsters part of the system?"

"Hmm, doesn't seem like it. In a sense, these are real people. They're artificial fluctlights loaded onto the Lightcube Cluster... They've got souls."

"Really?! Oh my God!" Vassago abruptly screeched, leaning forward. "These hobs are humans?! They've got souls, just like us?! If my grandma back in Frisco heard that, she'd fall over dead on the spot!!"

He smacked Critter on the head and continued, "Talk about research that spits in God's face! Does that mean everyone in those lightcubes is a goblin or an orc? Even our sweet Alice?"

"Obviously not," Critter replied, slapping Vassago's hands away in annoyance. "Listen up—the Underworld, as Rath created it, is split into two main areas. Just to the west of the middle is the Human Empire, where normal people live. And around it is the Dark Territory, which is chock-full of monsters. Alice is obviously going to be somewhere in that human realm, but it's super-huge, so finding her will be impossible if we're just peering in from out here."

"It should be easy. People understand words, right? So just dive into the Human Empire, ask around if anyone knows an Alice, and we'll find her in no time."

"You're an idiot. Hey, everyone, we've got a live one!"

"Shut the hell up!!"

"Listen, the Underworld was created by the Japanese. So obviously, the language those folks are gonna speak is Japanese, too. Can you speak Japanese?" Critter asked with a mocking smile.

But Vassago just grinned back. "*Namete moraccha komarunda yo na.*"

Instantly, Critter's smirk vanished, and the rest of the team was similarly stunned. Even Gabriel was stunned at his natural, fluent Japanese: *"We're gonna have a bad time if you underestimate me."*

The Hispanic young man switched back to English. "I got no communication problems. You got anything else you wanna say to me, Four-Eyes?"

"Y-yeah...I do." Critter snorted, recovering admirably. "There are tens of thousands of people living in the Human Empire. And you think you're gonna go around alone and ask every... last...one......?"

He trailed off, then shot upright as though reaching an epiphany. Vassago swore when the man's head struck him in the jaw, but the hacker ignored him. "Wait. Wait, wait, wait, wait. It might need to be alone..."

At that point, the vague suggestion of an idea inside Gabriel's head began to coalesce into a rough shape. "Ah...I see. The accounts prepared for logging in to the Underworld probably aren't all simple level-one commoners. Is that what you mean, Critter?"

"Yes. Yes, Boss!"

The hacker banged on the keyboard as if it were a percussion instrument, scrolling through a number of lists on the big screen. "They should have accounts that correspond to all different classes so that Rath's operators can log in and observe or manipulate the simulation. Military officers...or commanders... or nobles, royal families...Maybe even the emperor himself..."

"Damn, that'd be pretty cool," Vassago muttered, stroking his chin. "So you could log in to play the shogun or president or whatever and just order everyone around? Full military procession! Right face! Search for Alice! That would be so easy."

"...Y'know, after *you* said it, my brilliant idea sounds so stupid now," Critter grumbled, scrolling through the lists as fast as he could. After a few seconds, he came to a stop and swore, which was rare for him. "Shit—no good. Direct input or logging in on a high-level account from this point on has a friggin' password on it, too. Sadly, it looks like the only way for us to dive into the Human Empire is in a low-level commoner account."

"...Hmm..."

Critter and Vassago were clearly disappointed, but Gabriel merely inclined his head without twitching a single facial muscle.

The amount of time they had left to work with was limited. But that was only a limit prescribed in real-world time. The Underworld displayed on the screen ran on incredibly compressed time, hundreds of times faster than the real world.

In other words, the twenty-three hours they had in real life would be over an entire year in the Underworld. With that much time, it was certainly possible to log in as a common person, find and secure Alice, then eject to the real world from the common console within the simulation.

But it was also a very tedious and unnecessary approach. If anything, trying it from outside the Human Empire might be faster.

"Critter, are there any high-level accounts outside the empire... in the Dark Territory?"

"...Outside? Wouldn't the likelihood that Alice is on that side be way, way lower?" Critter wondered, even as he tapped at the keys to figure out the answer to the question.

Gabriel glanced up at the new window and said, "I suppose it would be. But the boundary between the two areas isn't completely impregnable, is it? Depending on the access level of the account, there might be a way to pass that boundary."

"Oh, hell yeah, Bro! You got all the best ideas! So you're saying... rather than being some human boss, we'll be the monsters' boss instead and invade them?! That sounds way more exciting!" Vassago hollered, whistling in excitement.

As usual, Critter was the one to dump cold water on him. "You're free to get as excited as you want," he deadpanned, "but if you log in to the Dark Territory, you're gonna have to be a hobgoblin or an orc or whatever. I mean, it suits you...Oh, hey, I found it!"

He smacked a key with a flourish, and two more windows appeared.

"Let's see. Unlike on the human side, there are only two super-accounts here…but hey, no password! Let's see…One of them is apparently a dark knight. Its access level is…seventy! That's pretty good!"

"Yeah, very nice! I'll use that one!" Vassago clamored. Critter ignored him and brought the other window on top.

"And the other one is…What is this? The status field is blank, and there's no listed level, either. All it has is the account name. It says…how do you read this? Emperor…Vecta?"

"Holy crap, an emperor? Never mind, I'll take—," Vassago started to say, until Gabriel clapped him on the shoulder from behind.

"No, I will use that one."

"Huh? But, Bro, can you even speak Japanese?"

"*Omae hodo janai gana,*" Gabriel replied, the result of three years of Japanese study. While he might not speak it as well as Vassago—as he had just said—and he'd given up on reading or writing, he knew he was good enough at speaking it for casual conversations.

"Ohhh, damn. Okay, Bro, you can be the emperor, and I'll take the dark knight. Yeah, this is getting fun now! Can we log in yet, Four-Eyes?!"

Critter just typed away, completely ignoring Vassago. He was absorbed in the information popping up on the monitor. Gabriel approached him and quietly asked, "What is it, Critter? Is there another problem?"

"…It's not really a problem, more of a curiosity…I'm seeing some strange terms popping up in the data files. I just don't exactly know what it means…"

"Oh? What would that be?" Gabriel asked.

Critter took a deep breath.

"…Final stress test."

3

Higa hesitantly broke the heavy silence that shrouded the sub-control room.

"Um, well…His body—that is, Kirigaya's physical situation in the real world, as I just explained…does not leave room for optimism."

When he saw how Asuna Yuuki flinched with Rinko Koujiro's hands still on her shoulders, he hastily added, "B-but there's also a slim hope!"

"…Meaning?" Rinko asked sharply but with a note of pleading as well.

"Kirito continues to be logged in to the Underworld."

Higa looked up at the monitor, which was much smaller than the big one in the main control room they'd been chased from. With a few clicks of the mouse, the display turned into a full map of the Underworld with the circular human lands and the Dark Territory surrounding it.

"In other words, while his self-image might be damaged, his fluctlight itself continues to be active, and it receives and reacts to stimuli. So while it might not be possible here, maybe his soul can be healed in the Underworld instead. He damaged his own soul by excessive self-flagellation. So if someone else provides him with forgiveness…then maybe…"

Higa was aware that what he was saying was vague, unscientific. But it was also his honest, true opinion.

After the NerveGear and the Medicuboid, the Soul Translator was the latest evolution of brain-machine interface. But when it came to the fluctlight, the form of human quantum consciousness as discovered by the very machine Higa had helped develop, what he didn't know vastly outweighed what he did.

Was the fluctlight a physical construct?

Or was it some kind of conceptual phenomenon that couldn't be explained with modern science?

If the latter, perhaps Kazuto Kirigaya's wounded and exhausted soul could be healed by some other power that surpassed science.

Such as, for example, love.

"…I'll go."

The tiny but determined voice filled the sub-control room just as the thought had entered Higa's mind.

Everyone in the room held their breath as they looked at the one who spoke. Asuna Yuuki nodded to Rinko Koujiro to indicate that she was all right and took a step forward to repeat herself.

"I'll go into the Underworld. I want to go in there and tell Kirito that he did good things. That through all the hardships and sad things that I'm sure happened, he did everything that he could."

Higa was the kind of person who was prepared to be married to his work for life, but even he had to admit that the sight of Asuna, her light-brown eyes filled with tears, was indescribably beautiful.

Kikuoka appeared to have been struck by this sentiment, too, but after a moment, his lenses hid his eyes, and he looked at the door to the adjacent room.

"We do have another Soul Translator open," the officer admitted, his face pensive. "But the Underworld is not in a peaceful state at the moment. Within a few hours by our time, it should be entering its final stress test phase, as we had planned it out."

"Final...stress? What's going to happen?" Rinko asked.

Higa cut in with a gesture to explain. "Well, um...to put it simply, the shell's going to crack. The human territory and Dark Territory have been separated for centuries by the Eastern Gate, which is going to fall to zero durability and allow an army of monsters into the human lands. If humanity has built up a sufficient defensive structure, they should be able to drive back the invaders in the end. But in this experiment, Kirito mostly destroyed the Axiom Church, which is the ruling body, so...I'm not sure if that will happen..."

"In a sense, it might be necessary for one of us to dive in there, regardless," Kikuoka muttered, crossing his arms. "When the invasion begins, it's possible that wherever she is in the human lands, Alice could be killed. If that happens, then the entire locking of the main console to buy time will be for nothing...But if we take a high-ranking account, provide protection for Alice, escort her to the far altar, and eject her lightcube to Subcon, then..."

"Yes...that's what you asked Kirito to do right before the accident," Rinko noted. Kikuoka nodded powerlessly.

"Yes. If he had been well, I know he would have done it. He was right next to Alice at the time..."

"So even though months have passed on the inside since that point...you think it's likely that they're still together?"

Higa considered that question. "Yes...I think we can make that conjecture. So maybe we *should* ask Asuna to do the dive...Not only will she be best at communicating with Kirito, but combat ability will be needed to protect Alice. And out of all the people here, Asuna's easily the most experienced at virtual movement."

"Then the highest-level account we can provide would be best," Kikuoka suggested.

Higa nodded and ran his fingers over the keys. "Well, you've got the pick of the litter. Knights, generals, nobles...We've got a whole variety of high-ranking accounts to use."

"Um, hang on," said Rinko, sounding slightly anxious.

"What's up?"

"...Is there no possibility that the people who attacked us are thinking the exact same thing? What did you just say? The secret to securing Alice is an internal operation?"

"Ah...yes, it is possible that they could do the same thing. Maincon down below has two STLs as well. But they don't have the time to crack the login to use any high-level accounts, I bet. Only level-one civilians. That's not the kind of character profile that will help them in the fray of the final stress test," Higa explained, speaking rapidly.

But he had a brief moment of anxiety—a feeling that he was forgetting something important.

Unfortunately, the sight of the high-speed list of accounts scrolling past distracted him, and that concern never reached the surface.

Sword Ar

The 4th Episode
Project Alicization
The New Chapter
War of the Underworld

t Online

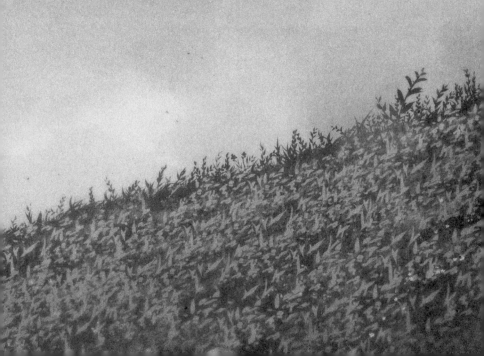

Ocean Turtle Interior

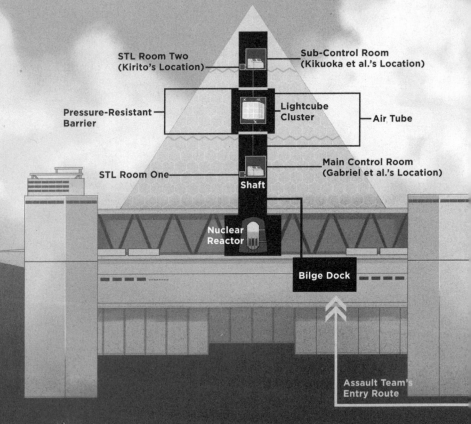

STL Room Two
(Kirito's Location)

Sub-Control Room
(Kikuoka et al.'s Location)

Pressure-Resistant
Barrier

Lightcube
Cluster

Air Tube

STL Room One

Main Control Room
(Gabriel et al.'s Location)

Shaft

Nuclear
Reactor

Bilge Dock

Assault Team's
Entry Route

The *Ocean Turtle* is an autonomous megafloat craft that also acts as
a base for Rath, the business front of Project Alicization, which is a
top-secret plan to create a true bottom-up artificial intelligence. The
giant pyramid-shaped craft has four Soul Translator machines in two
special rooms that are used to connect to the Underworld. The STL
Kirito is using to log in is located in STL Room Two.

In the center of the *Ocean Turtle* is the Lightcube Cluster, which
contains all the artificial fluctlights, or souls, of the Underworld's
residents. Gabriel's mission is to eject the precise lightcube that
contains Alice's fluctlight so it can travel down the air tube to them.

Illustration: Tatsuya Kurusu

CHAPTER SEVENTEEN

1

The dark knight Lipia Zancale leaped off the back of the dragon before it even came to a stop, and she took off at a sprint down the elevated walkway that connected the landing platform to the Imperial Palace.

Immediately, her breath came up short, and she reached up to rip off the helmet that covered her head and face. Her long blue-gray hair flew wild until she tossed it behind her back with her other hand and was finally comfortable enough to speed up. She wanted to get the heavy armor and cape off, too, but she had no intention of giving those scheming consuls that skulked around the palace even a glimpse at her bare skin.

As she raced down the curving walkway, the sight of the dark, looming palace jutting through the red sky came into view between the pillars on the right side.

Obsidia Palace was easily the tallest object—aside from the hateful End Mountains, of course—in the endlessly vast dark wasteland, carved out of a rocky mountain over a period of a hundred years.

From its throne room on the top floor, one could supposedly see the faint sight of the End Mountains on the far western horizon and the vast gate carved into them. Of course, no one actually knew whether that was true or not.

The throne of the dark nation had been empty ever since the first emperor, Vecta, the god of darkness, had descended into the void beneath the earth in ancient times. The great doors to the top floor were locked with a chain that had infinite life and would thus never open.

Lipia tore her eyes away from the top of the black castle and called out to the ogre guards at the gate she was rapidly approaching.

"I am Zancale, eleventh knight! Open the gate!!"

The wolf-headed, human-bodied guards were mighty, but slow to think, and it wasn't until just before Lipia reached the cast-iron gate that they finally began to rotate the crank that opened it.

She waited until it had ponderously rumbled open with just enough space to squeeze through sideways and slipped inside.

The castle welcomed Lipia on her first time back in three months with its usual frosty ambience. The kobolds kept the hallways absolutely spotless with their daily cleaning. Her boots pounded against the obsidian floor as she ran. Eventually, two scantily clad women with bewitching proportions appeared ahead of her, walking over so silently that they seemed to glide across the floor.

The large, pointed hats that rested atop their long hair identi-fied them as dark mages. Lipia kept running, intending to pass them without eye contact, but one of the women called out in a loud, teasing voice: "My goodness, what rumbling! Are the orcs stampeding nearby?"

The other one screamed with laughter. "Why, not at all. I rec-ognize this vibration: It's a giant!"

If it wasn't forbidden to draw your sword in the palace, I'd cut their tongues out, Lipia thought, racing past with no more than a flare of her nostrils.

Human women born in the land of darkness typically joined the dark mages guild after they graduated the training academy. It was a hedonistic group, where one learned excess instead of discipline, and all it produced were people like *them*, interested in nothing but their appearances.

And yet, they had a fierce rivalry with the women who chose to be knights. When she was a child in school, there was one magician who was her worst enemy, and the girl had put a horrible poison-bug curse on her. Lipia had gotten her back by cutting off her beloved braided hair, however.

In the end, the people of this land were all idiots who refused to look ahead.

Organizations and individuals were constantly bickering. A land that only knew how to separate good from bad through strength had no future.

For the moment, the Council of Ten maintained a fragile balance, but that would not last long. If one of the ten lords who made up the council died in the imminent war against the human land—what the orcs and goblins called the Ium Nation—the balance would be lost, replaced by chaos and bloodshed once more.

It was one of those ten who painted this picture of the future for Lipia—her direct superior, the commander of the dark knights brigade, and her lover.

And it was at this moment that Lipia carried the top-secret information he'd been waiting for. So she didn't have a single second to waste with the taunts of stupid mages.

She rushed straight across the empty hall and up the great stairs, skipping two at a time. She was in excellent shape, but even she was starting to run out of breath when she reached the proper floor at last.

The Council of Ten that collectively ruled the entire Dark Territory consisted of five humans, two goblins, an orc, an ogre, and a giant. After a hundred years of internal strife, they had finally reached a treaty of sorts, with the official understanding that none of the five races were above or below the others.

So the ten lords had their own private rooms on the eighteenth floor of Obsidia Palace, close to the top. Lipia ran down the hallway, trying to moderate the sound of her footsteps, turning to one door near the end and rapping on it three times with the back of her hand.

"Come in," said a deep voice.

She glanced both ways, confirmed that no one was watching, then slipped quickly through the door.

Inside the room, which was minimally decorated, the air was musky and familiar. She went down on one knee and lowered her head.

"Knight Lipia Zancale, returning from travel."

"Very good. Be seated," said the deep voice. Conscious of the quickening of her heartbeat, she looked up.

Sitting on one of the lounge chairs facing the round table was a man with his legs raised and crossed—the dark knight commander, or general of darkness, Vixur ul Shasta.

For a human, his size was tremendous. While they might not be similar in breadth, his height on its own was comparable to an ogre's. His black hair was cut short, and the whiskers around his mouth were well-groomed.

His simple hemp shirt rippled with muscles so burly, they threatened to pop the buttons clean off, but there was no extra flesh around his waist whatsoever. His body was perfect, especially for a man over forty, but few were aware that it was the product of a vigorous daily training regimen that he'd continued dutifully even after becoming the highest of knights.

Lipia sat on the sofa across from Shasta, fighting the urge to jump into the arms of her lover now that they were finally together again after three long months.

Shasta straightened up and gave one of the crystal glasses on the table to Lipia before opening a bottle of aged wine.

"I snuck it out of the treasure repository yesterday, thinking I'd share it with you," he said with a wink, pouring the fragrant deep-red liquid into the glass. He always looked like such a scamp when he made faces like that. Just like the old days.

"Th...thank you, my lord."

"How many times must I tell you not to do that when we are alone?"

"But I *am* still on duty."

Shasta shrugged in exasperation. They shared a quiet toast, and she downed the rich wine in one gulp, feeling her exhausted life value begin to recover after the long journey.

"And now," said the knight's commander quietly, his own glass empty and expression sharp, "I must ask you about the nature of this emergency that you sent a familiar to warn me of."

"Sir..."

Lipia couldn't help but glance back and forth before leaning over. Shasta was a bold and open man but also a scrupulous one. The chamber was placed under a number of defensive arts, such that even the "witch" who headed the dark mages guild would not be able to listen in. Even still, the importance of the secret information she was carrying forced her to speak in hushed tones.

Lipia stared into Shasta's dark eyes and said, "The supreme commander of the Axiom Church in the human realm...is dead."

Instantly, the general of darkness's eyes flashed. He broke the silence with a long, heavy sigh.

"If I were to ask if that was the truth...I would only be shaming you. I do not doubt your information...it is just...That undying one..."

"Yes...I understand your feeling, my lord. I found it hard to believe and took a full week to confirm the information. It is the truth. I sent an 'ear bug' into Central Cathedral and heard it for myself."

"That was a reckless move. If they'd traced the art, you would have been trapped in their city and torn to pieces."

"I know. But given that they could not even detect my art, I think the information is accurate."

"...Hrm..." Shasta sipped from his second glass of wine, his menacing face downcast. "When did it happen? What was the cause?"

"Roughly half a year ago..."

"Half a year. Yes, around that time, the security in the mountains was more lax than usual."

"Correct. As for the cause of death...well, I find it hard to believe on its own, but it was said to be defeat by sword in combat..."

"By sword? You mean someone cut the undying one in two?"

"It is not possible," Lipia replied, shaking her head. "I believe she must have finally reached her natural end, despite her reputation. But in order to preserve the holy reputation of their supreme pontifex, they must have spread that false story instead..."

"Yes...I suspect you are correct. But still...Administrator, dead..."

Shasta closed his eyes, folded his arms, and leaned against the backrest. He was silent for a long time, until his eyes snapped open again.

"It's an opportunity," he said simply.

Lipia held her breath, then asked hoarsely, "For what?"

"For peace, of course," he answered immediately.

It was a dangerous word to speak aloud in this castle. It instantly faded into the air of the room.

"Do you think...it is possible, my lord?" Lipia whispered.

Shasta concentrated on the red liquid inside his glass and slowly but firmly nodded. "Whether it is possible or not, it must be achieved at all costs."

He downed the wine and continued. "The life of the great gate that has separated the lands of humanity and darkness since the time of creation is finally running out. The armies of the five races of darkness are like a kettle about to boil over just before the invasion of the Human Empire with its bounties of sun and earth. At the last Council of Ten, there was great debate about how to divide the lands, riches, and slaves of that realm. Sometimes it is hard to fully fathom their greed," Shasta said bluntly. His tone made Lipia tense.

Unlike the Human Empire, where a great text called the Taboo

Index reigned supreme, the Dark Territory had just one rule: Take what you want with strength.

That meant that to the nine lords who had nearly limitless greed, which drove them to the very heights of success, Shasta, with his thoughts of peace with the human realm, was an outsider, a heretic.

But it was because of those strange, alien thoughts that Lipia felt herself so drawn to him. And unlike the women who served the other lords, Lipia had never been taken by force. Shasta had knelt and offered her flowers. He had wooed her with sincere words and feelings.

Shasta had no idea that his lover was lost in reminiscence. He continued, his voice deep and heavy, "But...the lords overlook the humans. Particularly the Integrity Knights, who have protected their borders for three hundred years."

Lipia nodded, feeling her mind sharpen at the mention of that name. "Indeed...They are all fearsome opponents."

"Warriors worth a thousand men, as the saying goes. Countless members of the dark knights brigade have been slain by them, but never has the reverse been true. Their combat is shrewd and precise, and the divine weapons they utilize are peerless in strength...Even I have never fully bested one in combat, although I have been close on multiple occasions. And I have had to retreat many, many times."

"But...that is only because of their bizarre abilities to shoot fire and light and such from their swords..."

"Perfect Weapon Control arts, you mean. I had the knighthood's articians study them for a long time, but we never reached a full understanding. You would need more than a hundred goblin soldiers to counteract even a single one of those attacks."

"But still, our military numbers are over fifty thousand. And there are only about thirty of those Integrity Knights. Couldn't we win with sheer numbers...?" Lipia wondered.

The edges of Shasta's manicured mustache curled sardonically.

"Warriors worth a thousand, as I said. We would lose thirty thousand of our number by that calculation."

"You don't think…they would fell so many?"

"Perhaps not. While I don't like it as a tactical choice, if we stacked our knights, ogres, and giants along the front row and hurled dark arts remotely from the rear, even the Integrity Knights would eventually fall. But I can't imagine how much damage we would suffer to slay even a single knight. It might not actually be thirty thousand, but I would believe half of that number."

He set the crystal glass down loudly on the table. Lipia made to pour another cup, but he motioned her off, then leaned his broad back against the lounge chair.

"…And the result of that, naturally, would be unequal distribution of power among the five tribes of darkness. The Council of Ten would be meaningless, and our equal treaty would be a shell of its former self. The Age of Blood and Iron from a hundred years past would return. In fact, this would be worse. In this case, the gates to the sea of milk and honey that is the Human Empire would be thrown open. A hundred years would be too short to end the fighting over control of that prize…"

This was the worst possible future: the vision that Shasta had feared and explained to Lipia time and time again. And none of the other lords saw it as the worst option—in fact, they seemed to welcome it.

Lipia looked down at the full-body armor that she'd been given in exchange for her knighthood vows. Its scuffed but polished black surface shone in the light. She had been a small child, and during the Age of Blood and Iron, she would never have been made a knight. She'd have been sold to slavers or dumped in the wilderness outside town, where her short life would have come to a miserable end.

But thanks to the peace treaty (such as it was), she'd spent her childhood in the youth training academy rather than in a slave market, and it was there that her late-blooming skill with the sword had been discovered, and she'd reached what was about the highest status that a human woman could possibly hope to gain.

Since becoming a knight, she had spent nearly her entire monthly salary on gathering abandoned children in the outer regions where the slavers still reigned, running something like a nursery for them until they were old enough to enter school.

She hadn't told Shasta about this, much less her other comrades. It was because even she couldn't exactly explain why she was doing it.

It was just...a feeling that made its home in a corner of her mind—a sensation that something about this land, where the mighty were meant to seize what they wanted, was wrong. Unlike Shasta, she wasn't knowledgeable enough to put her doubts into clear, concise words, but she most certainly felt that there was a better way for this land—and for the entire Underworld itself—to be.

Lipia had a vague sense in her mind that this new world she envisioned probably existed far into the future of the peace that Shasta sought. And of course, as a woman, she wanted to help the man she loved.

But...

"But how do you intend to convince the other lords? And... would the Integrity Knights even entertain a negotiation for peace?" she asked, her voice quiet.

"...Mmm..." Shasta grunted, closing his eyes and rubbing his smooth mustache. When he spoke, his voice was laced with bitterness. "I sense that there is ground to be made with the Integrity Knights. If their pontifex is dead, then it would be old Bercouli calling the shots over there. He's a shrewd fellow, but he can be reasoned with. No...the problem is with the Council of Ten. This might seem to be a contradiction, but..." His eyes lifted, gazing into space with a fierce glint. "They might need to be killed. At least four of them."

Lipia gasped, and against her better judgment, she asked, "When you say four...you mean both goblin leaders, the orc leader, and...?"

"The head of the dark mages guild. She is hoping to find the secret to Administrator's longevity and one day rise to becoming empress. She will never accept a pathway to peace."

"B-but—!" Lipia protested. "It's too dangerous, my lord! I'm sure the goblins and orc are no match for you...but I cannot imagine what sort of wicked tricks the dark mage will use against you!"

She stopped there, but Shasta did not reply at first. He held his silence for a long while, and when he finally did speak, it was not what she'd expected to hear.

"Say, Lipia. How long has it been since you came to me?"

"Huh? Er...w-well...it was when I was twenty-one...so four years."

"That long already? I'm sorry for leaving things so...uncertain for all these years. What do you think...? Is it time, at last?" His eyes wandered, and he scratched his head. At last, the head of the dark knights muttered brusquely, "Will you...officially be my wife? I'm sorry I can't be younger."

"M...my lord..."

Lipia's eyes bulged—and she felt something hot blooming around her heart, growing until she was ready to leap over the table and into the arms of her beloved on the other side—

Beyond the thick, heavy door, a tense, high-pitched voice cried, "Emergency! It is an emergency! Oh, this is a disaster! Come quick, my fellows, come quick, come quick!!"

The voice was vaguely familiar to her. It belonged to the head of the commerce guild, one of the ten lords. Lipia remembered a large, broad fellow who looked the picture of wealth—only now his voice was shrieking and panicked, unbefitting of that mental picture.

"It is an emergency!! The ch-chains! That seal the imperial chamber! They *tremble*!!"

2

As Gabriel Miller made his appearance in the imperial chamber as Emperor Vecta, he viewed the artificial fluctlights prostrating themselves before him with a kind of wonder.

They were light quantum information, trapped inside a lightcube two inches to a side. But in this world, they were real humans with intelligence and a soul—even if half of the ten arrayed before him were monsters with grotesque appearances.

These ten generals, who styled themselves as feudal lords, the knights and mages behind them, and the army of fifty thousand stationed outside the castle were all units given to Gabriel for his use in battle. He had to use these pawns as he saw fit to vanquish the defenses of the Human Empire and capture Alice.

But unlike a real-time strategy (RTS) game in the regular world, these units could not be moved about with a mouse and keyboard. He had to lead them with speech and character and give them their orders.

Gabriel stood up from the throne without a word, took several steps, and glanced at a mirror set into the wall behind him. He saw himself dressed in a truly hideous outfit.

The features of his face and the nearly white blond hair were Gabriel's as they existed in real life. But now he wore a crown of black metal with inlaid red jewels, a leather shirt, and trousers similar to black suede, as well as a luxurious pelt gown, also pure black. A slender, faintly glowing longsword hung from his waist, and there was fine silver stitching on his boots and gloves. On top of all that, a long cape the color of blood hung from his back.

To the right, about a step lower than the throne, there was a knight with his hands casually pressed behind his head, looking around.

That was Vassago Casals, who had logged in at the same time as Gabriel, dressed in an amethyst-purple suit of armor. He'd warned the man not to get carried away and do anything until they got a handle on the situation, but Vassago's fingers were tapping away at the back of his head, expressing his desire to voice his feelings about such an incredible experience in his usual slang.

Gabriel shook his head and looked back at his reflection. For someone who was so used to wearing tailor-made suits, he looked rather uncomfortable now. But in the Underworld, he was not the CTO of a private military contractor.

He was the emperor who ruled over the vast Dark Territory.

And he was a god.

Gabriel closed his eyes, inhaled, and let the breath out.

Somewhere in his mind, the switch flipped to take his acting role from the tough, calm commanding officer to a merciless emperor instead.

His lids rose, and Gabriel—the god of darkness, Vecta—swept his crimson cape aside to view the ten generals imperiously. With a voice devoid of all humanity, he intoned, "Raise your heads and name yourselves. Starting with you at the end."

A plump middle-aged man, who practically had his face rubbing against the floor, bounded upward with surprising agility and spoke in fluent Japanese.

"Y-yes, Your Majesty! I am the head of the commerce guild, and my name is Rengil Gila Scobo!"

He lowered his head again, and then a figure like a small mountain next to him budged.

At a full height, this creature was at least twelve feet tall, his torso crisscrossed with gleaming chains and a string of animal pelts around his waist. He lifted his abnormally long-bridged nose and said, in a bass that practically shook the ground, "Chief of the giants, Sigurosig."

As Gabriel chewed on the fact that even this monster had intelligence and a soul, the third figure spoke in an unpleasant rasp.

"Head of the assassins guild...Fu Za..."

Next to the striking giant, this slight figure, frail and unassuming in a hooded robe, was of indeterminate age and gender. Gabriel considered ordering this one to show their face but then figured it was probably the assassin's code never to give away appearances.

Instead, he focused on the next general—and had to keep himself from scowling.

A creature that seemed designed to define the word *hideous* was plopped down on the steps; its legs were too short for it to properly kneel. Its belly was round, bloated, and shiny, and around a neck that threatened to sink into its shoulders hung a string of what looked like small mammal skulls.

The head atop its body was about seven parts pig to three parts human. It had a flat, jutting nose, a large mouth exposing tusks, and beady eyes, but they gleamed with cruel intelligence that just made it that much more grotesque.

"Chief of the orcs, Lilpilin."

The orc's voice was high enough in pitch that Gabriel couldn't be sure whether it was male or female, but he did not find himself curious in the slightest. An orc was bound to be an inferior unit. It would have no use but as a sacrifice.

Next to lift his head, in one smooth motion, was a young man barely more than a boy. His reddish-gold curls and tanned skin featured nothing more than a leather belt on his upper half. Below, he wore tight-fitting short pants and sandals. On his hands were a pair of gloves with square metal studs.

"Tenth champion of the pugilists guild, Iskahn!!" the youngster shouted. Gabriel found this a bit confusing. By pugilist, did he mean boxing? Was it possible to be a good soldier if unarmed?

His line of thought was interrupted by a sudden growling.

It was coming from another demi-human of considerable size, if not as large as the giant. This one's upper half was almost entirely covered in long furs. He only realized that they were not clothing but his *actual* fur when he noticed that the creature's head was that of a beast itself.

It looked like a wolf: extended snout, rows of sharp fangs like saws, and triangular ears. Its long tongue hung from its mouth and formed words that were hard to make out.

"*Grrr...Ogre...chief...Furgr...rrr...*"

Gabriel wasn't entirely sure whether that was the ogre's name or just more growling, so he merely nodded and looked to the next person. He was greeted by an awful, screeching voice.

"This one is Hagashi, chief of the mountain goblins! Your Majesty, I beg you to give the honor of first spear to the brave warriors of my clan!!"

It was a smaller humanoid, with a bald, monkey-like head sprouting long, thin ears from the sides. It was shorter than the giant, the orc, the ogre, and even the humans.

According to what Critter had said before the dive, there was only one law in the Dark Territory: Those with the power rule. So what was it about the goblin, which looked so weak, that gave it equal status with the other races?

They'd clearly be inferior soldiers even to the orcs, but this interested Gabriel. He stared at the mountain goblin's face and came away with his answer. The ugly creature's tiny eyes were swirling with ferocious greed and desire.

No sooner had the mountain-goblin chief finished his greeting than the leader next to him, a similar humanoid with a different color of skin, screeched, "Absolutely not! We will be ten times more useful to you than these bunglers! I am Kubiri, chief of the flatland goblins!"

"What did you call me, you slug slurper?! All that humidity has waterlogged your tiny brain!!"

"And being closer to the sun has dried out yours into a husk!!"

Before the two goblins could sink any further into argument, there was a snapping sound and a burst of blue sparks, sending the goblin chiefs screaming out of the way.

"You are in the presence of the emperor, you two," said a sultry voice belonging to a young woman wearing a revealing outfit. Her outstretched hand had produced the sparks with a snap as easily as if her fingers were the flint of a lighter.

She got up slowly, leaning over to accentuate her full figure and bewitching beauty, and gave an affected salute. Vassago whistled softly, and Gabriel could not entirely blame him.

Her light-brown skin shone as if oiled, covered by just the bare minimum of black enameled leather. Her boots had high heels like needles. On her back was a fur cloak shining black and silver, over which her voluminous platinum-blond hair hung nearly to her waist.

The woman's eye shadow and lipstick were brilliantly bright blue, and her eyes were nearly the same shade, narrowed coquettishly. "I am the chancellor of the dark mages guild, Dee Eye Ell. My three thousand mages—and my body and mind—belong wholly to you."

It was quite an act of seduction, but Gabriel, who was never controlled by sexual urges, merely nodded in response. The witch named Dee blinked and seemed to consider saying something else but decided better of it and bowed again before kneeling.

This was a wise decision, Gabriel thought. Now there was only one general unit left to be introduced.

This man, who merely bowed in silence, was rather tall for a human and looked to be in the prime of his life. His full black armor glinted softly with countless scrapes and cuts. Faint scars were also visible on what Gabriel could see of his forehead and nose.

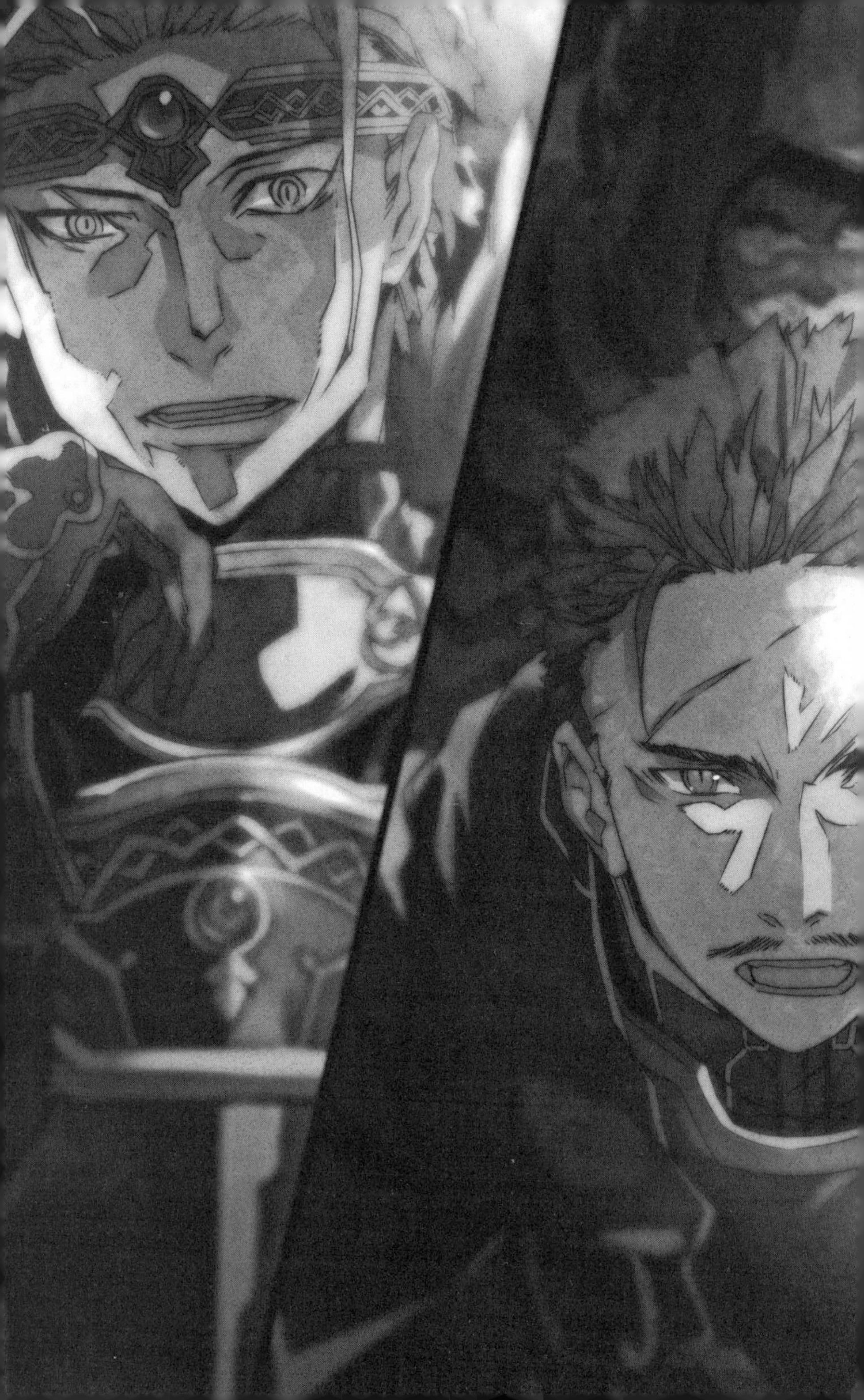

Without lifting his face, the man spoke in a rich baritone. "Commander of the dark knights brigade, Vixur ul Shasta. Before I pledge my sword…I have a question for Your Majesty."

When he looked up at last, Gabriel saw that his features were as hard as those of the few "true soldiers" he'd met over the course of his life.

Unlike the other nine generals, this knight named Shasta dared to stare at him with a fierce determination of some kind. Even deeper, he asked, "What desire brings you back to the throne at this time?"

Ah, I see. Yes, they are indeed more than just simple programs. I ought to keep this in mind at all times, Gabriel told himself. He gave his answer coldly, playing the role of the merciless emperor.

"Blood and fear. Flames and destruction. Death and screams."

When they heard his voice, hard like metal, the generals' expressions tensed.

Gabriel looked at each of them in turn, then swept aside his fur cape to raise his arm to the western sky. Words of false conquest fell from his mouth, easy and automatic.

"…The great gate that protects the land to the west, overflowing with the power of the gods who exiled me from their celestial realm, will fall very soon. I have returned…to make my might known to all corners of the land!"

Critter had given him as much information as possible about the so-called final stress test that was approaching in a week of in-simulation time. He explained the topic in the same adopted, grandiose tone.

"The moment the gate falls, the lands of man will belong to the people of the darkness! My only desire is for the priestess of the gods who resides within that distant land! You have my blessing to kill and steal from as many other humans as you desire! This is the moment that all the tribes of the darkness have longed for—the promised time!!"

There was a brief, ringing silence.

Then a fierce, high-pitched bellow broke through it.

"*Giieee!!* Kill them! Kill all the white Iums!!" screeched the chief of the orcs, its beady eyes full of greed and resentment. The goblin chiefs picked up the cry next, thrusting their stringy arms into the air.

"*Hooooh!!* Battle!! Battle!!"

"*Uraaaaa!!* Battle, battle, battle!!"

The war cries spread to the other generals—and from there, to the officers lined up behind them. The black-robed figures of the assassins guild twirled and swayed like the tree branches their limbs resembled, and the witches of the dark mages guild cheered and shot sparks of all different colors.

The vast throne chamber was full of the primitive roar of war and blood.

And then Gabriel noticed that only the knight named Shasta remained kneeling and perfectly still.

It was impossible to tell from the statuesque figure whether this was simple military decorum or the manifestation of some other emotion.

"Damn, Bro, I didn't know you could pull that off! Why didn't you decide to become an actor instead?" Vassago said with a grin as he tossed the bottle of wine.

Gabriel snorted. "I merely met the demands of the situation. You ought to learn how to give a proper speech when the time calls for it. You're in a position one step higher than that lot, remember."

He popped the cork out of the bottle and took some of the ruby liquid into his mouth. It then occurred to him that this might actually count as imbibing alcohol in the midst of a military operation.

Vassago seemed to think it was a waste if they *didn't* drink. He slugged the fancy vintage down as if it were beer and wiped his mouth afterward. "I don't give a shit about orders or speeches—I just wanna kill guys at the front line. We're on a dive in this incredible VR world, so why not take advantage of it...? I mean, look at this wine and that bottle. They're practically *real*."

"And in exchange, every wound you suffer will hurt and bleed. There is no pain absorber in this simulation."

"That's the best part." Vassago smirked. Gabriel shrugged, put the bottle down, and got to his feet from the sofa.

The imperial chamber on the top floor of Obsidia Palace was far bigger than the executive rooms at Glowgen DS's headquarters, and the enormous windows offered a full view of the night sky over the castle town below. It wasn't quite as bright or colorful as San Diego's, but that just made it more fantastic.

The generals who styled themselves lords had left to prepare for the coming war, and the fires of the supply train transporting materials from storage stretched down the road as far as the eye could see. He had commanded the head of the commerce guild to use the castle's entire stockpile of food and equipment, so the soldiers would not starve or freeze anytime soon.

Gabriel turned away from the abundance of lights and strode to the corner of the room to place his hand on the purple slab of crystal there—the system console.

He made a few commands in the menu and hit the button to call an external observer. There was the strange sensation of time decelerating back to its normal speed, and then Critter's high-speed voice came through the screen. "Is that you, Captain?! I just got back to the main control room to keep tabs on you and Vassago in your dive!"

"We're already in the first night. I knew how it worked, but this time acceleration is a very strange thing, regardless. For now, the situation is proceeding as planned. Within the next day or so, I will have all the units supplied and ready, and in two days, we will begin marching on the Human Empire."

"Fantastic, sir. Now, when you get Alice, you'll need to bring her back to where you are and perform the menu option to eject her to the main control room. Then Alice's lightcube will be ours. Also, this is something you should tell that idiot Vassago."

Gabriel heard a muttered curse over his shoulder—Critter's voice had been loud enough for all parties to hear.

"Since we don't have full admin privileges, you cannot reset accounts. If either of you die while you're in there, you can't continue using those super-accounts. You'll have to start over as a typical grunt!"

"Yes…I'm aware. I will ensure that we're not fighting at the forefront for now. What is the JSDF doing?"

"Nothing, as of this moment. Doesn't seem like they're aware you guys are in a dive."

"Good. I'm going to cut communication. I'd like to save the next one for after I've secured Alice."

"Roger that. Looking forward to it."

Gabriel closed the communication window, and the usual accelerated-time sensation returned with another slightly unpleasant shift. Vassago was still spitting and grumbling as he fought with the fasteners of his armor, until at last he had hurled all of it onto the floor and was standing in leather shirt and trousers.

"So, Bro…I'm guessing that if I wanted to go kick it downtown, that would be…not cool with you?"

"Have patience for now. I'll give you a night to yourself after the operation is finished."

"Got it. So no killing or women for now…Guess I'll just get a good night's sleep, then. I'll take that room."

Vassago disappeared into an adjacent bedroom, cracking his joints. Gabriel exhaled and removed the crown from his forehead. He put the ostentatious cloak and gown on the sofa and tossed the sword on top of them.

In the other VR games he'd played, removing a piece of equipment returned it to item storage, but this world did not have such a convenient feature. If he lived like this for a month, the room would become a pigsty, but he'd be leaving the castle in two days and returning only so he could log out.

Gabriel undid the top button on his shirt, opened the door on the opposite side of the room from Vassago's—and froze, eyes narrowed.

In the bedroom, which was also frightfully large, there was a small figure prostrated next to a bed of almost comical extravagance.

He had ordered that no one, not even servants, come to the floor above the castle's throne room. How could someone have defied the orders of their god?

He considered going back for his sword, then thought better of it and chose to enter the room, closing the door behind him.

"…Who are you?" he demanded.

The female voice that answered was a bit on the husky side.

"…My role is to attend to your bedside this night."

"Ahh." His eyebrow perked up. He crossed the darkened room toward the bed.

It was a young woman in a sheer gown, her hands on the floor. Her ashy-blue hair was tied up top with a decorative string. The shape of her body, subtly visible through the material, did not suggest the presence of any weapons.

"On whose order?" he asked, sitting on the sheer silk sheets.

The woman paused, then quietly answered, "This is…my duty, Your Majesty."

"I see."

Gabriel looked away and lowered himself onto the middle of the bed. A few seconds later, the woman got up and silently slipped to his right. "Pardon my intrusion…"

Even Gabriel had to admit that she had a striking, exotic beauty. Her skin was dark, but the shape of her cheekbones suggested a certain Scandinavian-style regality. As he watched her undo her clothing and pull at the string that held her hair up, Gabriel was even moved, in a way.

So artificial fluctlights will act to such an extent?

Even this woman was incomplete as a true AI. So what heights must Alice, the completed version, be capable of?

It was not that the woman was offering up her body that had so impressed Gabriel.

No, it was that he knew and foresaw that when her hair fell down, she would whip out the knife that glinted in the air overhead.

Gabriel saw it coming and had plenty of time to hold back her right arm with one hand and quickly grab her around the throat with the other, throwing her down to the bed.

"Rrrgh!!" the woman grunted, flailing wildly and trying to stab him with the knife. She was stronger than she looked, but not enough to cause Gabriel to panic. He immobilized the elbow of her dominant arm and held his left thumb hard against her windpipe to keep her in place.

Despite the obvious pain on her features, the woman's gray eyes never lost their determination. Based on the ferocity of her expression, the clumsiness of her makeup, and her musculature, she did not seem to be an assassin by trade. So this act of rebellion had come not from the leader of the assassins named Fu Za but from one of the other generals—probably one of the humans.

Gabriel leaned closer to the woman and asked again, "On whose order?"

As she had done before, she rasped, "It was…my decision."

"Then who is your commander?"

"……I have none."

"Hmm."

Gabriel considered this, emotionlessly and mechanically.

There was a limit to artificial fluctlights that Rath was trying to overcome, and that was their inability to defy any rule, law, or order from a higher person or body.

Compared to the people in the Human Empire with their many overlapping law systems, the Dark Territory seemed to be much freer, but at its heart, it operated no differently. It only looked that way because there was simply one law that ruled the fluctlights here.

And that law was "Take what you want with your own power."

It was survival of the fittest, where those with the greatest battle power ruled over the weak. If Rath's test had gone as planned, the ordered world of the humans and the chaos of the dark lands would've clashed without Gabriel's help, and the ensuing war would've provided the results they used to find that breakthrough.

But for whatever reason, before the project reached that stage, a fluctlight appeared in the human realm that broke through that limit. The informant at Rath did not say there had been a similar breakthrough on the dark side.

In other words, even the woman who attempted to assassinate the emperor with a mere knife was still a soul bound by the absolutes of law. Yet, when Gabriel asked—no, ordered—she did not reveal the name of her master. In other words, this woman prioritized her fidelity to her master more than the orders from Gabriel, her emperor and god. Or rephrased yet again, she thought her master was stronger than the emperor was.

In order for this operation to go smoothly, Gabriel—Emperor Vecta—would need to demonstrate his fighting ability to the generals and officer units so they understood that he was indeed the strongest being in the world. But he certainly couldn't slaughter every last one of those generals. So what could he do?

No...in any case, he would need to eliminate only *one* of the generals: whichever one gave this woman the intent to kill him.

How could he expose the traitor? Contact Critter again and have him observe the generals from the outside? No, that would force him to fix the acceleration factor at one-to-one for a while, eating up valuable real-world time while he waited.

Instead, Gabriel gazed back into those steel-colored eyes and demanded, "Why did you attempt to take my life? Were you given money? Were you promised status?"

He didn't put much thought into the questions themselves. But the answer he got was nothing like what he expected to hear.

"For good cause!"

"Oh...?"

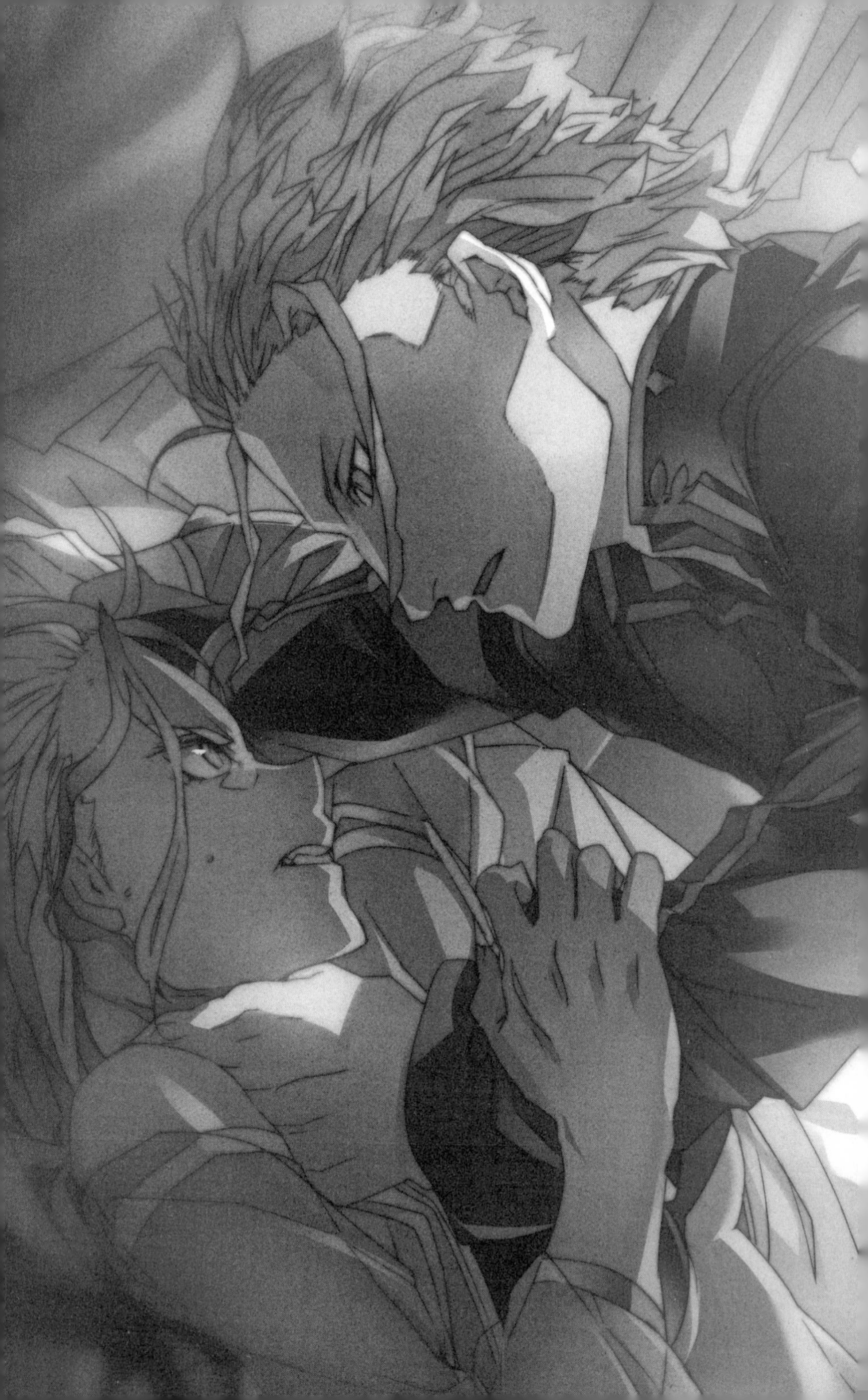

"If you start a war now, history will lose a hundred—no, two hundred years of progress! We mustn't go back to the days when the powerless were tortured!!"

Once again, Gabriel was mildly surprised. Was this woman really at the stage before the AI breakthrough? If so, was it this woman's master who'd put those words in her mouth?

He leaned closer, staring directly into those gray irises.

Determination. Loyalty. And hiding beyond those things…

Oh. I see.

In that case, he did not need this woman anymore. Or more accurately, he did not need her fluctlight.

Following his decision, Gabriel spared not another word, squeezing harder with the hand he had around her neck.

He could hear her vertebrae cracking, and the woman's eyes bulged. Her mouth opened in a silent scream. As he weighed down on her flailing limbs and mercilessly strangled her, Gabriel was filled with a different kind of surprise than before.

Was this really a virtual world? The sensation of muscle and cartilage being destroyed through his fingertips—the fear and agony exuding from her bare skin—all of it stimulated his senses in a more tangible way than the "real" world ever had.

Before he knew it, his body convulsed, and his left hand clenched on reflex.

There was a dull crunch, and the unfamiliar woman's vertebrae snapped.

And then Gabriel saw it.

Protruding from the woman's forehead, with her eyes closed and teeth gritted, came a radiant, colorful light.

It was the same thing—the cloud of the soul that he had witnessed when he murdered young Alicia.

Gabriel instantly opened his mouth to suck in the woman's soul.

Bitterness born of fear and pain.

The sourness of frustration and sadness.

And then, upon his tongue, the indescribable nectar of Heaven.

A vague, hazy light flickered against the back of his closed eyelids.

Young children frolicking in the front yard of an older two-story house. Humans, goblins, orcs, too. They looked to him, faces shining and arms outstretched as they ran closer.

The image vanished and was replaced by the torso of a man. His chest was broad and strong, warm, and powerfully enveloping.

"I love you...my lord..."

The faint voice echoed and faded away.

Even after all the visions passed, Gabriel continued to clutch the woman's corpse.

Sublime. What a truly sublime experience.

The majority of Gabriel's consciousness trembled with pleasure, but the remaining bit of rationality attempted to add a kind of logic to what he'd just experienced.

The woman's lightcube-encased fluctlight had made contact with Gabriel's own through the Soul Translator. So perhaps, as her life (or hit points) reached zero, a fragment of the quantum data that was released flowed back into him through his connection.

But at this point, that rational reason did not matter to him.

At last, he had again experienced the phenomenon he'd dedicated his life to finding. He absorbed the final emotion, the last fleeting love the dying woman felt, and savored it to the fullest. It was like manna from Heaven amid the barren wastes of the desert.

More.

I must have more.

I must kill more.

Gabriel rocked back, shaking with silent laughter.

—◆◆◆—

The ten generals and their various lieutenants were lined up, all bowing obsequiously, much to Gabriel's satisfaction.

As he'd ordered, they had fully prepared for the march in just two days. In fact, it might even be possible that these general units were more capable military officers than the ones found lounging around the executive offices of Glowgen DS.

At this rate, they might as well be finished products. On top of their excellent management skills, they were utterly loyal. You couldn't ask for anything more from an AI to be loaded onto battle robots.

And yet, it mustn't be forgotten that the fealty of the generals was an effect of the very flaw in the artificial fluctlights that Rath was so concerned about. It was because the concept that the one with the most power should rule was etched into their souls that these ten were so blindly obedient to Gabriel—to Vecta. It also meant that the moment they had any reason to doubt the emperor's power, any one of them could betray him.

That concern had already shown itself to be very real.

The woman who'd tried to sneak into his bed as an assassin two nights ago.

She had attempted to kill the emperor, the one with the highest authority in the land. In her heart, there was a master on a level higher than Gabriel. Someone whom she'd called *my lord* in her dying thoughts. And it was practically certain that it was one of the ten generals lined up before him now.

To her, this master was stronger even than Emperor Vecta. Which meant that it was highly likely this lord, whoever he was, secretly did not swear fealty to Gabriel, either. If he went into battle with such a unit under his command, the possibility of betrayal when he least expected it was undeniable, no matter how unlikely.

He had to find this lord from among the ten and eliminate him. That would be his final mission before their march began.

It would also display the emperor's power to the remaining nine. Their fluctlights would eternally understand who was truly the mightiest of all.

*   *   *

At this time, Gabriel Miller did not consider even the most infinitesimal probability that he might be shown inferior in battle to any one of the ten units before him. To him, the Underworld was another VR world, one that existed as an extension of video games. He was still under the belief that all the units around him were nothing more than unusually complex NPCs.

———

The dark general, Vixur ul Shasta, knelt and hung his head as the words of his master echoed in the back of his mind. It was a moment from over twenty years ago in the sparring room of the headquarters of the dark knights brigade.

"The master of my master before him died instantly by way of beheading. Master's chest was slashed, and he perished on the path back to the palace. But while I lost an arm, I made it back alive. It's not much to brag about, I know."

And from his formal sitting position on the polished dark floorboards, Shasta's master had displayed his right arm, which was cut clean off above the elbow. The wound had been healed with herbs and bandages but nothing else. It was hideous to behold.

The cause of that injury, just three days before, was the dark knight's oldest foe and the greatest swordsman in the world—or the greatest monster—the Integrity Knight commander, Bercouli Synthesis One.

"But do you know what this means, Vixur?"

As a young man of barely twenty, Shasta didn't have an answer. His master had placed his good arm back on his lap, closed his eyes, and muttered, *"We are catching up at last."*

"Catching up...to him, you mean?"

Young Shasta couldn't keep the note of disbelief out of his voice; such was the overwhelming power of Bercouli's combat. The sight of his master's severed arm spraying blood as it flew through the air lodged into Shasta's spine like ice, and the sensation still hadn't melted after three days.

"I will be fifty this year. But I still feel as though I have not mastered swinging the sword or even my grip. And doubtless I will say the same when I die in another five or ten years," his master said quietly. *"Our lives are too short. We are not meant to reach the territory of a man like him, who has lived over two hundred years already. It is shameful to admit, but until we actually traded blows, a part of me was already resigned to this. But now that I have been roundly defeated and come back alive in retreat, I realize that I was wrong. It wasn't a waste…Not my master's attempt on his life nor all the other masters before him. Vixus, what is the ultimate sword technique?"*

The question was so sudden that Shasta had answered without thinking.

"The Empty Sword, master."

"Correct. After many years of training, the sword becomes one with the body. And the greatest of all techniques happens when one does not think to strike or think to draw or even think to move. That is what my master taught me—and what I taught you. However… it was not so, Vixur. There was something beyond it. And I learned this when that monster struck me down."

There was a faint flush of excitement on the man's weathered face. Without realizing it, Shasta was leaning forward in his formal sitting position.

"Something…beyond?"

"The opposite of emptiness. Unshakable certainty. The power of will, Vixur." Suddenly, his master swung the stump of his right arm out. *"You saw it happen. I swung level at the right. It was an Empty slash—the fastest attack of my life and completely unthinking. My first movement gave me the advantage over Bercouli."*

"Yes…I thought so, too."

"However—however. When he put up his sword to receive the blow, which should have rebuffed it, he somehow pushed back my swing instead and chopped off my arm. Can you believe this, Vixur? In the moment, his sword was not even touching mine!"

Shasta was stunned. Then his disbelief set in. *"That...that cannot..."*

"It is truth. It was as if the path of my swing itself was pushed aside by some invisible force. Not arts. Not Perfect Weapon Control. There is only one way to describe the phenomenon. My Empty Sword lost in battle to the willpower he refined over two centuries. He envisioned the path his sword was meant to take so powerfully that it became unshakable truth!"

In the moment, Shasta could not believe what his master was saying. How could it be possible that something without form, like the power of will, could have that effect on a real sword—hard and heavy, something that truly existed?

But his master had expected Shasta's reaction. He returned to a formal position atop the shining floorboards and quietly said, *"Vixur, I give you my final instruction. Strike me down."*

"Wh-what do you mean?! When you just..."

Shasta couldn't get the word *survived* out of his throat. Not when his master's eyes were full of such fierce determination.

"Now that I have prolonged my life, you must strike me with your blade. After he defeated me with a single blow, I am no longer the most powerful figure in your mind. As long as I am alive, you cannot fight him on equal terms. You must cut me, kill me...and stand on the same level as Bercouli!!"

His master got to his feet and took a stance, as though holding his sword with the arm that was no longer there.

"Now stand! And draw your blade, Vixur!!"

Shasta cut down the master and ended his life.

And in doing so, he understood the meaning of his master's words.

The invisible blade clutched in his right hand—the blade of will—produced a profusion of sparks when it intersected with Shasta's, and it even cut open his cheek, leaving a scar that had never healed.

Face wet with tears and blood, young Shasta stood at the

doorway of the secret that surpassed the Empty Sword—the Incarnate Sword.

Time passed, and five years ago, Shasta had finally challenged Bercouli, the head Integrity Knight and sworn enemy of the dark knights. At age thirty-seven, he sensed that his sword had reached the limit of what it could achieve.

His master had returned from the fight alive at the cost of an arm, but Shasta was not intending to come back at all if he lost. Shasta had never taken a disciple to be his sword heir. He did not want to burden a young soul with the fate of killing his master and being killed one day in kind. It was his decision instead to end the cycle of blood with his own life.

With all the willpower and determination he possessed—in other words, his Incarnate power—he met Bercouli's first strike head-on and was not rebuffed. But even at that moment, Shasta sensed his coming defeat. He did not think he could summon a strike with the same power and weight a second time.

But as their swords locked, Bercouli just laughed and muttered, "*A very good swing. No sword forged of desire to kill could stop my blade that way. Think upon that and come to me again in five years' time, boy.*"

The commander of the Integrity Knights created some distance and leisurely left the scene. It seemed like his back was open to attack as he went, but for some reason, Shasta couldn't take the opportunity.

It took a long time for him to understand what Bercouli had meant. But after those five years, he now felt that it made sense. If Shasta had put nothing but murder and hatred into his swing in that fight, he would have lost the ensuing clash. The fact that he managed a draw for that single moment was because more than the desire to kill gave weight to his determination.

In other words, it was the gratitude to his forebears who had given their lives to pass down their skills, as well as a prayer for those who would follow in his footsteps.

It was why Shasta instantly decided to launch a negotiation for peace when he heard the news of the pontifex's death. He was certain that the Bercouli he knew would accept the offer.

And for the same reason, he knew that when Emperor Vecta descended out of nowhere onto Obsidia Palace and decided unilaterally to prepare for war, he would have to kill the man.

Even as he knelt and bowed his head, Shasta was preparing the Incarnation he would put into his killing blow.

In his return after centuries of absence, the emperor appeared to be a young man with the pale skin and golden hair of a human from that distant realm. His size and features did not inspire fear or imply great menace.

But those piercing blue eyes alone spoke to the extraordinary nature of the emperor. There was a void behind them—an endless abyss that absorbed all light. This was a man who possessed an unfathomable, evil hunger.

If that void swallowed whole his Incarnation, the sword would never reach him.

If so, Shasta, the dark general, would die. But his will would be carried over to those who followed.

He had only one lingering concern. Because Lipia had not come to his room last night, he had not been able to express his will to her. Either she was too busy with the various tasks to be done before the journey, or she had gone to visit the special "home" she cared so much about.

If he revealed his plan to kill the emperor to her, she would insist on joining him and refuse to hear his reasoning against it. So in that sense, it was a good thing.

Shasta drew a breath and held it.

He reached out with his left hand to brush the sword he had taken off and placed on the floor.

It was fifteen mels to the throne. Two strong steps, and he would reach it.

He mustn't allow his first move to be read ahead of time. His mind must be empty when he drew the blade.

His power of Incarnation was refined to the limit of what he could achieve, and he let it flow from his fingers into the sword. Then he emptied his body.

His left hand reached for the sheath.

But then the emperor spoke, almost incidentally, in a voice as hard and smooth as glass.

"By the way, an interloper snuck into my bedchamber the night before last. With a knife hidden in their hair, in fact."

A murmur of muted surprise swept through the chamber.

Some of the nine feudal lords to the left of Shasta held their breath; others growled or sank deeper into their thick robes. More than a few gasps went up from the officers waiting behind them.

Shasta was just as stunned as the others were. He thought quickly, not budging from his combat stance.

Someone else had reached the conclusion that the emperor should be eliminated. Given that he was perfectly alive and well, that attempt had sadly failed—but which of the nine had sent the assassin?

It wouldn't be any of the five nonhumans. The giants, ogres, and orcs were beyond question, but even the relatively small goblins would not be able to sneak to the top floor past the many guards.

Out of the four human lords, young Iskahn, the pugilist, and Rengil, the head of the commerce guild, could be ruled out. Iskahn's entire purpose for living was to master the art of unarmed combat, and Rengil stood to gain enormous wealth should a war erupt.

Given the method of sending a killer to the bedchamber, Fu Za of the assassins guild was most suspicious, and to be fair, the man could be absolutely inscrutable, but the use of a dagger did not make sense.

After much research and experimentation in the ways of skulduggery, the assassins guild were masters not of arts or weapons but of a third means: poison. Fu Za's clan were a people who banded together to survive because they were not blessed with a high arts-usage privilege or weapon-wielding privilege. They had their own rules, which stipulated that hidden needles and blowguns were the weapons of choice for administering poison. They did not use daggers.

For the same reason, the dark mage leader, Dee Eye Ell, on his left must also be ruled out. The woman was nothing but ambition, and she seemed like the type to consider climbing to the top of the land of darkness by killing off its emperor, but any of Dee's assassins would use arts, not a dagger.

But that meant none of the nine other lords sent the killer.

Only Shasta, commander of the dark knights, was left.

But of course, he did not order this. He knew that when the time came to depose the emperor, he would give up his own life and sword to do it. He had never ordered any of his knights to perform an assassination, nor had he even spoken of his hidden decision…

No.

No…

It couldn't be.

It had taken Shasta no more than the blink of an eye after the emperor mentioned the assassin to reach this point. He felt the tips of his fingers against the sheath growing cold.

The willpower in his hand abruptly shifted into something else: warning, unease, fear, and the dread of certainty.

It was then that Emperor Vecta made his second statement.

"I will not condemn whoever sent that assassin after me. There is nothing wrong with the use of one's power to gain greater power. If you wish to stop me, then I welcome your skulking attempts."

He gazed out upon the murmuring crowd in the great hall, and for the first time, he wore what might be called an expression of emotion: a faint smile on his pale lips.

"But only, of course, if you understand that your actions will be met with the appropriate consequences. Such as…this one."

His hand stretched out from the long-sleeved black outfit and gave a signal.

From the side of the throne, on the right-hand wall from Shasta's perspective, a door opened silently, and a little serving girl snuck forward. There was a large silver tray in her hands, holding something rectangular that was covered by a black cloth.

The servant set the tray down before the throne, bowed deeply to the emperor, and scurried back to the doorway.

In the tense silence that followed, Emperor Vecta reached out with the long tip of his shoe, a twisted smile at the corners of his mouth, and stepped on the cloth covering the tray to slide it away.

And then Shasta, frozen in place, saw what was underneath.

A cube of ice, pure and translucent.

And trapped inside it, laid to an eternal rest from which she would never wake, was the face of the woman he loved.

"Li…pi…"

His lips only formed the shape of the last *a*.

Even the chill over his body vanished, leaving nothing but an impossibly deep, dark void filling his chest.

Shasta knew about the orphanage that dark knight Lipia Zancale secretly operated. She took in children of all races without parents or siblings—children fated to waste away and die—and raised them herself. Shasta saw that action as a sign of hope for the future.

It was why he told his secret ideals only to Lipia. An endless dream in which the stagnant, ever-present war with the human realm ended, and they created a world of nurturing and sharing rather than slaughtering and stealing.

And all that did was cause Lipia to make an attempt on the emperor's life, bringing about this hideous result. It was the emperor who'd killed her—but it was also Shasta. Of this, there could be no doubt.

For the span of an instant, a storm of unfathomable regret and shame tore through the emptiness in Shasta's heart. That was all the time it took to transform into one dark, black emotional response.

Murder.

Kill him. Do anything you can to kill the man with his legs folded on the throne, smugly smiling down.

Even if it had to come at the cost of his own life and the entire future of the Dark Territory.

—◦◦◦—

So which of these lords is the problem?

Gabriel surveyed the ten kneeling leader units before him, feeling just the slightest hint of entertainment from the situation.

The woman had loved her master with all her heart. When he had drunk the emotions she exuded on her death, that sweet flavor like nectar from Heaven, Gabriel understood not just her love but also the love her lord gave to her—as a kind of data pattern only, of course, a mere fact.

So he was certain that if he showed them the woman's head, the one she'd called *my lord* would act. Then he just had to mercilessly eliminate the traitor unit, fostering the loyalty and fear of the remaining units. It was just like any other sim game he played in the real world to pass the time.

What a pathetic and entertaining bunch.

Given real souls, yet limited in their intelligence. No matter how many times he killed them, they could be regenerated at will. On the day he had the entire mainframe of the Underworld and its lightcubes, he would be able to satisfy the unbearable hunger that had plagued him since childhood at last.

Gabriel relaxed and waited with his cheek resting against an arm propped up on the armrest.

The distance between him and the units was a bit over fifty feet. It was enough distance that he could use the sword at his left side to block any kind of weapon from there.

Of course, system calls were insufficient to block a command-based attack. But Gabriel's concerns in this regard had been wiped away before he even logged in.

Dark God Vecta's super-account was set up so Rath's engineers could control the Dark Territory directly. Therefore, his hit points—or life—were vast, his sword was the best, and most of all, Vecta had a certain kind of cheat code: He could not be designated a target in any kind of command-based attack.

Given all this protection, when the knight in black armor on the left end of the list of ten arched his back—

When the aura gathered around him like a pale shadow—

When his hand darted to the sheath on the floor like lightning, when his face suddenly lifted, the bold eyes in the center of it visibly glowing with a kind of inhuman red color—

Gabriel was unable to fully understand what was happening.

This world was not just a program being calculated on a physical server, but it was also a kind of living dream constructed from the same light quantum particles as the human fluctlight.

He didn't realize that the pure, powerful hostility the knight in black exuded was traveling from his lightcube to the Main Visualizer, then through quantum pathways to the STL Gabriel was using to connect to the simulation.

—〰—

Shasta's bloodred eyes saw nothing but the emperor.

With the fastest movement he'd ever made in his life, he drew his blade.

From the sheath came the Divine Object his master had left to him, the long katana Oborogasumi, but it was no longer the familiar gray blade he had seen so many times. Now the thick night mist that gave the long blade its name was swirling fiercely around it.

Shasta did not realize that the logic of this transformation was the same as that of the Integrity Knights' Perfect Weapon Control, which he had studied for so many years but never understood. But even if he did, it would not matter to him now.

"Shaaa!!"

Shasta hissed, infusing all the rage, hatred, and sadness of the world into one great overhead swing.

3

She flew from the northern end of the human realm to the far-thest east.

Eastavarieth was the most enigmatic of the four empires, and it was the first time Alice the Integrity Knight had ever visited it—as it was for Amayori, who was born in the west.

A rushing river as blue as lapis rushed between strange, jutting rock formations. When the occasional town or village appeared on its banks, it was built not of the familiar stone as in the north, but mostly of wood.

Nearly all the people who looked up to the sky and pointed at her had black hair. Alice recalled that Vice Commander Fanatio, whom she'd never quite seen eye to eye with, was from this region.

Directly in front, Kirito leaned back against her and stared mutely into the sky as she held the reins. His hair was black, too, so perhaps he was from this area—and maybe an encounter with the people below would even cause him to open up again. But sadly, she had to reach their destination as quickly as possible.

They'd been traveling for three days, setting up camp away from civilization and eating fish Amayori caught nearby and the dried fruit she'd brought along for the trip.

On the afternoon of the second day of the eleventh month,

they reached the End Mountains, which looked no different from those in the far north, and a ravine that looked as though the gods themselves had split the range vertically in two.

"...We can see it now, Kirito," she murmured, brushing the neck of her dragon, who had carried the load over their long journey. Now that most magical beasts had all but vanished from the world, dragons were the creatures with the highest natural life values, but even then, carrying two humans and three Divine Objects had to be a great burden. It seemed to have exhausted all the energy it had stored up from eating fish to its heart's content for half a year.

She whipped the reins, promising that she'd give her mount its favorite boiled mutton when they reached the camp. Amayori called back and beat its wings powerfully, showing no signs of fatigue.

The ravine looked like just a narrow crack from far away, but as they grew closer, its scale soon became apparent. By her eye, the span of the ravine was nearly a hundred mels. It was certainly wide enough for an army of orcs and ogres to march in standing abreast.

In the grassland surrounding the entrance to the ravine running straight through the rocky mountains, there was a massive camp made up of countless white tents. Smoke from campfires rose here and there, while soldiers engaged in training exercises. Even from the sky, she could see the glint of swinging swords and hear their shouts.

Morale wasn't as bad as she'd feared, but the total number of soldiers was still abysmally low. By a rough estimate, there couldn't be as many as three thousand in the camp. Meanwhile, the Dark Territory's invading army was at least fifty thousand. "Soldier" and "guard" were callings given to only a small fraction of the populace here, but beyond the mountains, everyone who was capable of fighting became a soldier.

It was impossible to imagine that Alice's presence alone was going to change anything. What kind of defensive strategy was Commander Bercouli envisioning…? As she considered this, Alice urged her dragon past the camp and toward the ravine, which was sinking into darkness.

"I'm sorry, Amayori. Just a bit farther," she said, and the dragon purred in response, just as the peaks passed in front of the dying light of Solus.

As soon as they entered the ravine, her body was hit by a shiver-inducing cold. The stone walls on either side were so smooth and sheer that they could have been carved only by the gods. She couldn't find a single blade of grass, much less a living creature, below.

After a few minutes' flight at slow speed, the trailing mists gave way at last to a gargantuan structure.

"Is this…the Eastern Gate…?"

The towering gray gate was a good three hundred mels from bottom to top. It was shorter than the five-hundred-mel Central Cathedral but every bit as imposing in person.

Most stunning of all was that the two doors of the gate were carved from single slabs of rock, with no parts or fittings. It seemed that such a thing was impossible not just with human hands but even with sacred arts' ability to harness natural materials. Administrator's greatest creation was the Everlasting Walls that divided Centoria into four sections, but they were a series of walls, each one being far smaller than this great gate.

The gate had been placed here by the gods from the moment the world began. In order to separate the human realm from the land of darkness—and to lead them to this terrible tragedy some three hundred years later.

"Stop, Amayori," she commanded the dragon, staring up at the gate from a close distance.

At about two hundred mels up, there was something written across the gray rock of the vast double doors in sacred script. She tried sounding it out.

"De…stroy…at…the last…stage…," she read from one of the middle lines, but she did not know what the words meant.

Just as she considered this, a terrible sound of destruction filled the air, startling Alice and Amayori. She rubbed the dragon's neck to calm it down and saw that along the gate, where it had been perfectly smooth before, there was now a narrow crack like a static bolt of black lightning through its surface.

The fissure grew to a length of a few dozen mels before it stopped. A number of pieces of rock peeled off and disappeared into the depths of the ravine. She looked up and examined the massive gate once more. Then she noticed the web of small cracks and fissures over almost the entire surface of the flat rock.

Alice swung the reins and brought her flying mount as close as possible to the gate.

She reached out, hesitant, and traced the mark of Stacia in the air, then struck the surface of the rock. The purple-colored window that appeared listed the maximum and present life values of the Eastern Gate.

The number on the left was the largest of any that she had ever seen—and they were many—at over three million. But the value on the right was just 2,985, less than a thousandth of the total. Even as she stared at it in shock, the number dropped by one.

Sweat on her palms, Alice measured the time until it went down again. From there, she calculated how much time they had until it was totally depleted.

"...Oh no..." She couldn't believe the answer she arrived at. "Five days...We only have five days left...?"

The gate that had firmly separated the two worlds for over three centuries would crumble to the ground in just five days' time. Was it even possible?

She thought of Selka's radiant smile, the craggy features of Old Man Garitta's face, and the troubled look of her father, Gasfut. It was just days ago that she had driven back the attacking goblins and blocked the cave with ice. She believed this would leave Rulid at peace for the time being.

But if the gate crumbled in five days, and the defending force was unable to stop the invading army of darkness, those bloodthirsty monsters would tear through this land like a flood. Its waves would reach those distant northern lands, too, and swallow the village of Rulid.

"I have to do…something…," she mumbled to herself, pulling on the reins without realizing what she was doing. Amayori turned away from the crumbling gate and slowly flapped its wings, gaining altitude. When they reached the top portion of the gate, at three hundred mels, she had the dragon hover again.

Beyond the gate there were ravines splitting the mountains, just as there were on this side. But beyond that were not blue sky and green grassland, but bloodred sky and Dark Territory soil that looked more like charred ash.

Alice made to look away from the hideous sight until something caught her eye. From what little she could see of the black earth, there were tiny, flickering flames.

She had Amayori gain altitude so she could look closely. It wasn't just one light. They were clustered irregularly, not spread evenly, and extended as far as she could see.

They were campfires.

It was a camp. The lead forces of the dark army were waiting in great number, just beyond their reach. Waiting for the moment that the gate fell, and they had a path into the human lands.

"Five…days…," she mumbled again, voice hoarse.

Then she turned the dragon around. If she kept staring at the sea of campfires, she was going to be consumed with fear and rush among them to fight on her own.

She knew that against simple goblin and orc foot soldiers, she could easily dispatch a hundred or two of them and return safely. But if they had ogre archers or a contingent of dark mages, it would not be nearly so simple.

Even an Integrity Knight with the might of a thousand was still just one person. She would not remain unharmed by ranged attacks from the rear, where sword techniques and sacred arts would not reach, and a sufficient number of small injuries would still eventually prove to be fatal. That was what Commander Bercouli had feared for so many years: the greatest weakness of the Integrity Knights and thus of humanity's protection itself.

Administrator, who had demanded that their power be concentrated into an elite group of individuals, was now dead, and the weapons and armor gathering dust in the cathedral had already been distributed to the impromptu defensive army. But the time they had remaining was far too short. If only they had ten thousand and a full year to prepare...

Alice sighed, cutting off that fruitless line of thought, and ordered Amayori into a descent.

The guardian force's camp had a large empty space left in the center. Based on the extra-large tents adjacent to it, this was clearly where the dragons were meant to land and take flight.

Amayori circled around as they descended, and before the beast's claws had even brushed the green, it was stretching its neck toward the tents and gurgling with excitement.

An emotional response came right away—that would be Takiguri, Amayori's brother. Once the dragon came to a stop, Alice picked up Kirito, hopped down to the grass, and removed the heavy bags from the dragon's legs. Amayori promptly plodded toward the tent and began rubbing against the neck of the other dragon, who popped its head out from under the thick fabric.

Alice found herself smiling at the sight, then heard footsteps approaching from the other direction and hastily made her expression neutral. She straightened out the hem of her simple skirt and pulled her wind-bedraggled hair behind her head.

But before she even turned around, a familiar man's voice rang out across the landing area.

"Alice, my mentor! I always believed in you!"

Sliding across the grass into her view was the Integrity Knight with whom she'd just shared a drink ten days ago, Eldrie Synthesis Thirty-One. Despite being in a camp, his wavy lilac hair and shining armor were both utterly spotless.

"...You seem well," Alice noted drily, which did not dissuade Eldrie from his state of bliss—but he froze in the act of saying something.

He had noticed the black-haired youth Alice was supporting with her left arm. One cheek tensed, and he drew his head back in a show of disbelief. "You...brought him here?" he groaned. "Why?"

Alice arched her back to the best of her ability. "Of course I did. I swore an oath to protect him."

"B-but...when the battle comes, we Integrity Knights must stand at the front line at all times. What will you do with him while you are exchanging blows with the enemy? You cannot bear him on your back, surely."

"If necessary, I will."

Alice drew her foot back, trying to keep Kirito's gaunt, limp body away from Eldrie's skeptical gaze. But other soldiers at rest and lower Integrity Knights were gathering in small groups around the landing area, glancing inquisitively at the way Alice and Kirito stood together.

As a swell of murmurs rose around them, Eldrie issued a sharp rebuttal. "You mustn't, Mentor! If you'll permit my forwardness, heading into battle with so much extra weight will not only reduce your ability to fight, it will surely expose you to greater danger! In the coming battle, you will have to..."

He paused, then gestured to the other soldiers in the area with a shining silver gauntlet. "You have a duty to lead them into combat! How can you choose not to make use of every last bit of your strength?!"

He was right. But she couldn't just admit that it was so. Alice ground her teeth together, trying to find the right words to explain how both fighting for the realm and protecting Kirito were equally important to her.

But at the same time, her disciple's impassioned argument startled her.

Compared to their time in Central Cathedral, when Alice was

teaching him to use the sword, he was clearly different now. At the time, Eldrie had practically worshipped Alice, and he'd never once talked back or argued with anything she told him.

The people of this world were given a secret seal in the right eye from the mysterious "God from beyond" that made them unable to disobey any order from the law or a higher being. As far as Alice knew, she and Eugeo, the late owner of the Blue Rose Sword, were the only ones to successfully break that hold. Even Administrator and Cardinal, who were practically gods themselves, had been unable to defy the seal.

Eldrie must still be under its influence. But though he didn't clearly disobey anything she said, he was no longer blindly obedient as he once was. He was thinking for himself and offering his own opinion.

And it was most likely Kirito—and Eugeo—who had brought about this change in him.

The two swordsmen, proud despite being the world's greatest rebels, had found a way to shake Eldrie's soul in a powerful way through their momentary encounter.

Now that she considered it, her sister, Selka, back in Rulid also complained constantly about the stubbornness of the old-fashioned village rules and the ideas of the influential members of town. There were also the two female students who'd approached when Alice had taken Kirito and Eugeo from North Centoria Imperial Swordcraft Academy. Young girls like them would never dare to hail an Integrity Knight.

Of course, Alice herself was part of that list.

Until she fought Kirito and fell partway down the exterior of the cathedral, she had never held the slightest doubt about the structure of the world, the church's power, or the infallible holiness of its pontifex.

But when she was forced to accept a truce and work with him to climb the walls and escape their peril, Kirito continually shook Alice with his words, his sword, and his pitch-black eyes—until she was finally able to break through the seal in her eye…

Kirito was like a hammer swung down to smash a world full of false harmony. With the power hidden in his soul, he made the world tremble and quake, and he had finally succeeded in smashing the huge old rusted nail at the center of it all named the Axiom Church. The price he paid was the lives of his friend Eugeo and the wise sage Cardinal—and even his own heart and mind...

Alice clutched the thin body she was supporting with her left arm. She stared directly back into Eldrie's eyes.

She wanted to tell him. To say, *You're only who you are now because you fought him.* But he would not understand, of course. To the knighthood, Kirito was still an unforgivable traitor and heretic.

Alice just stood there in silence. Eldrie had a face like he was suffering some kind of dull pain. He was about to say something further when the gathering crowd suddenly parted, as though a giant invisible fist pushed them apart.

What emerged from its midst was a voice that was so nostalgic it nearly brought tears to Alice's eyes but also set her on a painful, nervous edge.

"Don't get so worked up, Eldrie."

The young knight promptly straightened up. Alice looked away from him and turned to face the speaker.

He wore a loose, eastern-style outfit that opened in front. A wide sash tied around his midsection at a low point. On his left hip was a simple longsword that had been thrust carelessly into his belt. And on both of his feet were odd wooden shoes.

Compared to the knights and soldiers around him, he was dressed very lightly. But the pressure that emanated from his perfectly chiseled body was thicker and heavier than any armor.

The man rubbed at his short-cropped hair, a faded blue color that matched his clothes, and smirked. "Yo, little lady. You look better than I feared. I'm glad. Have your cheeks filled in a little bit?"

"...It has been too long, Uncle," Alice said, doing her best to fight back tears. She saluted the world's oldest and most powerful swordsman—commander of the Integrity Knights, Bercouli Synthesis One.

In the six years she'd lived as an Integrity Knight, this was the one person whom Alice had opened her heart to, revered as a mentor, and considered a father figure. And he was also the only person—aside from Kirito—whom she was certain she could never beat in a sword battle.

She couldn't let him see her cry now.

If Bercouli said that she couldn't leave Kirito here, she would have to obey him. Of course, in her present state, Alice was not forced to obey his commands. But if she defied him in front of this crowd, it would threaten the order of the knighthood and the guardian army. With the final battle approaching in just five days, she couldn't afford even the tiniest scratch on Bercouli's ability to lead.

Bercouli gazed upon her—his all-seeing eyes full of understanding and a smile of simple kindness on his lips as he approached. He looked her straight in the eyes, then gave her a forceful nod.

Eldrie was about to say something, but the commander silenced him with a look, then faced Kirito where he hung in Alice's arms.

His lips pursed. There were pale fires glowing in his piercing eyes.

Bercouli sucked in a long, slow breath. Alice could sense the air around them getting colder.

"…Uncle…," she whispered, barely audible.

Bercouli was focusing his sword spirit. He was going to utilize an Incarnation technique taught only to Integrity Knights… something that surpassed even Incarnate Arms. The ability to move objects with the power of the heart—this was an Incarnate Sword.

He would infuse his blade with the power of concentrated will and unleash it. At times, that invisible blade could even deflect the actual blades of the enemy. The commander's Time-Splitting

Sword, with its Perfect Weapon Control ability to cut into the future, was possible only because of the overwhelming power of his will.

So was Bercouli going to attack Kirito?

If he was literally planning to cut this problem in half, she could not allow it. She would have to draw her sword to protect Kirito, if need be.

Overwhelmed by the extreme power in Commander Bercouli's sword, the nearby soldiers, Eldrie, and even the dragons at the tent fell silent. With the air so heavy that breathing felt difficult, Alice worked her hardest to move the fingers of her right hand.

But before she could touch the hilt of her sword, Bercouli's lips moved, and she heard a voice that was more mental than spoken.

It's all right, young lady.

"…?!" Alice held her breath.

Then, without budging a muscle, Bercouli's eyes unleashed a fearsome flash of light. In the same moment, Kirito's body jerked and twitched in her arms.

There was a sharp *ting!* and a silver flash in the air between Bercouli and Kirito.

What was that?! Alice wondered, gasping with shock. But Bercouli was already wearing a broad smile. It was as though that display of ferocity had never happened.

"U-Uncle…?" she stammered. But the commander merely rubbed his chin with his fingers like they had just finished a practice exercise.

"Did you see that, young lady?"

"I…I did. Just for an instant…but it looked like…the glint of a swordfight…"

"Indeed. I hurled an Incarnate Sword at him—well, more like a dagger. If it hit him, it would've at least cut the skin of his cheek."

"*If*…it hit him? Meaning…?"

"That's right—he caught it. With his own willpower."

She couldn't help but crane her neck to glance at Kirito, whom she was still cradling.

But her hopes were dashed at once. The only thing in his half-open black eyes was empty darkness. There was no expression on his face.

But I felt his body twitch. I felt it.

She brushed his hair with her free hand and looked back to Bercouli. The commander just shook his head. "Seems like his mind is elsewhere," he said firmly, "but he's not dead. Listen: He was trying to protect you, young lady, not himself. So he *will* return someday. That's what I think. And it will probably be whenever you really need him most."

Alice had to work twice as hard as before to keep the tears from blurring her vision.

Yes. He will come back.

Kirito is... Well, he's the greatest swordsman in the world. With his two swords, he defeated that half-godly being.

Come back...not for me. For the sake of all the people who live in this world...

Then she couldn't take it anymore, and she clutched Kirito tight in her arms. Over her back, the commander's understanding voice explained, "And that's why, Eldrie. Don't get hung up on the little things. We can look after one young fellow, easy."

"B-but..." With admirable spirit, the newest of the Integrity Knights spoke his mind openly to the oldest. "I can see how even the slightest bit of increased strength might help. But in this situation...even if he returns to normal, I cannot see how a student with a sword will make any difference..."

"Are you kidding?" Bercouli asked. While his smile was warm, it also had the edge of a blade itself. "Have you forgotten? That boy's partner bested me in a fight. He beat Bercouli Synthesis One, commander of the Integrity Knights."

The air around them went abruptly silent.

"That boy by the name of Eugeo was powerful...Unbelievably so. I even used the Perfect Control arts of the Time-Splitting Sword—and I still lost. Just the way that you lost and Deusolbert lost and Fanatio lost."

At last, Eldrie seemed to have lost his tongue. Of course he had—there couldn't be a swordsman who could defeat Bercouli in a one-on-one duel, not among the knighthood or in the Dark Territory beyond the gate. It was what everyone in the Axiom Church believed.

But in that sense, wasn't this a very dangerous thing to admit?

Commander Bercouli had put together this rushed, impromptu defensive army on the strength of his reputation as the greatest warrior alive. But by telling everyone about Eugeo, a swordsman who had defeated him—and claiming that Kirito was Eugeo's equal in skill...

Alice was just regaining the strength to look at him again when Bercouli's head snapped up toward the sky.

"U-Uncle...?" she prompted. His reply changed the subject in the most unexpected of ways.

"Very far away, I sensed a swell in the spirit of someone's blade before it disappeared a moment later...Someone I know has just died..."

4

The genders, personalities, and hidden ambitions of the ten lords who made up the Council of Ten in the Dark Territory were varied, but there was one thing they all shared in common.

It was that they understood, better and clearer than anyone else, the one law that power rules all.

In a sense, their proof was in the fact that this law was carved into their souls from childhood, and that their unceasing efforts—whether in personal improvement or elimination of rivals—had ensured that they were the fittest to survive and reach the top of their dog-eat-dog world.

And so, when the commander of the dark knights brigade, kneeling at the right end of their line, launched himself at the emperor with his sword drawn, none of the other nine lords were truly surprised by his actions.

If anything, more of them were impressed at the particulars—*He's doing it now? How bold.* Even the chiefs of the orcs and ogres, whose intelligence and language ability had stagnated over the last three centuries, flashed their beady eyes as they realized they would get a chance to see just how strong their emperor actually was. The young pugilist, who respected Shasta as a fellow devotee of the art of combat, even secretly rooted for the knight to cut down his opponent now that he had committed to battle.

Of these figures, there were two who predicted this would happen, seconds before it did.

One was Dee Eye Ell, chancellor of the dark mages guild. She was a fierce rival of Shasta's and recognized Lipia because she herself had plotted to kidnap the dark general's lover.

So she was more shocked when she saw Lipia's head encased in ice than when Shasta made his move. She had a hunch that he might draw his blade in anger, and she began to consider what she would do when it happened.

She could cast her arts on him from behind and attempt to ingratiate herself to the emperor. But ultimately, Dee chose to watch. If Shasta lost, that was all well and good, and if he somehow actually won, he would be gravely injured, and she could burn her fiercest rival alive so that *she* had control of the land of darkness. On the inside, Dee grinned, then licked her lips to hide her rising excitement.

There was one other figure who sensed the dark general's rebellion ahead of time.

And this one acted instantly.

—⁓—

Shasta swung back his blade, his entire being dedicated only to the act of killing.

Judging by the toughness of the Incarnation in his blade alone, it was indeed greater than the time he had attempted to kill Commander Bercouli. The ferocity of his rage and mourning brought about the Perfect Control state instantly, when it typically required a long chanted command first.

Shasta's long katana Oborogasumi was a Divine Object automatically generated about two hundred years ago by the Underworld from its VRMMO package assets. Its natural element was water, and in responding to Shasta's overwhelming urge to kill, it transformed its deadly power into a kind of misty shadow form.

Under Perfect Weapon Control, Oborogasumi completely

shortcut the normal, accepted attacking process of any sword: to deal damage by severing or piercing the target with the edge of the blade. Any target that made contact with the long strip of mist suffered slashing-type damage to their life value. In other words, no method of defense worked, aside from avoidance altogether.

Emperor Vecta (aka Gabriel Miller) drew his own blade the moment Shasta drew his, and the god of darkness attempted to strike back at his opponent's swing.

If it had happened in this way, Shasta's blade of mist would have passed through Gabriel's and delivered its payload of compressed murder directly into his body.

But just before his lightning-quick strike could leap forth, Shasta simply froze where he was standing.

Somehow, there was a throwing needle sunk deep into the left flank of the dark general's armor in a tiny gap between its thick plates. Behind him, a man as thin as a ghost stood up, his body covered by dark-gray robes.

It was the head of the assassins guild, Fu Za. He was the least noteworthy of the ten lords, preferring to stay quietly in the shadows with hardly a word at the council meetings. He slipped silently forward, drawing the most attention he had ever received in his life.

Fu Za recognized Shasta's rebellion because he was the most cowardly and sensitive of all the lords.

The assassins guild was a place where those without power stuck together. Those who were given life without physical or magical strength, without money, without any kind of power to their names—and who also refused to live the tortured life of a slave—came together to advance the ways of poison, which was despised even in the Dark Territory.

The small number of insects, snakes, and plants with poisonous qualities in the Underworld had been placed there for the sake of the final stress test. So their effects were limited and easy enough for the residents to avoid with a proper amount of knowledge.

In other words, poison was not strong enough to counteract the power of the dark arts or swordfighting.

But the ones who created the assassins guild developed a process of concentration that Rath never envisioned to produce ever stronger poisons over years and years. The guild's headquarters, deep below the slums of the castle town, featured rows and rows of massive pots that had been boiling poisons continuously for over a century. Other pots held snakes found from all over, which were placed together so they would eat one another and develop greater venom.

However, when they finally perfected a lethal poison, it led to tragedy: assassination within the guild. Unlike with swords or arts, slow-acting poison made it very difficult to identify the aggressor.

Naturally, the one who led the guild would have to be extremely cowardly to survive. Enough to cower away from the sight (or presence) of others and so sensitive as to pick up the tiniest buds of malice in others.

And when Shasta saw Lipia's head in the ice, Fu Za sensed his instant rush of rage more keenly and strongly than the smell of fresh blood itself. Shasta, the dark general, was also the single greatest target of Fu Za's hatred.

How many times had he drawn up assassination plans and scrapped them? He was certain that he could perform the actual killing. But once it became clear that poison was the cause, everyone would know it was the assassins guild's work. Within an hour of Shasta's death, the mighty dark knights brigade would charge into the headquarters and slaughter them all. The assassins didn't stand a chance in a direct fight.

But perhaps now, in this very moment...

He had a very good rationale for piercing his hated enemy with a sharp, poisoned needle. The act of drawing his weapon in the emperor's presence instantly meant Shasta was no longer the dark general or a council member, just a simple outlaw.

Fu Za pulled out and threw a weapon that had been passed

down continuously through the leadership position of the guild
over the years. It was a very thin needle made of a dangerous
metal called Ruberyl's poisoned steel that contained a paralyz-
ing substance of its own. The needle was hollow, so it could store
other poisons as well.

Held within the weapon was a poison that was the apex of the
guild's efforts. They took fifty thousand of a rare creature called
the bloodcurdle leech and ground them into a liquid, then fil-
tered and concentrated the result many times, until they were
left with just a single drop of poison. Because all their attempts
to breed and raise the leeches themselves had failed, it took an
unfathomable amount of effort to produce this tiny drop.

Fu Za, of course, had no way of knowing that the animals that
lived in the Underworld were generated by the system to meet
certain determined density levels across an area, and therefore,
any animal that fell outside of livestock units like sheep and cows
could not be intentionally bred by humans whatsoever.

So the poisoned needle that Fu Za hurled, both in material and
poison content, represented the concentrated work of the entire
assassins guild in one item. It was the synthesis of the collective
hatred of the weak, distilled over centuries of torment.

—◊◊◊—

Because Shasta had put all his willpower into the sword in his
hand, he was not conscious of any pain from the poison needle
embedded deep into his flesh.

All he knew was that the moment he tried to leap for the throne,
he was stunned to find that his entire body felt as heavy as lead.
The strength went out of his legs, and he fell loudly to one knee
before finally noticing the foreign object lodged in his left side.

Poison...

Before the icy chill could paralyze his hands, he quickly pulled
the needle free. It was so thin and fragile—barely a weapon—but
when he saw how it shone a vicious green color, Shasta recognized

Ruberyl's poisoned steel and immediately began to chant a counter-art.

But the chill spread from his left flank through his whole body with terrifying speed, reaching his mouth. Before he could even say the system-call prompt, his tongue was numb, and he could not even grind his teeth together.

Finally, his right arm gradually lowered the sword, undoing the Perfect Control status. The gray mist returned to its physical form: a long blade with its tip dragging on the floor.

Shasta wound up in the exact same position—lowered head and left knee on the ground—as he'd been in before he'd made up his mind to attack the emperor. A dark robe passed silently through his vision.

Fu Za. To think it would be this man, of all people.

"...Undone by such a minor, insignificant person. Is that what you're thinking, Vixur?" said a hissing, sibilant voice from overhead. The only thing Shasta could move on his body was his eyelids, which he squinted.

How dare you call me by that name...

"You're probably thinking, 'You have no right to refer to me by name.' But actually, this is not the first time I've called you Vixur."

The assassin bent his knee so he could crouch next to Shasta, putting his face into view. But the heavy hood blocked the light, leaving everything but his jutting chin hidden in darkness.

The chin trembled, and that raspy, haunting voice said, "You probably...don't remember. You wouldn't recall the faces of all the children you beat in the youth training academy. Nor the one who threw himself into the canal out of sheer shame, never to return."

What? What is he talking about? Youth training academy?

Shasta was the child of a simple knight, so from the age he was old enough to hold a wooden sword, he was forced into the children's training academy attached to the dark knights brigade. After that point, his only memories were of training all day to survive. He won in every selection test, was eventually made an officer of the brigade, and was taken under the wing of his master, the previous commander. Half his life had passed in such a rush that he never had the time to reflect on it.

Of course he could not remember. How would he remember the names of the children he'd swung swords with over thirty years ago?

"...But you see, I've never forgotten you for a day of my life. The assassins guild picked me up out of the culvert where I washed up, and I was worked like a slave for years and years. I still never forgot. I gained knowledge, developed many new poisons, and finally clawed my way up to head of the guild. I lost many things in exchange...but it was all in search of vengeance against you, Vixur."

When the twisted voice paused, the hood tilted just a tiny bit, and Shasta saw Fu Za's real face.

He did not receive a flood of old memories. In fact, even if Shasta perfectly remembered all his old classmates, he would not have recalled this one's name. Perhaps it was the effects of poison—Fu Za's face was horribly melted and disfigured, a countenance that would frighten even an orc.

The hood fell forward again, leaving only two glittering eyes under its darkness.

"The poison I injected into you was developed to kill you and created drop by drop through an excruciatingly long process. Our tests found that even a great land dragon with a life of over thirty thousand could be killed in an hour with it. Based on your strength and total life, I would give you another two or three minutes. So...now it is time for you to give back the hatred and humiliation I left with you."

Hatred? Shasta looked away from Fu Za's eyes and down at the poison needle on the black-marble floor. *I put my anger and hatred into attempting to kill the emperor. Fu Za put the same power into this needle in an attempt to kill me. That's why my blade came to a stop. Murder Incarnate cannot defeat Righteous Incarnate. Years ago, I grasped the secret after my battle with Commander Bercouli...and at the very, very end, I forgot that lesson...*

He couldn't even maintain his kneeling position anymore. Shasta fell hard to the stone on his left shoulder.

Through his hazy vision beyond that poisoned needle—there was a block of ice resting on a silver tray.

—⁂—

The avenger Fu Za, once known as Fuelius Zargatis, watched very closely, intent on savoring the moment of his greatest delight now that it was finally here.

Shasta, the dark general, who had taken every glory he ever wanted, now lay at Fu Za's feet. His skin, smooth for one his age, was now ashen, his formerly sharp eyes were dull, and his breath was short and shallow.

It was a miserable, pathetic death.

And Shasta's end was also proof that poisoning techniques were superior to sword techniques or dark arts. The confluence of Ruberyl's poisoned steel and bloodcurdle leeches was powerful enough to leave a target instantly unable to fight or chant—and to kill them soon after.

Emperor Vecta on the throne would have realized the value of the assassins guild from this incident. When they figured out a way to mass-produce this new poison, there would no longer be any need to worry about what the knights and mages thought. He could take his real name back and return to the Zargatis family, which had abandoned him, as the rightful conqueror...

So absorbed was Fu Za in his long-awaited moment of pleasure that he failed to notice Shasta's sword at the corner of his vision turning back into mist.

—⁂—

Lipia.

Just before his life hit bottom, Shasta silently spoke the name of the one woman he had ever loved.

Lipia had almost certainly attempted to kill the emperor because she was praying for the arrival of the new era Shasta spoke to her about. She surely believed that if the three-hundred-year war ended and a new law and order shone upon the land of darkness, even the orphans whose only options in life were starvation or slavery might have the right to live happily.

Fu Za...You claim I beat you in the youth training academy? And unable to bear the shame, you threw yourself into the river?

At least you had that opportunity. Your parents put you in school and gave you three meals a day, along with a warm bed and a roof to stave off the elements. How many lives in this world are deprived of even that minimum right, treated like garbage, and fated to vanish while they are still young?

Lipia gave up her life in an attempt to make this world right. I cannot allow that Incarnation of hers to come to nothing. Your petty personal grudge...

"...will not stop me!" roared Shasta, who should have been completely paralyzed. Something like a gray whirlwind swirled around the dark knight's hand.

This was the Memory Release phenomenon that only a few of the Integrity Knights could command. Shasta's mental Incarnation of unparalleled strength began to overwrite the Main Visualizer, that machine that stored and calculated all the information in the Underworld.

The gray whirlwind was a phenomenon of pure destructive force without any particular affinity—it simply broke down everything it touched. Fu Za was swallowed by the tornado before he could leap away. His thick black robe was blasted into nothing, dying like smoke in the air.

The scrawny, middle-aged man within it lifted his arms to hide his disfigured, melted face. His arms were torn into a cloud of flesh—and then his entirety was nothing but a thick swarm of blood in the air.

—⁓—

The moment the strange whirlwind rose from the dying dark general's body, Dee Eye Ell leaped away, seized by an awful premonition. She generated wind elements in both hands and used them to fly backward at top speed.

When the rapidly expanding whirlwind touched her right leg, removing all of it below the knee without a trace, that premonition turned into the ultimate shock.

Whether bathing or sleeping, Dee always kept herself protected by dozens of defensive arts. She should have been surrounded by a perfect wall that kept out not just other magic, but all thrown weapons, swords, poison, and every other kind of attack imaginable.

Of course, it was possible that an all-out attack from one of the ten lords who shared her level of priority could break through that defense and harm her directly. But it was not possible for it to act like her defensive wall was nothing and tear away the flesh with a simple touch. It just wasn't possible.

But no matter how she tried to deny it, the whirlwind of death continued advancing on her faster than she could retreat, carving up her right leg. Dee was an accomplished enough dark mage that she could re-create a lost limb with healing arts, but only if she survived the ordeal first.

"Aaah...*aaaah*!!"

At last, a scream burst from Dee's mouth.

But it was drowned out by similar screams from the two goblin chiefs. On her left side, Hagashi, chief of the mountain goblins, and Kubiri, chief of the flatland goblins, were racing as fast as they could from the whirlwind on their stubby legs. But even Dee could not escape its wrath at full flight speed; they stood no chance.

"Kgyaaa!!"

Hagashi slipped and tumbled to the floor with a hideous shriek. With his outstretched left hand, he caught Kubiri's ankle like a vise.

"Hiyeaaah!! Let 'ooo!! Let g..."

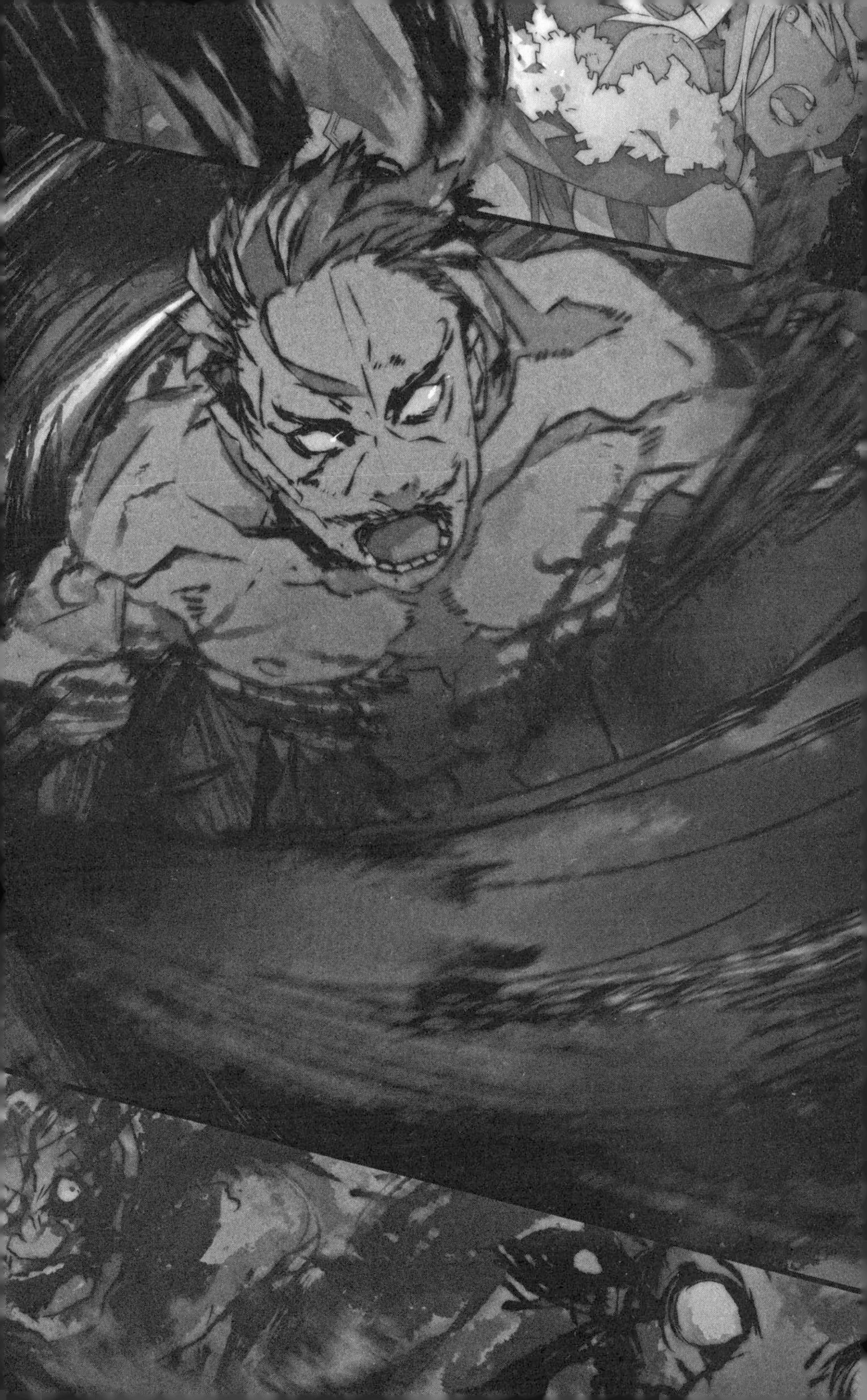

Splurch.

The rulers of the goblin tribes turned into bloody mist.

Zhurnk.

The remainder of Dee's leg was blown to pieces.

Before the eyes of the dark mages guild's chancellor, her beautiful features twisted with shock and terror, the whirlwind's expansion miraculously came to a stop.

Shasta's fallen body was no longer visible. The inverted cone of his raging storm was already a good twenty mels across and in height. The five lords who'd been far enough away had retreated to the western wall. The other military officers lined up along the south end of the chamber were safe, too, but just barely.

Dee's mind was beset by confusion, but she had just enough rational power left to vaguely understand why the whirlwind had stopped expanding.

It was protecting the dozen or so high-ranking dark knights in the room. The whirlwind was something created by Shasta's own will.

As if to back up her suspicion, the upper half of the whirlwind began to change shape. It formed a man's torso made of translucent mist.

While it was incredibly huge, it was also clear that it was a representation of Dark General Shasta.

—◦◦◦—

Gabriel Miller stared up at the oncoming tornado giant with something that indeed resembled shock.

When he had revealed the assassin's head, he'd expected that the knight on the left end would draw his sword in response. When the head of the assassins guild used some kind of poison to paralyze the man who tried to attack Gabriel, that was not exactly a shock, either.

His plan was to crush the traitor at once and instill absolute obedience into the remaining nine. That wouldn't happen now, but a spontaneous act of protecting the emperor was worthy of praise, he decided, so he allowed events to unfold.

But then, a gray whirlwind suddenly erupted from the fallen rebel unit, and it obliterated the head of the assassins guild and the two goblin generals in an instant. That caught Gabriel off guard.

The general units should have all been roughly equal in status. So if they fought one another, it shouldn't be quick. It should be a long series of chipping away at HP and healing, back and forth.

But three units had just been destroyed in mere seconds. Perhaps there was some kind of logic to the Underworld that neither he nor Critter understood yet...

At that point, the giant in the whirlwind opened its mouth and let loose with an earthshaking bellow. Unable to withstand the intense pressure, a majority of the glass windows around the royal chamber gave way and broke outward.

The giant lifted a fist the size of an engine block—and swung it down at Gabriel.

It was pointless to block it with his sword, and he could tell that there wasn't enough time to evade it on his feet. Noticing Vassago leaping nimbly out of the right corner of his eye, Gabriel stood at the throne and awaited the gray fist.

—◌◠◌—

The deadly whirlwind of Incarnation that Shasta produced in his final moments transcended even the system of the Underworld.

He did not eliminate the life value of Fu Za and the goblins with numerical attack power to kill them. Instead, he forced the mental image of death directly into their lightcubes, thus destroying their fluctlights—and in reverse order, this caused their flesh to be obliterated.

So his attack against Gabriel similarly had no effect on Emperor Vecta's vast store of life.

But the aura of death that Shasta's fluctlight produced passed through the quantum circuits and into the STL machine where Gabriel's organic body lay—and so the pure concentrated blood-lust of Shasta, the dark general, one of the greatest warriors in the Underworld, scored a direct hit on the core of Gabriel Miller's fluctlight: his ego.

In the moment, Shasta's consciousness fused with his unstoppable attack, so that he felt as though he were plunging inside Emperor Vecta.

It was clear that the life of his actual body was long gone. Shasta knew this was the last attack he would ever make.

He regretted that he would never fulfill his promise to cross swords with Integrity Knight Bercouli again. But the man would understand. He would know what the dark general wanted, and why he struck back against the emperor.

He had killed both Fu Za of the assassins guild and the two goblin chiefs, who were the most combative of all the lords. It was a shame that Dee, chancellor of the dark mages guild, had escaped, but she could not recover instantly from such a terrible wound. If the head of the dark knights brigade and Emperor Vecta himself both died, the remaining lords would surely reconsider their final war against the Human Empire.

If they could just form a temporary truce with the people of that side, who had recently lost their own ruler. If they could trade words instead of blows, perhaps some common understanding would arise.

And he could only hope that somewhere down that line, the world of peace that Lipia had desired would arrive.

Completely fused with his Incarnation, Shasta split Emperor Vecta's brow and plunged into the core of the soul that existed within. If he destroyed this, even the god of darkness would be erased just as completely as Fu Za and the rest of them.

With a silent roar, Shasta's will collided with the emperor's soul—

Only to be met with the final shock of his life.

Nothing.

At the center of the cloud of light that was the soul, the place where the pure essence of consciousness and being should have been, there was nothing but dense, choking darkness.

But why? Even the soul of Fu Za, the recluse, had been glowing with a perverse fixation on life.

The infinite darkness at the center of the emperor swallowed Shasta's Incarnation.

He was vanishing. Evaporating.

This...this man...

Does he not know life?

A man who knew nothing of the shine of life, of soul, and of love. No wonder he was starving. No wonder he wanted others' souls.

No matter how powerful his ability to Incarnate, no sword built of murderous anger could defeat this man.

The man's soul was dead, even as it lived.

He had to tell someone. Whoever was fated to fight this monster in the future.

Someone...someone...

But that was the moment Shasta's consciousness was enveloped in the infinite abyss.

.........Alas.........

.........Lipia.........

And with that final thought, the soul of Vixur ul Shasta, general of darkness, was obliterated at last.

—◇◇◇—

At the moment of that overwhelmingly powerful soul shine piercing him, Gabriel Miller felt more joy than fear.

The dark knight's soul, even more than the woman's he'd devoured two days ago, was brimming with thick emotions. Love for the woman. And a kind of beatific love that was much broader in nature and harder to understand. And using those as a source of power—an untamed drive to kill.

Love and hatred. Could there be anything more delicious in this world than those two concepts?

Gabriel was completely unaware at this time that his own life was in terrible danger. Even after seeing the three units fragged to pieces by the dark knight's attack, Gabriel was more interested in devouring the knight's soul than in his own safety.

If Gabriel feared the attack and wished for his own survival, Shasta's deadly drive would have crushed Gabriel's instinct for survival through the STL and, by extension, obliterated his fluctlight itself.

But Gabriel Miller was a man who did not understand life. To him, all life, including his own, was like that of the many insects he slaughtered when he was a young boy—automatic and mechanical. All he wanted was to unlock the secrets of the soul that powered the machine—that mysterious shining cloud.

So the destructive signal of Shasta's fluctlight simply passed through the empty void at the center of Gabriel's fluctlight and vanished without colliding into anything at all.

Gabriel had no way of knowing all this, but as he chewed on the knight's soul, two things stuck in his memory.

First, that there were ways of attacking in this world beyond just the weapons and magic spells of normal VRMMOs—and that this kind of attack did not have any effect on him, apparently.

He would have to make Critter study the logic of the phenomenon he witnessed, Gabriel thought. He slowly rose from the throne.

—◈◈◈—

The six surviving lords—the dark mages guild chancellor, Dee Eye Ell; the head pugilist, Iskahn; the leader of the commerce guild, Rengil; the giant chief, Sigurosig; the orc chief, Lilpilin; and the ogre chief, Furgr—were either pressed back against the wall or flat on their backsides or attempting to stanch their bleeding. But all of them were staring up at Emperor Vecta.

The only feeling in their hearts at this point was fear.

Dark General Shasta's stunning mega-attack, which had reduced three of their number to a bloody mist in an instant and ripped off the leg of the fearsome mage Dee, had not left so much as a scratch on the emperor.

The one with the power makes the rules.

It was clear to the six lords and hundred-plus officers behind them that even if they all fought together, they could not overcome the power of Emperor Vecta.

Like a wave rippling across them, they all bowed their heads, signaling acquiescence to the emperor. Even the dark knights brigade, who had just witnessed their beloved commander's death, were no exception.

The emperor's voice rang out loud and clear over the scene.

"…For each army that has lost its general, the next-highest officer must immediately take command. We will begin the march in one hour, as planned."

He did not rage about the outlaw or point a finger in blame. This fact only brought a fresh wave of fear to the remaining officers.

Dee finally succeeded in stopping the bleeding of her leg. She thrust her hand high in the air, fingers splayed, and shouted, "Long live the emperor!!"

After a brief pause, voices echoing her cry poured forth from the crowd over and over, a flood of sound that threatened to shake Obsidia Palace to its foundation.

5

Alice looked around the tent that had been assigned to her, and she sighed.

The simple bed was neatly turned down, and the sheepskin leather on the floor was brand-new. Even the air inside smelled of sunflowers. That was all well and good, but it was clear at a glance that this tent had not been hastily arranged for her after her arrival. Commander Bercouli had prepared for her presence and ordered an extra knight's tent in advance.

Perhaps she should have taken it as a sign of trust, but knowing what the commander was like, it was hard not to feel like he could read her mind and actions like a book.

No—that couldn't be entirely true. Even the commander hadn't seemed to guess in advance that Alice would be bringing Kirito along. There was only one bed in the tent.

She brushed Kirito's back, leading him over to the bed to sit down. Instantly, the young man was moaning, trying to reach out with his left hand.

"Yes, I know, just a moment."

She hurried back to the pack she'd set down by the entrance and pulled out two swords, one black and one white. Then she went back and laid them across his lap. Kirito put his arm around the swords and became quiet.

Alice sat next to him and thought as she removed her boots.

She'd told Eldrie that if necessary, she would fight with Kirito strapped to her back, but if it actually came to that, it would be difficult to do. Kirito alone was scrawny enough, but the weight of both the Night-Sky Blade and the Blue Rose Sword would limit her mobility in battle.

She could leave him on Amayori's saddle, but there were dark knights on the other side who hunted dragons, so air battles were likely. She wanted to keep her mount's burden as low as possible.

Sadly, the most realistic option at the moment was to leave Kirito in the care of someone back in the supply train during the battle. The problem was whether she could find someone trustworthy enough in time.

The Integrity Knights that she knew were, of course, all going to be in the midst of the fighting, and she didn't know a single soldier among the common people. She also wasn't in the state of mind to ask Eldrie to point her to a suitable person.

"Kirito..."

Alice stared at him right in the face and brought her hands up to cup his cheeks.

She was not going to treat him like a burden. If he could just get his old self back, he would be the best possible protector of the realm that anyone could ask for. She had brought him here to the brink of the battle because she thought there might be a chance it would be the spark that healed his mind.

Commander Bercouli claimed that Kirito had deflected the Incarnate Sword he'd hurled. Even in his current state, he had tried to protect Alice, supposedly.

Should she believe that?

When they first met at Swordcraft Academy, they were apprehender and criminal. When they met again on the eightieth floor of the cathedral, they were executioner and rebel. Even in the moment they traded their final words on the top floor, the most favorable view one could take of them said they were potential enemies in the midst of a truce.

If he hasn't had his mind ever since that battle, how is it that he tried to protect me from Uncle's sword technique?

Tell me…what do you think of me?

Her question bounced right off Kirito's lightless eyes and back to her. What did *she* think of this young man?

If there was any single word she'd felt about Kirito in the cathedral, it would probably be *detestable*. Before and since, no one else had ever called Alice Synthesis Thirty an idiot so many times.

But the way Kirito had looked in the final battle, as he'd bravely stood up to the all-powerful Administrator…

The sight of the swordsman—black cloak flapping in the buffeting wind, a sword in each hand—had made Alice's heart tremble. It was a powerful image, one that pierced her chest with sadness.

She still felt it in her chest, a bittersweet throbbing.

But she was afraid to learn the reason for that and thus kept her heart shut tight.

I mean, I am only a creation. A puppet created to fight, occupying the body of Alice Zuberg. I am not allowed the luxury of possessing any emotions aside from the will to battle.

But what if…?

What if my voice isn't reaching you because I'm holding myself back?

If I unleashed the Incarnation of all my being, would you respond in kind?

Alice sucked in as much air as her lungs could bear and held it.

Kirito's cheeks were cold in her hands. No—it was her palms that were hot.

She drew his cheeks closer and stared into those black eyes right in front of her. Dark as midnight. But somewhere in the distance, she felt she could make out tiny, blinking stars.

She stared at those stars, getting closer, closer…

At the abrupt tinkle of a small bell, Alice leaped back into a standing position. She looked around the tent in a panic, but no one else was there. Finally, she realized that it was the bell on a string attached to the entrance flap of the tent.

There was a visitor. Alice cleared her throat, straightened her hair, and crossed the tent. It was probably just Eldrie coming to complain again. She wasn't going to kick out Kirito, no matter what he said, and she was going to let him know that.

Alice stuck her head through the thin inside flap of the doubled entrance curtain, then pushed aside the heavy fur exterior to the outside.

Her half-opened lips froze in place.

Standing before her was not an Integrity Knight or even an ordinary soldier. She couldn't help but stare.

"Um...," the little visitor said, voice timid, holding up a covered pot with both hands. "I...I brought your supper, Miss Knight."

"...Oh, I see." Alice glanced at the sky. Somehow the red of the sunset was already retreating toward the western horizon. "Thank you...for bringing it to me."

She took the pot and gave the visitor a proper examination from head to toe. She was still just a girl, maybe fifteen or sixteen years old. Her hair was a brilliant red color and hung to just below the shoulder. Her large eyes were a similar reddish-brown color, which, combined with the pale color of her skin and thin bridge of her nose, indicated she was from the northern empire.

The girl wore light armor, suggesting she was part of the defensive army, at least, but the gray jacket and skirt underneath it looked more like some school uniform.

A poor child, here on the battlefield, Alice thought at first—but then she blinked in surprise.

She recognized the girl's face. But while she'd been stationed at Central Cathedral, Alice had almost never had any contact with ordinary people.

Just then, a second girl bashfully popped out from behind the back of the first. "Um...w-we brought bread and a drink."

This girl had dark-brown hair that was nearly black and

deep-blue eyes. Her voice was barely audible. Alice accepted the basket she offered, trying to hold back a smile. "You don't have to be afraid. I won't bite."

But just then, Alice's memory jogged itself. She recognized that nervous voice. These were the girls who—

"Pardon me...are you two...from North Centoria Imperial Swordcraft Academy...?"

For just a moment, the nervous faces of the two girls relaxed, but then the duo hastily straightened up and snapped into a salute.

"Y-yes, Miss! I...I am Primary Trainee Tiese Schtrinen of the Human Guardian Army, Supply Corps!"

"P-Primary Trainee Ronie Arabel, of the same!"

Alice returned the salute out of habit and realized that her hunch was correct. They were the ones who had rushed up when she was taking Kirito and Eugeo away from the school and requested permission to say their good-byes.

Just because the guardian army was shorthanded didn't mean they were about to conscript students. These two must have enlisted of their own accord and traveled from the familiar city out to this dangerous place of battle. The girls were still so young. Why would they do this...?

Alice stared at the two, pot in her right hand and basket in her left. The brown-haired girl named Ronie slipped behind the red-haired girl named Tiese's back to hide again. Tiese hunched up a bit smaller herself, but soon, she decided to go for broke and opened her mouth to speak.

"I...uh...I'm well aware that...this is, uh...a most inappropriate and impertinent matter to inquire about..."

Alice had to stifle a groan at her awkwardly grandiose vocabulary. Instead, she put on as understanding a smile as she could and interrupted, "Listen, you don't have to try to be so formal. Here in this camp, I'm just one more warrior to help protect the realm. Call me Alice, Tiese...and Ronie."

Tiese looked stunned by this, as did Ronie when she poked her head out from behind her companion again.

"...Wh-what's the matter?"

"Er, it's just...wh-when we saw you back at Swordcraft Academy, you seemed, um...different..."

"Oh...did I?" Alice asked. She couldn't tell for herself, but perhaps the six months she'd spent in Rulid had changed her somehow. The commander had said some kind of nonsense about her cheeks filling out, after all.

On further reflection, perhaps there were some times that she was a little too excited about Selka's cooking and overate a bit... but surely it wasn't enough to change her appearance...

Cautious not to let her doubt show, Alice had to favor them with a friendly smile. "So...did you want something?"

"Oh...uh, y-yes," said Tiese, a bit less nervous than before, perhaps. She bit her lip briefly. "Um, Miss Kni—er, Miss Alice, we heard that when you arrived on your dragon...you were with a young man with black hair...and we were wondering if it was someone we know..."

"Oh...I see. Yes, of course." Alice nodded, understanding their reason for being here at last. "You were good friends with Kirito at school, then..."

The moment the words were out of her mouth, the two girls' faces lit up. Ronie's blue eyes even started brimming with tears.

"It...it really was Kirito...," she whispered.

Tiese took her hand and said, voice full of hope, "Then...is Eugeo also...?!"

Alice sucked in a sharp breath at the mention of that name.

They didn't know. They didn't know about the fierce battle half a year ago at the cathedral—or the outcome of it. They couldn't have known. Everything surrounding the pontifex's death had been kept a secret from all but the Integrity Knights.

Alice's stunned silence left the two girls confused. She looked into Tiese's and Ronie's eyes, back and forth, then closed her own.

She could not hide the truth from them.

They had a right to know everything. In fact, they had probably come all this way and joined the guardian army just for the hope of seeing Kirito and Eugeo again...

She steeled herself and opened her mouth. "This might be...too difficult for you to bear. But I have faith that if you learned from Kirito and Eugeo, you will be able to endure it."

She took a step back, lifted up the pelt flap, and beckoned the girls into the tent.

Counter to Alice's faint hopes, Kirito did not display any reaction whatsoever to the sight of Tiese and Ronie. She stood at the tent's wall, hiding her disappointment, and watched the tragic sight play out.

Ronie knelt in front of Kirito, who sat mutely on the bed, and held his left hand in both of hers, allowing the tears to fall freely down her cheeks.

But even more painful was Tiese, who slumped onto the leather mat on the floor, staring at the Blue Rose Sword. Her face was as white as paper, and she hadn't moved the tiniest bit since Alice had told her the news of Eugeo's death. She just gazed at the broken sword in silence.

Alice herself had barely had the chance to exchange any words with the young man named Eugeo. They had been together only while she took him from the school to the prison, when she fought him and Kirito on the eighteenth floor, and when they fought on the same side against Administrator.

She had boundless respect for him, not only for winning against Commander Bercouli but also for turning his own body into a sword to destroy the Sword Golem and cut off the pontifex's arm. But most of what she knew about Eugeo came from what Selka told her from memory.

According to her, Eugeo was a quiet but thoughtful boy, who was often dragged out on adventures by his childhood friend Alice Zuberg. Given his personality, it was no wonder he made such a good partner to Kirito.

Kirito and Eugeo must have caused all sorts of trouble at the academy. Tiese and Ronie would have found them fascinating, and the boys would have influenced the girls in a huge way. Just as they had done to Alice.

So please, understand and accept your sadness. Kirito and Eugeo fought, hurt, and lost heart and life to protect things they cared very deeply about, Alice silently willed as she watched the two.

The people of the four empires, when faced with a mental shock like overwhelming terror or grief, had a tendency to falter and grow mentally ill. The recent attack on Rulid Village had left several villagers bedridden, even though they had no physical injuries.

Tiese must have loved Eugeo.

To lose a loved one at that young age must be a terrible shock, one hard to withstand. Alice watched as Tiese's hand twitched and began to creep toward the Blue Rose Sword bit by bit.

Alice felt her hackles rise. The Blue Rose Sword, though broken in half, was still a Divine Object of the highest caliber. Tiese couldn't possibly use it, but such deep grief and desperation could bring forth unexpected power at times. She couldn't predict what might happen.

Tiese's awkward, outstretched fingers finally made contact with the pale-blue weapon. She touched not the edge of the blade itself, but the smooth, polished flat.

And just then, the broken sword began to glow, faintly but surely, overcoming the dim-red light of the sunset through the skylight of the tent.

At the same moment, Tiese's body twitched. Ronie sensed something and turned to look at her friend. In the tense silence, clear drops formed on Tiese's eyelashes and silently fell to the floor.

"…I just…," she whispered through pale lips, "heard…Eugeo's voice…saying…*Don't cry…I'll always…be…here…*"

The tears continued to fall, one after the other after the other, until Tiese hunched over the sword at last and began to sob

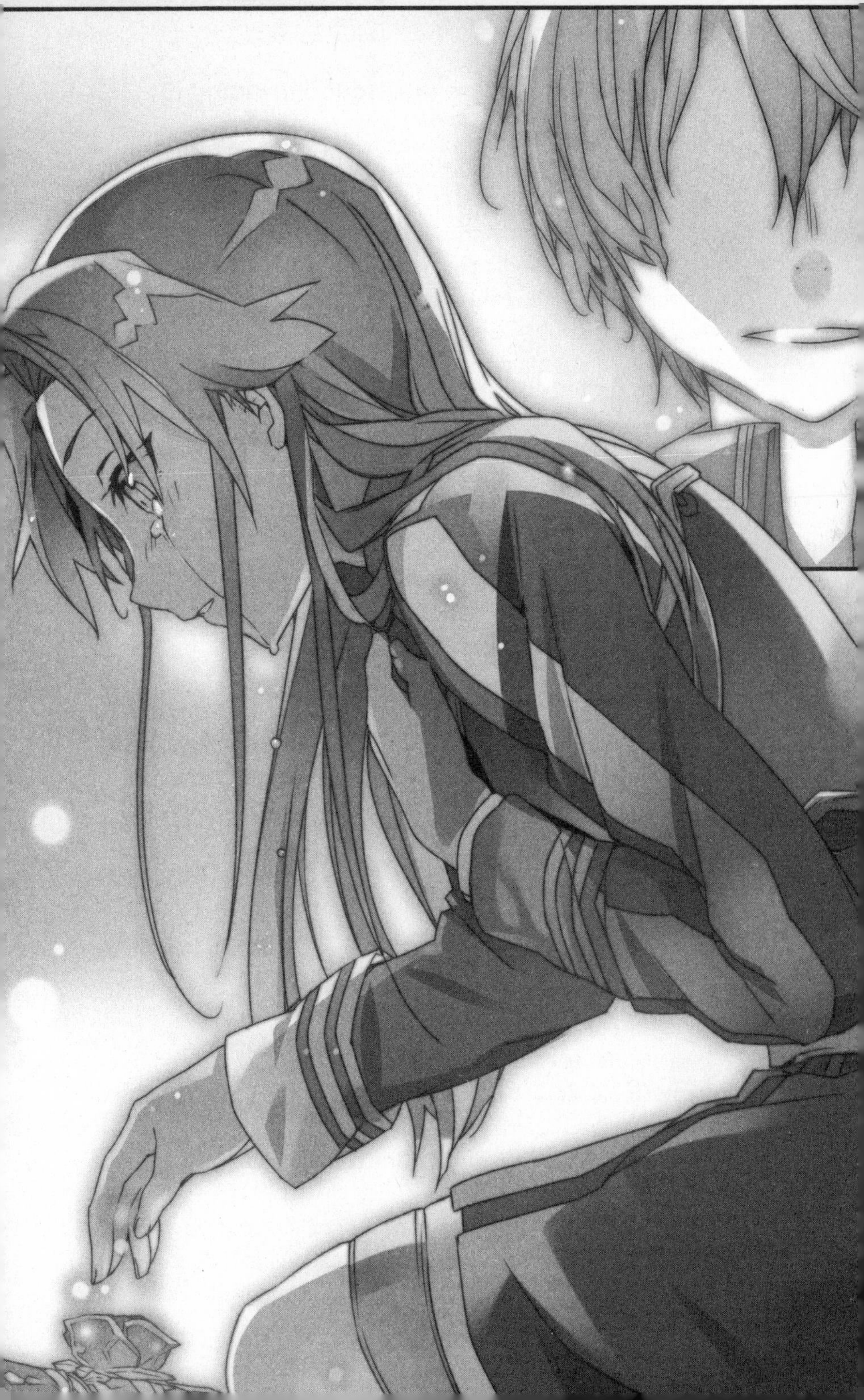

violently, like a young child. Ronie had her face pressed into Kirito's knees, bawling.

Alice felt her own eyes growing hot at the painful but pure display before her, and a part of her wondered whether this was something that had really happened. She hadn't heard Eugeo's voice, but the sword had indeed glowed for a brief moment. So she couldn't claim that whatever Tiese had heard had been in her imagination.

Could the Blue Rose Sword have something like Eugeo's soul still within it…?

When Alice activated Perfect Weapon Control, she felt a sensation like her mind becoming one with the Osmanthus Blade. And in Eugeo's case, he'd actually fused his own body with the Blue Rose Sword—during which he'd suffered a fatal injury.

So perhaps it was possible that, in the remaining shard of the sword, some of its owner's will still lingered. But Tiese had said that Eugeo had called out to her. So what if it was not just a soulless echo in the sword, but a real will—even Incarnation?

Was it an illusion brought about by her love? Or…?

It was so frustrating. Kirito would probably be able to get to the bottom of the phenomenon. He'd fallen into this world from the outside—from the mysterious place where the gods dwelled.

On the surface of her thoughts, above the swirling fray, one term rose to the top like a bubble and burst into being.

World's End Altar.

At that place with the unfamiliar name, there would likely be a door to the outside of the world.

If she could reach it, would all the mysteries be thawed in an instant? Could she bring back Kirito's missing soul? But the altar was outside the Eastern Gate and far to the south, they said. It was a distant place, even in the Dark Territory ruled by the tribes of darkness.

If she was going to go there, she'd need to break *through* the army outside the gate, rather than defend against its invasion. And even if she succeeded, she'd have to abandon the defensive mission and head south. As an Integrity Knight with phenomenal power, Alice had a duty to protect the human realm.

What if she gave herself up to draw the enemy's attention and headed for the altar, pulling them away from the gate with her? On the other hand, the Dark Territory had been dreaming of invading for hundreds of years. There couldn't be anything more tempting to them than to rush inside…

No, if she was going to travel to that altar at the end of the world, she would need to utterly destroy the forces of darkness first.

Alice shut her eyes when she arrived at the conclusion. Obliteration was an admirable goal, but at present, they would have difficulty just pushing back the first line of enemy troops. Yet, it had to be done if she was going to protect Tiese and Ronie—and Kirito.

She exhaled, thought for several moments, then approached the crying girls.

6

The last rays of Solus had vanished to the west long ago, but the sliver of sky over the Dark Territory visible beyond the Eastern Gate was still stubbornly, eerily bloodred.

In the center of the grassy clearing the Human Guardian Army used for dragons to take off and land during the day, there was a pure-white enclosure that seemed designed to draw the eye away from that baleful red color. Just before the fence, under the proud flag of the Axiom Church, a group of about thirty Integrity Knights and army captains had their heads together, faces solemn.

Alice came to a stop, startled to notice that the knights and soldiers were not separated into distinct groups. A knight wearing shining silver armor and a military captain with less attractive but still effective steel plate stood drinking from the same pitcher of siral water, deep in discussion. From what she could hear from listening in, they had completely dispensed with any formalities that would have bogged down the conversation.

"Pretty good for a hastily assembled force, don't you think, little lady?" said a deep voice at her side, drawing her attention.

Commander Bercouli, hands thrust into the waist of his eastern-style clothing, shook his head to stop her from saluting. "I decided that all that tedious saluting and protocol was a waste of time for this army. Fortunately, the Taboo Index doesn't have an entry that says 'Normal folks must ensure that a knight is properly mollified before they speak to them.'"

"I...see. That is all well and good, but aside from that," Alice prompted, looking back to the military discussion, "where are the other Integrity Knights? From what I can see, there are only ten or so of them here."

"Sadly, that's about all of them."

"Wh-what?!" Alice yelped, then covered her mouth with her hand. She looked up at the commander, aghast. "You...can't be serious. There should be thirty-one members of the knighthood, including me."

It was easy to remember, because the latest knight was Eldrie, who was designated Synthesis Thirty-One. Bercouli sighed in acknowledgment and lowered his voice to explain.

"I'm sure you know that Prime Senator Chudelkin performed 'tune-ups' on any knight who was about to suffer from memory issues. When he died, there were seven knights undergoing retuning in the senate. None of them has awakened as of yet."

"...!"

Her eyes bulged. Bercouli looked away from her uncomfortably. He continued, "Only Chudelkin and the pontifex knew how to perform the art of retuning. Now that they are dead, we can't bring those seven back without working to decipher the command, and we don't have the time we need for that. There was just one knight who was in simple cryosleep there, not undergoing retuning, and we managed to get them awake, but..."

She sensed the awkwardness in his tone, so she asked, "And who was that?"

"...Sheyta the Silent."

"...!"

It was a name Alice knew from a number of stories, but she'd never actually met the knight in person. She held her breath, however, because they were terrible stories, indeed.

Bercouli just cleared his throat to suggest they could talk about that *later* and continued discussing numbers. "Ultimately…there are twenty-four Integrity Knights awake at the moment. Four of them are managing things back at the cathedral in Centoria, and another four are patrolling the End Mountains for safety. That leaves us with sixteen. That's the maximum we can have at this crucial line of defense. That includes you and me, of course."

"Sixteen…," she murmured, biting her lip not to include the word *only*.

And once she studied the lineup that was present, she realized that the majority of the fourteen here were lower knights without divine weapons—and thus without Perfect Weapon Control arts. They were still stout warriors who could kill a few hundred goblins in a battle, but they did not have the kind of overwhelming power that could alter the course of battle in an instant.

Bercouli filled in the silence by changing the subject. "By the way, about the question of what to do with the young man…I could have the rear guard take—"

"No…it will be fine," she said, responding to his awkward offer with a smile. "There are volunteers who were his pages at the training academy…Once the battle starts, I will leave his care to them."

"Aaah, that's good to hear. So…did the fellow show any response when meeting someone from his past?"

Her smile vanished. She shook her head.

Bercouli exhaled and grunted in acknowledgment. "Just between you and me…I can't help but get the feeling that he's the very person who will determine the course of the coming war…"

Alice was stunned to hear that.

"The fact that he defeated the prime senator and pontifex with his sword, even accounting for the help from his partner and you, is a hard thing to fathom. I might not even be a match for the sheer durability of his Incarnation."

"…I didn't think it was so remarkable…"

She had no intention whatsoever of doubting Kirito's strength at this point, but Commander Bercouli's Incarnation was an ability he'd spent over two centuries honing. And Kirito was just a student, not yet a full adult. If anything, Incarnation should be the one category in which he was absolutely unable to match the commander, regardless of his technique and stamina.

But Bercouli was certain in his assessment. "When I struck him with my Incarnate Sword, and he struck back, I could feel it. That boy's got just as much experience with true battle as I do, if not more."

"True battle...? What do you mean...?"

"Just what it sounds like. The trading of life."

Now, *this* she could not believe.

The people of the human lands were protected—or perhaps imprisoned—by the Taboo Index and Basic Imperial Laws. Duels with wooden swords were common, but it was typical for one to go from birth to death by old age without ever once experiencing a true battle to the death with naked steel.

The only exception was for the Integrity Knights, who did fight against goblins and dark knights attempting to breach the End Mountains. But these events happened only once or twice over the course of a long campaign, and the Integrity Knight was inevitably far superior to the other side, so it was hard to call that a real battle of life and death.

In that sense, the one person with the most bountiful battle experience would be Bercouli himself, who had been fighting the monsters of darkness since the knighthood was at its smallest. Apparently, soon after he had been made an Integrity Knight, he even lost to a dark knight at the time—hard as it was to believe now—and had to flee for his life.

And somehow, Kirito had more experience with fighting for his life than Bercouli?

If that was even possible, then it was not experience that came from this world.

His real home was in the "outside world." But that was also the place where the gods who truly created the Underworld lived. True battle? Who would he have fought for his life...?

Alice wasn't sure how to process all this information. Ultimately, she had to make a decision for herself: She would tell Bercouli everything. About the existence of the outside world—and the World's End Altar that led to it.

"Uncle," she said hesitantly, choosing her words carefully, "the truth is...during the battle against the pontifex..."

But she didn't get any further because a sharp voice interrupted over Bercouli's shoulder. "It's time, Commander."

She started and looked toward the owner of the voice.

It was an Integrity Knight, dressed in beautiful light-purple full armor that shone even in the twilight, with a silver rapier on her left hip. The moment she saw the full-face helmet adorned with wings like a bird of prey, Alice's instinctual emotion was...*Ugh*.

It was probably the one person in the world whom Alice got along with least: the vice commander and second of all Integrity Knights, Fanatio Synthesis Two.

On instinct, Alice made the knight's salute of a right fist across the breast and a left hand on the sword hilt, doing her best not to let her emotions show on her face. Fanatio made the same gesture, her armor clanking. But while Alice stood up straight, feet slightly apart, Fanatio placed her weight on her right foot and dropped her left shoulder in an affected way.

This is the exact sort of thing that drives me mad about her, Alice secretly grumbled, lowering her arm.

Perhaps she thought that her imposing helmet and tone of voice hid it, but to a member of the same sex, it was clear that Fanatio couldn't help but exhibit a flowery femininity. Having been taken to the cathedral at a young age, Alice had never successfully learned such a skill.

On the fiftieth floor of Central Cathedral, Vice Commander Fanatio fought Kirito and Eugeo and suffered nearly fatal wounds when Kirito's Perfect Weapon Control hit her directly. But despite the great effort it took him to win, Kirito used healing arts on Fanatio and then used some mysterious ability to teleport her away from the place, according to one of the lower knights who'd been present.

It did sound like something Kirito would do, but she couldn't help but be unnerved by it.

For one thing, Fanatio seemed to be utterly devoted to Commander Bercouli, and yet, she had four attendant knights who were clearly smitten with her. Didn't she pity the ones who admired her so much but would never be able to even touch her? She could at least show them her face, rather than hiding it at all times with that helmet.

So it was to Alice's great surprise, during Alice's secret griping about the helmet, that Fanatio actually reached up and clasped the sides of it with her hands. She clicked the fasteners to undo them and easily lifted off the light-purple piece of armor. In the firelight, her smooth black hair shone like spun silk.

The only times Alice had ever seen Fanatio's face at the cathedral were when they encountered each other in the great bath by coincidence. As far as Alice could remember, this was the first time she'd ever seen the vice commander remove her helmet out in the open.

Compared to before, her beautiful looks seemed somewhat softer, and upon closer examination, Alice understood why. Her plump lips were actually colored in, albeit subtly. The woman who tried so hard to hide that she was a woman was...wearing makeup?

Fanatio took the occasion to flash the stunned Alice a warm smile. "It's a joy to see you again, Alice. I'm ever so glad to see you well."

"..."

A joy? Ever so glad?

That added another three seconds to Alice's stunned silence before she recovered enough to return the greeting.

"I...it's been a while, Vice Commander."

"Please, call me Fanatio. By the way, Alice, I couldn't help but overhear...Did you bring that black-haired boy here with you?"

The question was framed innocently, but it replaced Alice's surprise with caution instead. It was Kirito and Cardinal who'd healed Fanatio's injuries, but she might not be aware of that. It was possible that she still harbored hatred for the boy who'd bested her in combat.

"I...I did," Alice replied. The vice commander deepened her bewitching smile and nodded.

"I see. Do you mind if I meet with him after this conference?"

"...Why do you ask, Fanatio?"

"Don't give me that look. I'm not going to attack him at this point," Fanatio said, her smile turning faintly sour. She shrugged. "I just want to thank him. I understand that he helped heal me when I was mortally wounded."

"...So you knew. But I don't think you need to thank Kirito. I've heard that it was actually a person named Cardinal, the previous pontifex, who saved your life. And sadly...she passed away in the battle half a year ago," Alice explained, feeling her hackles lower a bit.

Fanatio gazed into the sky and said, "Yes...I faintly recall it. I'd never felt such warm and powerful healing before that. But it was Kirito who sent me to her...and there is one other thing I wish to thank him for."

"Other thing...?"

"Yes. For fighting and defeating me."

...*Maybe she does mean to attack him*, Alice wondered again, backing up half a step.

But Fanatio only shook her head, her expression earnest. "It is my honest wish. For all the many years I have lived as an Integrity Knight, he was the only man who ever truly fought his hardest against me after learning that I was a woman."

"Huh...? What do you...mean by...?"

"In the past, I did not have this helmet. I fought with my face exposed, as you do. But one day, I came to understand that the male knights who fought me in mock battles, and even the dark knights I faced in true combat, had just the tiniest falter in their actions. To be pitied in combat for my sex is more humiliating than any defeat in the dust."

But surely that was an unavoidable thing. Very few men could completely ignore the potent allure of Fanatio's looks.

It wasn't until she set up in the cabin outside Rulid that Alice learned that almost no women received a calling that involved taking up the sword. The only exceptions were the daughters of noble or landowning families. Ordinary women were prevented from choosing any life for themselves other than as wives, home-makers, and mothers.

If it was this old-fashioned custom that bound men's hearts just as the Taboo Index did, it was an ironic thing indeed. The assumption that women were meant to be protected by men caused their abilities to weaken in the presence of her radiant beauty. If the knights in the Dark Territory had wives and children of their own, they would be no exception. At least the goblins and orcs, who had completely different appearances, were exempt from this belief.

But Alice, a fellow female knight, had never noticed or cared if male knights showed her favor or weakness. She had confidence that whether her opponent went easy or tried his best, she would be the victor, regardless.

Perhaps your anger is simply proof that you cannot move past your status as a woman, Alice thought right as Fanatio said something to the same effect.

"I used this helmet to hide my face and learned consecutive swordcraft techniques to keep foes away from close range. But that was because I myself was too obsessed with my gender. Not only did that boy recognize it immediately, he attacked me with all of his ability. I used every battle technique and art that I knew in the fight, and I lost. When I came to, thanks to Cardinal, that petty obsession of mine was simply gone…The entire time, the whole point was that I should be strong enough that no opponent would dare to go easy on me. Is it really so strange that I would want to thank the boy who showed me this simple truth and made sure I lived to understand it?"

At the end of that impassioned speech, Fanatio put on a little smirk and grinned. "And I must admit…I'm a bit chagrined that he never sensed any femininity from my bare face. I was thinking that I might try a few things to see if he wakes up from his fugue."

"Wha—?"

What kind of nonsense…?

If that actually worked on Kirito, everything she'd done would feel so empty and pointless. And when it came to Kirito, she couldn't completely rule out that possibility.

Alice did not bother to hide the stern furrow in her brow. "I appreciate your sentiment," she snapped, "but he is currently resting in the tent. Do not worry; I will relate your feelings to him later."

"Oh my," said the vice commander, her eyelid twitching. "I need your permission to visit him? When you sought an audience with the commander at the cathedral while he was on duty, I don't recall ever trying to stop you for personal reasons."

"That is because your permission is unnecessary for me to meet with him. And really, now that I think about it, if you wanted a man to beat you senseless, you always could have asked Uncle to do it."

"Oh, there's no reason for that. He's the strongest swordsman in the world, so of course he goes easy on everyone. He even showed mercy to the dark general."

"Oh, did he? When we trained together, Uncle always worked himself into a heavy sweat out of true exertion."

"…Is that true, my lord?!"

"Uncle, if you didn't always pamper her…"

Both of the women turned to the side—but the commander was not there.

Where Bercouli had stood just minutes before, there was now merely a pile of dried grass.

*   *   *

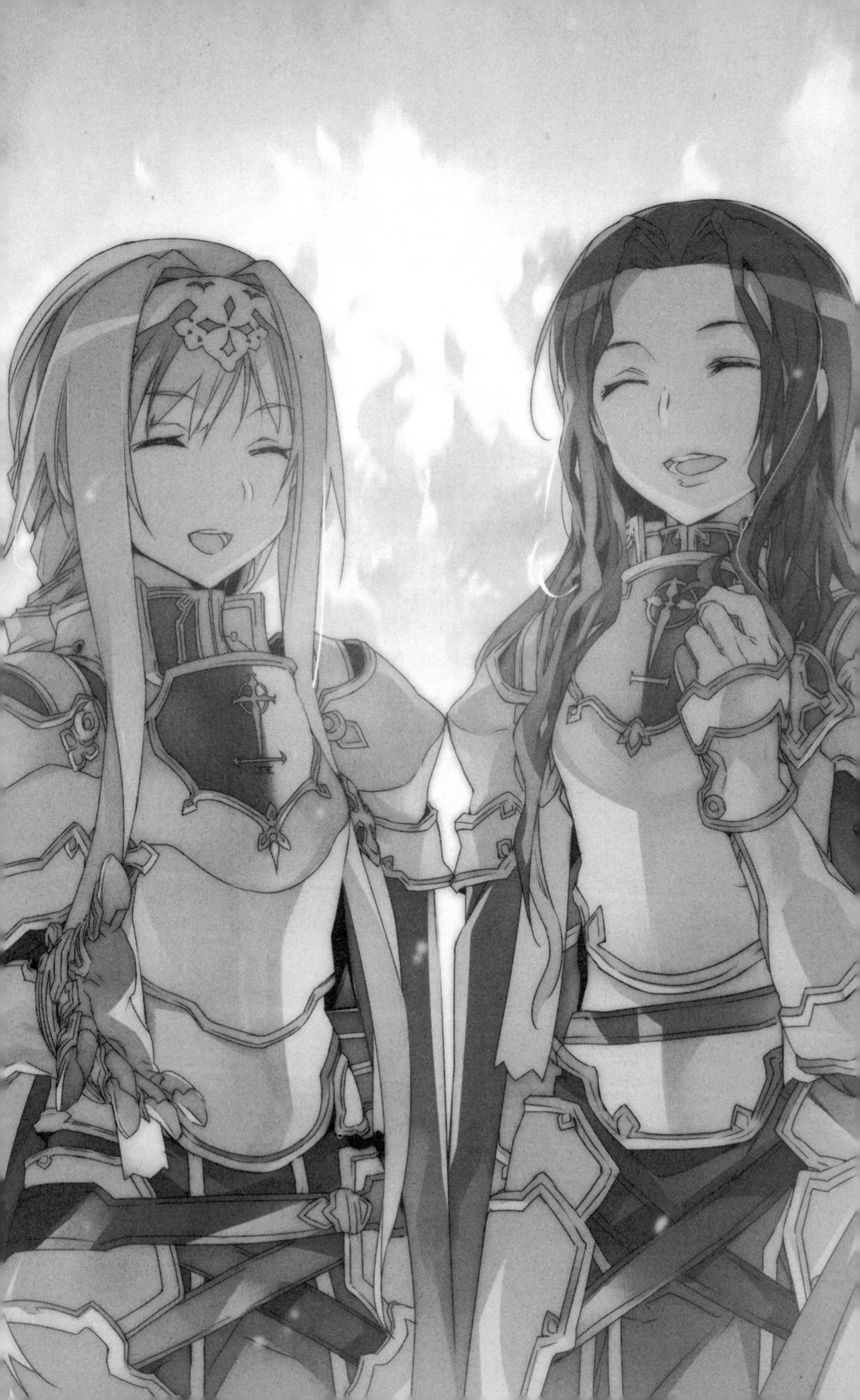

When the conference began at six o'clock, it was under rather tense circumstances, owing to the frosty air between the master of ceremonies, Vice Commander Fanatio Synthesis Two, and the newly arrived Alice Synthesis Thirty.

Alice completed a brief introduction and plopped into one of the chairs in the front row.

"...Miss Alice." Eldrie hesitantly reached over with a glass of siral water, which she snatched from his hands. She drained the cold sweet-and-sour liquid in one go. After a long, deep breath, she managed to shift to a different mental state.

Now that I get a good look...

There really were too few higher Integrity Knights with Divine Object weapons. The ones she knew and recognized were Commander Bercouli with his Time-Splitting Sword, Fanatio with her Heaven-Piercing Blade, Eldrie with the Frostscale Whip, and Deusolbert with the Conflagration Bow.

There were also Sheyta Synthesis Twelve, known also as Sheyta the Silent, and a very young boy knight named Renly Synthesis Twenty-Seven, both of whom had divine weapons, but she had hardly ever met them before and didn't know what they were capable of. At any rate, including Alice and her Osmanthus Blade, that was seven higher Integrity Knights in total.

The other nine, including the Four Whirling Blades who served under Fanatio, were lower knights without Divine Objects. And that included the infamous problem children, the apprentice girls whom even Bercouli had trouble managing—Linel Synthesis Twenty-Eight and Fizel Synthesis Twenty-Nine. They were seated obediently at the end of the row, but who knew whether they would behave and join the battle when it arrived.

That made sixteen in total, which was the grand sum of Integrity Knight power that they could actually apply to the ultimate line of defense.

Meanwhile, about thirty officers from the Human Guardian Army were also seated in attendance. Their morale didn't seem poor, but even at a glance, the difference in power between them and the knights was clear. Even one of the lower knights could take on all thirty of them in a consecutive match and win with ease...

"We've considered all potential strategies over the last four months," said Fanatio all of a sudden, pulling Alice back to the purpose of the meeting, "and the first conclusion is that with our current status, it will be very difficult to push back an all-out attack from the enemy, and if we are surrounded, we will not stand a chance of winning."

Using the long, slim scabbard of the Heaven-Piercing Blade as a pointer, Fanatio tapped a point on the strategic map set up at the back of the conference area. "As you can see, for ten kilors in all directions on this side of the End Mountains, it is nothing but grassland and rocks. If we get pushed back this far, their tens of thousands will surround us and defeat us. Therefore, we will have to maintain the fight in the narrow ravine to the Eastern Gate—a hundred mels wide and a thousand mels long. We'll set up a long, deep formation here to absorb the enemy's rush and grind them down. That will be the basic thrust of our strategy. Does anyone have any thoughts about this so far?"

Eldrie was the first to raise his hand. He got to his feet, lilac-purple hair waving, and kept his usual flowery formality to a minimum.

"If the enemy were only made up of infantry like goblins and orcs, fifty or a hundred thousand would be no matter. But they know that as well. They have units of ogres with powerful war bows and even more dangerous dark mages. How will we counteract the long-range attacks that will come from the rear of the infantry?"

"It is a dangerous gamble, I will admit," Fanatio said, pausing and looking to Alice. She straightened up and waited for the rest of the answer. "But the sunlight does not reach the floor of that ravine, even in midday, and there is not a blade of grass on the ground. In other words, the sacred power there is weak. If we can consume all of it before the battle, the enemy should be unable to utilize their powerful attack arts."

This bold idea brought a murmur to the knights and military officers.

"Naturally, the same will apply to us. But we only have a hundred capable of sacred arts in the first place. If it comes to a battle of arts thrown back and forth, the enemy side is bound to consume far more sacred power than we are."

That did make sense in its own way. But there were two problems with Fanatio's plan.

Eldrie was too stunned to speak, so Deusolbert, the archer, requested permission instead. The senior knight in his bronze-colored armor asked, "I believe you are correct. But sacred arts are not only used to attack. If the sacred power dries up, will it not be impossible to heal the wounded, too?"

"Which is why it is a gamble. We brought all the high-quality reagents and healing herbs from the cathedral's treasure repository here to this camp. If we reserve our sacred arts just for healing and use the herbs for extra support, the reagents should last us two...even three days."

This statement caused even louder gasps than the first one. The treasure room of Central Cathedral was known for having such tight security, there were fairy tales about it. Treasure was brought in—but this might be the first instance in history of anything being removed.

Even the imposing knight's stern face was slack with shock. Deusolbert sat down heavily with a grunt, and Alice took her turn to stand.

"There is one other problem, Miss Fanatio," she said, putting aside their earlier argument to offer feedback. "While the blessings of Solus and Terraria might be weak, the ravine is not perfect darkness, nor is it separated from the earth. I believe that a vast amount of sacred power has been stored in that place over the course of many years. What kind of person can use up all that power in the brief time we have before the coming battle?"

Now it was Fanatio's turn to be at a loss. The ravine through the mountain range was indeed more constrained than the grassland behind the camp, but it was still a hundred mels wide and a thousand long. It would take hundreds of people using high-level arts at once to completely sap all the sacred power in that vast space, and as Fanatio had just said, the guardian army did not have that many.

Perhaps a smaller group could achieve the same effect by casting some mega-scale art with cataclysmic effects, but no one was known to have that kind of power aside from the late Administrator and Cardinal.

But the vice commander stared at Alice with light-brown eyes and shook her head.

"I can tell you. We have just one person capable of that."

"...One...?" Alice asked, looking at the faces around her. But the name Fanatio said next was the last one she expected to hear.

"It is you, Alice Synthesis Thirty."

"What...?!"

"You might not realize it, but your present power surpasses the Integrity Knight's bounds. At this moment, you should be capable...of wielding true godly power that splits the heavens and earth."

7

"Is a higher Integrity Knight really that powerful?" asked Gabriel Miller as he sat in a large tank—which was really just a large four-wheeled vehicle without a cannon or treads—pulled by two dinosaur-like monsters.

Even the cushioned lounge chair couldn't eliminate the vibration, but compared to the deadly rumbling of the Bradley Fighting Vehicle he'd had to ride in as a soldier, this was nothing. At worst, it meant the glass of wine on the side table sloshed around a little bit.

Three days had passed since they left Obsidia Palace, a period of travel he'd never experienced in the real world, but he didn't feel tired at all. Perhaps that had more to do with the virtual nature of this world than the comfort of the tank's seating.

At his feet, a beautiful young woman reclined on the thick carpeting, rubbing her bandaged right leg. "But of course. In fact… over three hundred years of history, not once have our dark mages or knights ever succeeded in vanquishing an Integrity Knight. Does that convey the danger they pose? On the other hand, our own fallen are more numerous than the stars."

"Hmm," Gabriel murmured.

Vassago was sitting cross-legged along the spacious cabin's wall, cradling a bottle of distilled liquor. He wondered, "But,

Dee, if these Integrity Knights are so tough, why didn't they just come over here to invade?"

Dee Eye Ell, dark mage chancellor, gave Vassago a sizzling smile and raised a finger. "A very good question, Master Vassago. They are indeed warriors worth a thousand men, but each is only one person. If surrounded by ten thousand in a vast space, the little cuts and bruises will add up until their life is depleted. So the cowards never leave the End Mountains, knowing there is no danger of being surrounded."

"Oh, I get it. It's like when you're up against a really tanky mob, so you just chill at a safe distance and riddle 'em with DOTs until they kick the bucket…"

"Mob…? Dee-oh-tee…?"

Of course the artificial fluctlight would not understand Vassago's analogy. Gabriel shot him a look and cleared his throat.

"At any rate, the point is, if the Integrity Knights can be pulled into a wide-open arena, they can be surrounded and eventually overwhelmed, yes?"

"That would be the logic of it. But it would cost over ten thousand goblin and orc casualties, easily." Dee chuckled to herself and picked up a poisonous-looking fruit from the silver bowl on the floor and sensually placed it between her lips, of the same bloodred hue.

It hardly needed to be said that Gabriel did not care about the expenditure of grunt units. In fact, if he could defeat the enemy forces at the cost of Dee and every other soldier from the Dark Territory, he would take it without question. In a sense, this war was no different from the tactical simulations that Glowgen Defense Systems ran on a daily basis in its lab.

He would cross a mountain of bodies and rule over the Human Empire as their new sovereign, giving them just one order: to find the girl named Alice and bring her to him. Then his mission in this odd world would be complete.

The thought actually made the strange-flavored wine a bit more special. He would be sad to see it go.

Gabriel lifted his glass and downed the dark-purple liquid all at once.

At this time, the hunter of souls, Gabriel Miller, had an unconscious mental image of Alice that was very similar to his very first victim, Alicia Clingerman: innocent, young, and delicate. He assumed she would be a kind, beautiful—and helpless—girl living in a town just like Pacific Palisades.

So there was one thing that Gabriel failed to sense. He could never have imagined that the Alice he sought was going to lead the enemy army as an Integrity Knight.

The military train ahead of the command vehicle flying its imperial flag stretched endlessly to the west on its slow but sure advance. On the horizon against the crimson sky, a range of mountains as sharp and clear as the teeth of a saw jutted upward, growing slowly closer.

On the seventh day of the eleventh month, the fourth day of their march, the Dark Territory's main force reached the foothills near the giant gate that was soon to collapse. Around the flat mesa was a profusion of black tents prepared by the advance troops.

Du-du-rum.

Du-du-rum.

The beating of the giants' war drums kept the ground rumbling.

From the roof of the command vehicle, Gabriel watched as the single line of troops fanned out over a wide area, like blood cells pushed by the pulse of a gigantic heart.

The first regiment at the lead was fifteen thousand strong, consisting of a battalion of goblin light infantry and orc heavy infantry. They made a vertical formation sized just right to fit in the narrow ravine cut through the mountains. Here and there, individual giants loomed over the rest like siege towers—perhaps just a hundred in total, but they would be a valuable and active force to assist the infantry.

Behind the demi-humans was the second regiment, consisting

of a unit of five thousand pugilists and another of five thousand dark knights. The young knight who had been newly named to the position of dark general desired to fight on the front line to avenge the stain of his predecessor, but Gabriel ordered them back. The knight units were likely to have reduced morale now, and he wanted to eliminate uncertain variables.

The third regiment was seven thousand ogre archers and three thousand female dark mages. Their job was to enter the ravine behind the infantry and decimate the enemy with long-range attacks. According to Dee, as long as they could see the Integrity Knights, the primary source of the enemy's power, they could focus their fire on the target from a long distance and possibly defeat them.

For his part, Gabriel was intrigued enough by the supposed invincibility of these Integrity Knights that he wanted to battle one directly and devour their soul, just to sate his curiosity. But he couldn't afford to lose this account through some unforeseen accident, and he could always produce as many Underworldian artificial fluctlights as he wanted later. Right now, it was more important to seize Alice and escape from the *Ocean Turtle* with her.

Eight days had already passed inside since he'd logged in, which was about fifteen minutes in the real world. It would take roughly ten days to completely conquer the Human Empire and ensure the entire world knew about his order to find Alice. With that in mind, he wanted to get this battle over with as quickly as possible—within a full day at the longest.

"Damn. You think I'll even get a chance to shine?" complained Vassago.

Gabriel couldn't count how many whiskey bottles Vassago had downed today. He shot the other man a look and snapped, "I saw what you did. When that Shasta fellow turned into a tornado, you abandoned me and ran for cover."

"Heh-heh, I knew you'd be paying close attention, Boss." Vassago grinned innocently. "Listen, I've always been a PvP kind of guy. I'm not up for fighting against ghostly monsters without a corporeal body."

It wasn't clear just how serious or silly he was attempting to be. Gabriel stared at his subordinate, then asked, "Vassago, why did you enlist for this mission?"

"Mission? You mean the Underworld dive? Because it seemed fun, obviously…"

"No, before that. The mission to attack the *Ocean Turtle*. You're on staff at Glowgen DS, but you're a cyber-operations specialist. What's the reason you would take part in a mission that might involve live fire? You're too young to be a Middle East war dog like Hans or Brigg."

It was a long question by Gabriel's standards, but that did not mean he had any deep interest in Vassago Casals, of course. The thought merely occurred to him that something must lie beneath the young man's shallow exterior.

Vassago just shrugged and said, "Same thing. It seemed like it would be fun."

"Aaah…"

"Also, if you're gonna go down that rabbit hole, it seems a lot crazier for a fancy elite college boy like you to want to go into live combat. I don't care if you *do* have military training."

"I prefer a hands-on style," Gabriel replied. On the inside, he wondered, *What does "fun" mean to you, Vassago? A chance to shoot? Or…a chance to kill?*

He was deciding whether to go ahead and ask these questions or cut off the conversation there, when he was interrupted by the sound of high heels coming from the staircase at the rear of the command vehicle. The chancellor of the dark mages guild, Dee Eye Ell, appeared.

She gave an obsequious bow, licked her lips, and reported, "All units are now in place, Your Majesty."

"Good."

Gabriel unfolded his legs and stood up from his makeshift throne, then looked around. Aside from the main force of thirty-five thousand ahead, there was a reserve of ten thousand (mostly) goblins and orcs to the left of the command vehicle, plus five thousand members of the commerce guild's supply corps to the left and right.

This army of fifty thousand was what Gabriel had been given to work with. So if all his units were damaged without breaking the enemy's line of defense, he would have no choice but to give the plan a fundamental course correction. His chances of catching Alice would become infinitesimally small.

But according to the dragon scouts he'd sent out, the enemy's size was no more than three thousand. So as long as they could eliminate the Integrity Knights as he desired, their victory was all but assured.

"How long until the gate is destroyed?" Gabriel asked.

Without looking up, Dee answered, "Roughly eight hours, Your Majesty."

"Then one hour before collapse, move the first division into the ravine. Put them just in front of the gate and have them lead an all-out attack as it collapses. If that pushes the line, send in the second and third division behind them and wipe out the hostile force."

"Yes, Majesty. Before the day is out, you will have the head of the enemy leader. It may be slightly charred." She giggled and turned to pass on the orders to the messenger behind her before bowing and descending the stairs.

From the roof of the command vehicle, Gabriel surveyed the massive gate in the distance. It was more than two miles away, but it had such weight and presence that it felt as if it were practically hanging over his head. The crumbling of that mammoth structure would be something to behold.

But the true feast only started there. Thousands of souls would burst and vanish, releasing an indescribably gorgeous shine into the air. Perhaps the Rath engineers trapped in the upper shaft of the *Ocean Turtle* were gnashing their teeth, because the biggest spectacle they had scheduled in their system was going to happen, and they wouldn't be able to observe it.

Du-du-rum. Du-du-rum.

Dun, duh. Dun, duh.

The war drums' tempo rose, and with it the pitch of thousands of bloodthirsty roars.

8

"Well…I leave Kirito in your hands, then," said Alice, looking at the young girls in turn.

The primary trainees—really, they were full-fledged warriors by now—Tiese Schtrinen and Ronie Arabel, straightened up and bobbed their heads.

"Yes, Miss Alice, we will take good care of him."

"You have our word that Kirito will be safe with us."

Then Tiese took the left handle of his new wheelchair, and Ronie the right. The thin chair gleamed silver; Alice had used arts to change the shape of a leftover suit of armor from the supply tent. It was lighter and also tougher than the wooden wheelchair she'd used in Rulid.

But there was nothing that could be done about the weight of the two swords Kirito clutched in his lap. She was worried the girls might not be able to push the chair, but they worked in unison and did an admirable job of rolling it right up to her.

Now they wouldn't be left behind if they were given an immediate order to retreat. If they had to flee from the ravine, it would only be because the guardian army had been surrounded and crushed already.

Deep down, she wanted them to take Kirito and run to the west at the first sign of danger in the battle. But all that would do was delay their inevitable fate for a few months—or weeks, perhaps.

If the guardian army lost, the four knights guarding the End Mountains would withdraw from their posts, helping residents of the regional towns and villages evacuate and setting up the castle walls of Centoria as the final line of defense. But this would be a meager resistance, indeed. The invaders would trample all over them, and the beautiful city and chalk-white Central Cathedral would be burned to the ground. Within the prison walls of the End Mountains, there would be no real escape...

Alice crouched so she could look at Kirito at eye level.

For the five days they'd been in the camp, Alice had spoken to him when she had time, held his hand, and hugged him. But she'd never been able to get anything resembling a reaction.

"Kirito...I guess this might end up being our final farewell," she said, barely managing a smile for the black-haired boy. "Uncle said he had a feeling you would determine the course of this battle. I agree with him. You practically created this defensive army."

If it hadn't been for Kirito and Eugeo, in fact, it would be Administrator and the Integrity Knights set up behind the Eastern Gate right now—along with an army of those horrific Sword Golems.

Against two or three thousand golems and their tremendous fighting power, the fifty-thousand-strong Dark Territory army might as well be nothing. But the golems were also synonymous with the collapse of the human realm. They would be built out of thousands and thousands of residents. Kirito and Eugeo had sacrificed a heart and a life to prevent that tragedy.

But if Bercouli's Human Guardian Army was defeated, a great tragedy would happen anyway, just in a different form.

"...I'll try my hardest. I'm going to use up every last drop of the life you worked so hard to save. So...if I fall in battle, and I call for you with my last bit of strength, stand up and draw your sword. If you just come back to us, it wouldn't matter how many thousands the enemy has. You'll work another miracle...and protect everyone. I mean...

"You defeated the pontifex. You're the greatest swordsman alive," she whispered. She reached out and squeezed Kirito's scrawny body. After an embrace that could have been a second long or several minutes, Alice let go and stood up. Suddenly, she noticed that Ronie's gaze was concentrated on her, and in her blue eyes was a tapestry of emotions. Alice blinked, taken aback by this reaction, but she soon understood.

"Ronie, you...you love Kirito," she said, smiling. The girl covered her mouth with her hands, face going red from cheeks to ears. She looked away in embarrassment.

"N-no, I...," she stammered. "I couldn't...I'm not worthy of... I'm just a primary trainee and a page..."

"Worthiness has nothing to do with it. You're the heir of a noble family, aren't you? I was born in a tiny rural village, and I don't even know where Kirito came from..."

But suddenly, Ronie cut her off, shaking her head wildly. "No! It's not that! I...I'm..."

She lost her voice there, large droplets welling in her eyes. Tiese held out a comforting hand to support her friend. Her red eyes were wet, too. In a quavering voice, she said, "Miss Alice...are you aware of the taboo...that Kirito and Eugeo broke?"

"Er...yes. I heard there was a quarrel at school...and they killed another student."

Half a year ago, when Alice was a blissfully ignorant soldier of the Axiom Church, she was quite surprised to receive the arrest orders from the senate. She could still remember that now. There was no instance in the entire church record of such a serious taboo being broken before—a student in the city killing another student?

She motioned for Tiese to continue. The girl asked, "Then... do you also know how it was that they came to commit that crime...?"

"No, I didn't know that part," Alice said, shaking her head. But then a shouting voice replayed inside her mind. It was just after she and Kirito had been thrown out onto the cathedral walls, and she'd claimed that she did not need the help of a criminal.

He had shouted, *"Just because the Taboo Index doesn't outlaw it, should higher nobles be allowed to torment and defile completely innocent girls like Ronie and Tiese...? Is that what you believe?!"*

That's right. I heard him say their names back then.

The higher nobles he mentioned must have been the students Kirito and Eugeo attacked. And "defile"...?

Her voice trembling, Tiese explained to the wide-eyed Alice what that meant.

"...Elite Disciples Raios Antinous and Humbert Zizek repeatedly gave our friend Primary Trainee Frenica Cesky humiliating orders to obey. We protested to both disciples, but in our anger, we used words that were inappropriate for our station. Because of that, they executed noble judicial authority according to imperial law..."

Tiese choked up there, finding it painful to recall. Ronie was already sobbing faintly. Alice wanted to tell them it was okay and they didn't need to explain any further, but the redheaded girl shook off her weakness and continued.

"They were going to inflict...an unbearable punishment upon us, when Kirito and Eugeo used their swords to save us. If we had been just a bit smarter, it would not have come to that. They wouldn't have fought the church to fix the law, and no one would have died. We...we committed a crime with irreversible consequences. So...we don't have the right to express any love to them..."

Once she had finally admitted everything they'd been bearing, Tiese's eyes flooded with tears. The young girls hugged each other tight, sobbing with a regret far too terrible for their age.

Alice clenched her jaws and looked up at the skylight cut into the tent. She believed she understood the corruption and rot that was rampant in the higher nobles of the four empires. Gluttony, miserliness, and licentiousness.

But the former Alice the Integrity Knight had felt that knowing more would defile herself in turn, and she'd avoided learning of the deeds of the nobles. Whatever they did, she did not need to know—as long as no taboos were broached. She was the protector of the law, summoned from the celestial realm. As far as she believed.

That silence itself was a sin. It did not violate the Taboo Index, which Kirito hated so much, but that just made her crime more grievous. These two girls were many times braver than the one who looked the other way.

Alice inhaled a deep breath and said firmly, "No, you're wrong. You do not bear any sin."

Ronie instantly looked up. She usually seemed to be hiding in Tiese's shadow, so it was rare to see her look so intent and plaintive. "You would not understand, Miss Alice…You are a proud Integrity Knight! But they treated our bodies like their playthings, and now our dignity has been stained with sin!"

"The body is nothing more than a vessel for the heart," Alice replied, striking her chest with a clenched fist. "The heart…the soul is the one thing that truly exists. And the only one who can determine the nature of the soul is the self."

She closed her eyes and turned her mind's focus inward.

When Rulid was attacked about two weeks ago, Alice used the power of her heart—her power of Incarnation—to regain her lost eye. She herself had experienced that a strong, dedicated wish could bring about change in the body without the use of sacred arts.

But that alone was not enough now. She needed to change not her body, but the clothes around her, with Incarnate power.

She should be able to do it. Kirito had shown it to her before. When he faced Administrator with two swords, he was suddenly wearing a strange, foreign cloak of black leather that he hadn't been wearing moments before.

She had to go back. She had to be the old Alice, *before* she woke up in that unfamiliar white tower, fighting the unease and loneliness of lacking her memory and deciding to encase her heart in ice to protect herself from the pain.

I'm just like you, Ronie and Tiese. I was born a human, I made many mistakes, and I'm here now because I bore a terrible crime. If the death at Kirito's and Eugeo's hands was your fault, as you claim…then if I hadn't forgotten my taboos as a young child and touched the soil of the Dark Territory, they would never have had to go to the city in the first place.

Yes, that was my crime. Even if I have no memory of it, Alice Zuberg was not some unfamiliar stranger—she was me. My time in Rulid taught me that much.

Even with her eyes closed, she could sense that a warm white light was enveloping her body.

Alice's eyes slowly opened.

Her face had been downcast, so the first thing she saw was the skirt she was wearing. But it was not the pure white of the Axiom Church—it was a blue as clear as the autumn sky.

Over the skirt was a simple cloth apron. Her golden armor and gauntlets were gone. She brushed her head, and her fingers touched a large ribbon. It seemed like her hair was a bit shorter, too.

Then she looked up and into the stunned faces of Ronie and Tiese.

"…There, you see? Your body and appearance are entirely dependent on your heart."

This transformation was temporary, of course. The moment her concentration lapsed, she would return to her original knight form. But the girls would understand. They would realize Alice's and Kirito's and Eugeo's true feelings.

"Nobody can defile your heart. I should have grown up to look like this in the little rural village where I was born. But when I was ten, they took me to Centoria in chains, erased my memory with sacred arts, and turned me into an Integrity Knight. There were times that I cursed my fate…"

It was an enormous secret, something she had told only

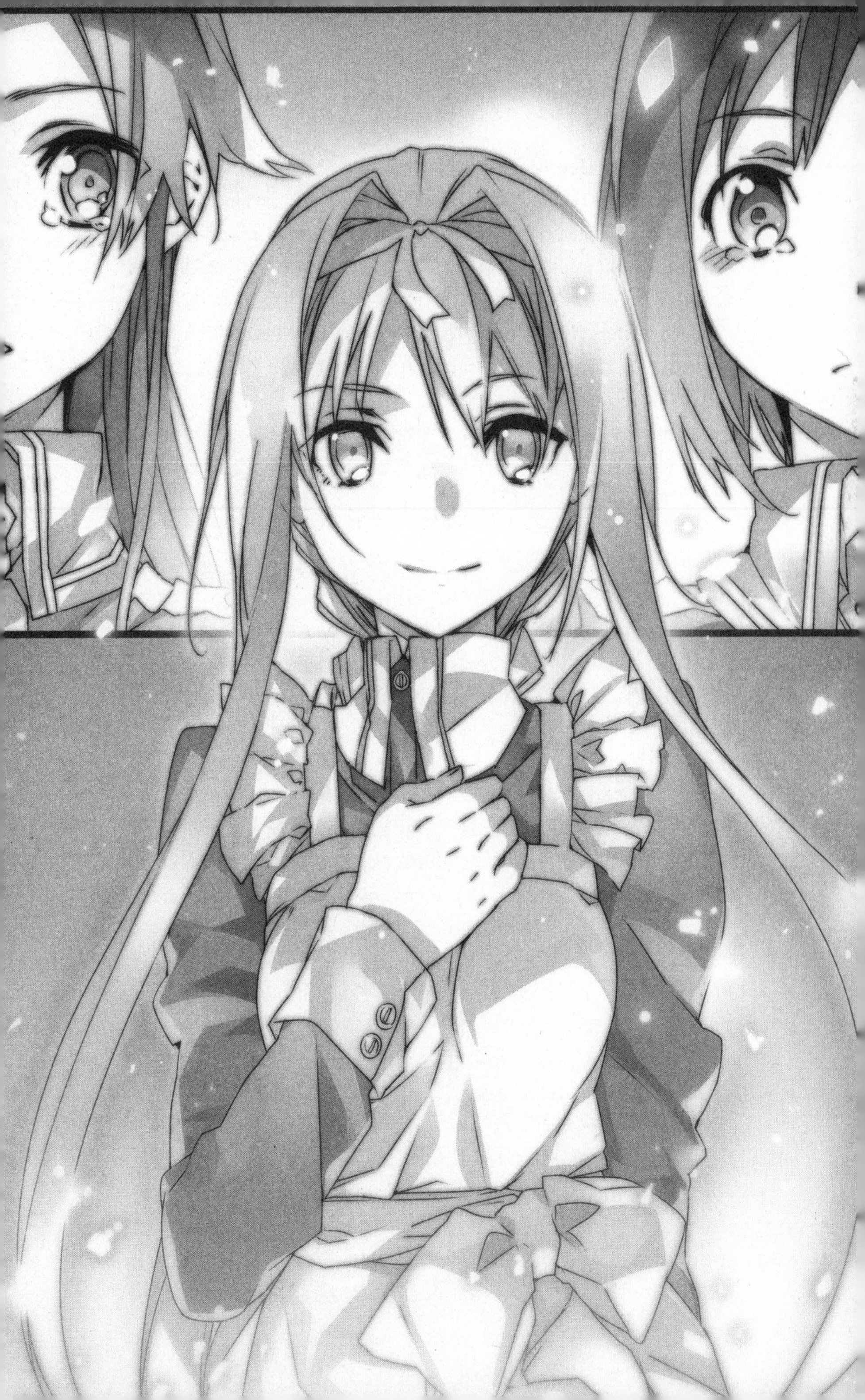

Commander Bercouli and no one else. She believed that these girls were able to bear her secret, too.

"But Kirito taught me that there were things I could and should do," she continued. "So I'm not lost anymore. I've decided to accept being myself and keep moving forward."

Alice lifted her hands and squeezed Ronie's and Tiese's together. "I know that you, too, have your own path in life—one that is wide and long and very straight."

A number of droplets fell on her hands. The tears ran down the girls' cheeks and fell, sparkling with a beautiful rainbow prism that had not been there before.

She gave Kirito one last hug in the wheelchair, then left him with Ronie and Tiese and exited the tent.

As though he'd been lying in wait, Eldrie suddenly bounded forward, bursting with compliments. "What a wondrous sight... like the concentrated blessing of Solus herself...You truly are my mentor, Lady Alice..."

"Don't worry—I'll be covered in dirt and dust again in an hour," she said, glancing down at her clothes.

The previous transformative effect was long gone; it was just her golden breastplate and white skirt, shining in the sun. She looked up at the western sky, thinking that if she came back from this alive, she'd add a piece of blue cloth somewhere to the outfit.

Solus was already on its descent. There was another three hours before it vanished over the horizon—and the moment that the Eastern Gate's life would dwindle to nothing. The three-hundred-year countdown would be over at last.

She had done all she could.

Alice took part in the guardian army's training exercises for five days, and she had to admit that for half a year of work, the soldiers' ability was admirable. To her shock, all the soldiers were using consecutive sword techniques that did not exist in the traditional styles of combat.

Apparently, Vice Commander Fanatio had taught them all the

secrets of her techniques she'd spent years upon years honing. The longest they could manage was only three strikes, but they would be a valuable tool against the free-swinging machetes of the goblins and orcs.

Of course, if any dark knights with their own combination attacks showed up, the soldiers might be outclassed. If you added the dark pugilists with their own speedy combos, only an Integrity Knight could match up.

The most important thing was not to be overwhelmed by the rush of demi-humans who were sure to be first when the gate fell. Next, they had to find a way to minimize the damage from the ranged attacks of the ogre archers and dark mages.

The success or failure of this strategy now rested solely on Alice's shoulders.

Her eyes traveled down to ground level again, where she could see several trails of smoke from the supply corps in the rear cooking up the final meal. Ronie and Tiese would be taking Kirito back there very soon.

She had to protect them. She had to.

"Miss Alice, it's about time," Eldrie prompted her. She acknowledged him and pulled back her leg to turn the other way.

But then she stopped and fixed her lone disciple with a firm gaze.

"...Wh-what is it?" the young man asked, a bit nervous.

Alice let her pursed lips relax just a bit. "You've served me well, Eldrie."

"Oh...wh-what?!" the knight yelped when she put her right hand over his left.

"It has been a great help to me to have you by my side. You sought out my instruction—a newer knight with little to show for herself—rather than a veteran man like Deusolbert. Was it out of concern for my mental well-being?"

"Wh-why, no! I would never do such an inappropriate thing—I swear it! I was drawn out of pure respect and admiration for the way you fought...!" Eldrie protested, shaking his head.

She squeezed his hand harder, then let go and smiled. "It was because of your support that I was able to walk my rocky path to this day. Thank you, Eldrie."

The young knight's eyes were huge—stunned. Suddenly, large tears welled in them.

"...Lady Alice...why...do you speak in the past tense?" he asked, his voice hoarse. "Why do you make it sound as though your path ends here and now? I...I have not learned nearly enough. Not of the sword, nor of the sacred arts. I am nowhere near your level. You must be around to train me and guide me to be better...!"

But just when his outstretched, trembling hand was about to touch her, Alice suddenly snapped, "Integrity Knight Eldrie Synthesis Thirty-One!"

"Y-yes, ma'am!" His hand froze, and he snapped to attention.

"As your mentor, I give you my final order: Survive. Survive and witness the coming of peace, then take back your true life and loved one."

Even now, the memory fragments belonging to the other Integrity Knights and their loved ones, transformed into swords, still remained on the top floor of Central Cathedral. There must be a way to return those things to their rightful places and forms.

Eldrie stood stock-still, shedding tears. Alice gave him a forceful nod and spun around on her heel. Her golden hair and white skirt cut through the chilly autumn air.

Just before her was the great ravine, sinking into darkness, and the Eastern Gate within it.

She was about to begin the command for a sacred art so unbelievably grand in scale that she had never experienced it before. It would be designed to use every last drop of sacred power in the ravine and deliver a painful blow to the enemy.

If she got a single word incorrect—or even just let her concentration lapse—the accumulated sacred power would misfire and likely wipe her from existence.

But she felt no fear anymore. The last five days had been fulfilling ones as an Integrity Knight, spent around Bercouli, Fanatio, and Eldrie. And as Alice from Rulid, she had been able to share half a year with her sister, Selka.

And most of all, by meeting Eugeo and Kirito, crossing blades with them, and coming into contact with their hearts, she had learned human emotions—sadness, anger, and even love.

What more could she ask for?

Her armor sliding and rattling, Alice proceeded forward, step by step, through the army waiting for the arrival of battle.

(To be continued)

AFTERWORD

Hello, everyone. I'm writing this afterword in an incredible rush right now. This is what happens when you completely forget that you need to write an afterword while several days trickle off the schedule!

But to get more to the point, thank you for reading *Sword Art Online 15: Alicization Invading.*

In the previous volume (*Uniting*), we beat Administrator, the big bad boss of the church, and yet, the book ended with "to be continued." This is the result of that shift...The story has now jumped outside the bounds of the human realm and into the vast and dangerous Dark Territory. In the real world, the *Ocean Turtle,* where Asuna and others are located, is under attack, and most ominous of all, Kikuoka changed from a *yukata* into a Hawaiian shirt...

After all that, the next volume should get into the war between the Human Guardian Army and the forces of the Dark Territory. The Alicization arc started in Volume 9, and we're rushing toward the climax, so just stick with me a bit longer!

As for personal news, I was invited to be a guest, with my illustrator abec, to the largest anime/manga convention in the United States, Anime Expo. It was my first time visiting Los Angeles (and only my second time in America), and not only is the city huge, so was the convention center! The passion from the American anime fans that filled the hall was overwhelming!

Of course, I was moved by how many *SAO* fans came to see me. It also made me think about how much *SAO* has grown, from being a simple website novel to being published by Dengeki Bunko, then being turned into an anime and video games—and it's all because of the incredible support you've given it for over a decade.

By the time this book comes out, the second season of the TV series should be airing. Unlike the first season, it's set in a world of guns, but the director, creative staff, and voice cast are working their hardest to create some awesome gunfight action and the usual *SAO* essence that you love, so please keep watching.

I get the feeling I'm running out of time, so I'll keep my acknowledgments brief! To my illustrator abec, who drew wonderful illustrations for so many new characters in this volume, to my editor Miki, who visited LA with us, to my assistant editor Tsuchiya, who kept Japan safe while I was gone, and to all of you who have read this far, thank you so much!

Reki Kawahara—July 2014